JOURNEY ADVENIA

Aiden Kinder

To you, the reader, for choosing my story amongst millions.

Chapter One

Kiro

Thirteen years had led to this day.

It was the crack of dawn. I had left my chambers and come to the meditation pedestal outside the temple some hours ago when I gave up trying to sleep. I was too excited, too nervous, to rest. So instead, I decided to train. I practised my forms and motions, again and again and again. I wanted to make sure I was ready. I *needed* to be ready. All it took was one mistake, one wrong step, one second misspent, to set me back another thirteen years.

When these nerves weighed down on me, I took a breath and focused my awareness on the present. My feet pressing into the cold stone of the pedestal beneath me. The light touch of my robes on my body. The crisp, cool wind of the Gentle Mountains flowing all around me.

The Gentle Mountains truly do deserve their name. Magnificent, rising monoliths of steep grey and white stone, layered with luscious pink, green, and amber forests growing on the plateaus and flourishing in the misty valleys below. Golden light was peering over the horizon in the east, piercing through the darkness of the passing night, heralding the most important day of my life.

The day I became a master.

I was halfway through my unarmed display, countering an invisible opponent's strike to my throat, when I heard my name.

'Kiro.'

Surprised, I fumbled the parry, and the invisible opponent stabbed me in the neck. I turned around.

'Master Shien.' I fixed my arms to my sides and bowed to my teacher. He was standing on the bridge to the pedestal, with a lantern swaying in his hand. I was shocked I hadn't heard him approach at all. I wondered how long he had been watching me.

'You stand well for a dead man,' he said, pointing to the invisible puncture in my throat.

My cheeks burned hot. I hoped that wouldn't affect his judgement later. 'My opponent caught me by surprise.'

A single, inward chuckle came from him. 'You didn't sleep well, did you?'

There was a warmth about him that put me at ease. 'Not at all,' I said.

A small smile appeared under his profound, white beard. 'Come. Join me. I wish to speak with you.'

I climbed down the pedestal and joined Shien on the bridge, following behind him as he led us back onto the outer deck of the Sanctuary, then inside the temple. Following at his side, we passed by the gardens, the workshop, the library, the eating hall. During this stroll, neither of us spoke. I understood that Shien would begin whatever lecture he had in mind when he decided, and I remained respectfully silent. But, knowing what he was going to talk about, I stayed quietly hopeful.

He returned us to the outer balcony of the Sanctuary, walking the wind-caressed deck that ran along the outer edge of the temple and gifted us with the sweeping views of the Gentle Mountains. The hanging chimes jingled delicately with the sway of the wind. Shien spoke without shifting his crinkly gaze from the valley. 'This is the day that marks your seventeenth year.'

I nodded.

'You understand what this means.'

'I can attempt my ordainment test,' I said, hiding my excitement and nervousness behind a calm tone.

'Indeed,' Shien said. 'Are you nervous?'

I smiled a little. 'Yes.'

We stopped, and for a moment, stood in silence. We savoured the gorgeous sights and listened to the wind.

'What is your earliest memory, Kiro?' asked Shien.

I thought for a moment, searching my mind, then answered, 'I remember meditating in the gardens as a young boy, and opening my eyes for a moment to peek at everyone around me. They were all sitting still, with their eyes closed. We were under a pink tree, on a clear sunny day.'

Shien hummed a note of acknowledgement. I wondered what he meant by the question. I was expecting it to lead into a long, profound lesson. But what it would be about, I was not sure yet.

'Your earliest memory is of this place,' Shien said, looking up and around at the pillars and the ceiling above us. 'But mine is not.'

'No?'

Shien placed the lantern down on the ground by his foot, then said, 'I remember my mother and father, preparing a slain animal for feast over an open fire just outside our home, a straw hovel. I remember feeling mud between my toes, and the smell of a storm before the rain comes down.' He was silent for a moment, staring off into a bygone world only he could see, before he looked back to me in the present, with his weary black eyes. 'It must seem like I have lived here all my life, but I was older than you are now when I first found our Sanctuary. I was a disciple for many years longer before I decided to commit myself to the Order through ordainment. Since the day I became a master, I have remained here in our sacred home. I have not seen the world below the mountain for decades.'

He laid a hand on my shoulder.

'And if you are ordained on this day, Kiro, you will never have the chance to see that world.'

I peered at his hand, then at his face. And then it became clear to me where this conversation was leading. A sick, heavy feeling sat in the pit of my stomach.

'Master... what are you saying?'

'The Masters and I have discussed it,' he said, looking into my eyes. 'You won't be completing your test today, because today is not the day you will be ordained.'

The words were final and as solid as the centuries-old stone beneath my feet. They hit me hard. 'But… Master, I…' It was hard to talk. '…But why?'

He went to the balcony and gazed out over the mountains. 'Who are you, Kiro?'

I had no idea how to answer that.

'I'm not trying to trick you,' he assured me.

'I am Kiro,' I answered, joining him at his side.

'What makes you special, Kiro? What sets you apart from your fellow disciples?'

I thought about it. 'I am the youngest one here.'

'And how did that come to be?'

'I have lived here all my life.'

Shien hummed. 'Precisely,' he said, pleased that I had found the answer he wanted me to find. 'There has been no one like you in our Order's history. You are the only person to have been raised in the Sanctuary since infancy.' He turned to me. 'That makes you special. While everyone else in our home has memories of life below the mountains, places they once called home, your whole world extends only as far as the walls of our temple.' He gestured with his hand to the walls behind us. 'As sublime as it is, all you have ever known is our Sanctuary. Because of that, there is knowledge you lack. Knowledge that you need to become a master.'

I gazed out over the sea of mountains. Doubts bubbled in my stomach. 'Does that mean I can never be ordained, Shien?'

'No. Not never. Just not today.'

'Then when?'

He rested a hand on the balcony. 'For you Kiro, we have decided that for you to prove yourself worthy of ordainment, your ordainment test will not be the traditional examination. Instead, you must complete one other task.'

He paused, and I listened on eagerly, an ember of hope flickering in my heart.

Shien joined his hands behind his back and looked out over the world below the mountains. 'To become a master, you must find the ultimate truth that will grant you enlightenment. Everything we can teach you here, we have taught you. The knowledge you need, you cannot find here.'

Realising what he meant, my eyes widened. 'Are you saying I must leave the Sanctuary?'

He nodded.

A breath escaped me. 'Where must I go?'

'To the one place where you will find the knowledge you seek,' he said, glancing at me. 'The end of the world.'

I was silent for a moment as I tried to comprehend what he meant. 'Forgive me, I don't understand...'

He explained. 'Far east of here, where the land of man ends and the skies and seas become one, there is a place we call the end of the world. Once you reach it, you will find the ultimate truth – the knowledge that will grant you enlightenment. And once you have that, you will be ready for ordainment.'

I paused to contemplate all of this, my eyes falling to the little cracks in the stone beneath my feet. 'How do I get there?'

'Any means possible,' Shien said. 'Travel east, through the land of Advenia. The journey is long, so we have preparations for you to leave today.'

I hesitated. 'Today?'

Shien noticed the doubts in my voice. 'Or, whenever you wish. It does not need to be today. You can simply continue your duties as a disciple and live here until you are ready. But until you find the ultimate truth, you will not be ordained.'

It felt very much like this was a test, even if Shien would not admit that. I wanted him to know I could do that, that I was worthy. 'No,' I spoke up, lifting my chin. 'I will go today.'

A small smile appeared under Shien's beard. 'Are you certain?'

'Yes, Master,' I said, standing as tall as I could. 'I am worthy of ordainment, and I will do whatever it takes to prove that. I will go to the end of the world, and I will leave today.'

Shien hummed a note of approval. 'Then come with me.'

He led me through the Sanctuary once more, taking us through corridors, up the stairwell, until we were approaching the two red doors.

Behind them was the Master's Chambers. Whenever I would pass these doors, I would always wonder what the room behind them looked like. It was forbidden for anyone but the masters to enter, and as a child, it had been a fascinating mystery. In my free time over the years, I had managed to find or stumble upon every little secret in this temple. But I did not know what it looked like behind these two red doors.

Shien opened them by just a crack, then turned to face me with a little smirk.

'Step inside, Kiro,' he said, aware of how curious I was.

I resisted the urge to grin and entered.

The Master's Chambers were dimly lit, and the air heavy with the smell of incense and weighty contemplations. An orange carpet draped along the stone floor laid a direct path from the doors to the end of the room, where the only window was obscured by a wooden lattice stand. Thin beams of morning light seeped through them, illuminating the invisible passage of dust in the air and casting little diamonds of light on the floor. The Sanctuary was quiet, but here it was doubly so, and every little sound that disturbed the stillness was almost deafening.

Shien went to an arranged assortment of trinkets, pots, and chests sitting in shadow by the wall, where he retrieved a faded leather satchel.

'Here, Kiro,' he said, handing it to me.

I opened it while Shien knelt to find something else. Inside the satchel was a rolled-up blanket, a sheathed knife, some gold and silver coins, two canteens full of water from the mountain springs, some bread and fruit, and a small red pouch that, to my surprise, contained four pomegen berries.

'Thank you, Master.'

'And one more thing.' Shien stood up straight and turned to me. In both his hands he held a small wooden box. It was of remarkable quality; smooth, and decorated with elegant, flourishing lines engraved in the lid. He held it out delicately and formally, like it was something sacred. 'In your journey, you will learn that the world is as beautiful as it is dangerous.' Shien's voice was slow and deeply serious. 'Should you find yourself, or others, in a circumstance where life may be lost, then I entrust you to use this wisely.'

He opened the box. Nestled in a little blue cushion was a silver ring, embedded with a single godstone. A tiny gasp slipped from me as I caught sight of the gem's heavenly blue colour.

'This is yours, Kiro,' Shien said. 'Take it.'

I looked up at him, unsure if I should have it. 'I thought only masters could wear these rings. Are you sure?'

He nodded slowly. 'I trust in you to have the respect and temperance to use it well.'

Carefully, I plucked the ring from the box and held it between my finger and thumb. I inspected it closely, noticing its smoothness, then slipped it onto my right hand. A faint tingling emanated through my skin from its touch, then disappeared.

Chapter Two

A Secret Letter

Synn,

To my understanding, you are a man with a fearsome reputation. Tales of your infamous streak of violence and mayhem reach as high as to grab at even my attention.

For this reason, I have decided to offer you a task that befits a man of your talents. I have but one simple assignment for you, and that is to find and assassinate a woman who bears the name Viella Vanclaude.

Though I will not disclose many details of myself to you in this letter, as keeping my reputation unimpeachable is imperative to both our interests, I will tell you that I am indeed from a very high place. In executing this task swiftly and discreetly, you will be rewarded quite graciously with ten thousand prences in gold coins.

Naturally, there are high expectations that come with such a magnanimous offer. First, your silence on this mission is of the highest importance. You will find the consequences of defying this to be most contrary to your interests. Second, I require irrefutable proof of her demise. The grotesque details of how you ensure this I will leave to your mind to imagine.

In assisting your search, I will share with you the details we know; Viella is hiding somewhere in the far west beyond Dagger Peaks in a small, obscure place. According to descriptions, she is tall, slim, and has white hair and blue eyes. The most valuable clue I can provide to identifying her is this; in her possession, she will have a rapier of supreme quality. It has a golden hilt in the shape of a spiral, adorned with a ruby. It is no ordinary sword that a commoner would come to possess, and it will draw your attention should you sight it.

If you intend to accept this task, my subordinates will meet you in Ceren in one week's time, under moonlight behind the Red Cathedral. They will equip you with more information and three thousand prences in gold coins as a sign of my goodwill. It is my hope you will be there to meet them.

The blessings of God be upon you,

Z

Chapter Three

The Journey Begins

Every descendant in the Sanctuary was at the gates to bid me farewell. Their encouraging words and parting hugs warmed me with hope and confidence. It made it a little easier to do what I was about to do.

The blue gates to the Sanctuary were the biggest doors I had ever seen and probably will ever see. They towered over everyone. When one of my fellow disciples wound the gears to open the gates, there was a thunderous creaking as the massive doors pulled apart. The light of day spilled through the gap, washing over me and the ancient floor. The warmth of the sunlight sank into my face and skin. I rolled my shoulders, feeling the weight of the satchel and my wooden staff shifting on my back.

I looked out over the world beyond the doors. The beauty of the view from our mountain home had not been lost on me over the years living here. Now, it was as clear and vast as I had ever seen it, and I was in awe. Beyond the many old steps beneath me, at the bottom of the stone staircase, was a faint dirt path that curved and weaved into the flourishing pink forest that laid beneath the mountain temple. Beyond them, a sheer decline. From there, I could see the land beneath the Gentle Mountains;

sweeping grassy fields, split by a dirt road that led to a town far in the distance. A shimmering river ran near the settlement and up through farmland that laid before a sprawling dark forest on the horizon.

I turned to face the people who became my family. I bowed to them one last time, and they did the same. All fourteen descendants of the Order of Light, bowing to me. They rose, and Shien spoke.

'Farewell, my student.'

'I will not fail you,' I promised. 'I will see you all again when I return. Farewell.'

Then I turned and made my way down the steps.

As I descended the stairs, it dawned on me that this was actually happening. I was going to see the world. I never thought I'd leave the mountains. But now that I actually was leaving, I was excited to see what Advenia would be like.

A deep, booming *bang* pulled me from my thoughts, and I glanced back at the massive doors to see them pulled shut.

I was on my own now.

I had never felt a silence like this. I had never truly been on my own. That warm confidence went cold. Doubts and questions swirled in my mind. *What if I'm not ready for this? What if I don't find the ultimate truth?* I couldn't put them out of mind, so I focused on just getting down the mountains first. *One step at a time, Kiro,* I reminded myself. *One step at a time.*

It was midday when I left the Sanctuary. I made my way down the mountain carefully, which meant slowly. I did not want to trample or ignore the precious beauty of the nature around me, so I was careful where I placed my steps. I never had the chance to be this close to all these trees, and I had often wondered what they were like up close. It was deeply calming to admire them as I walked, listening to the whistle of the summer breeze and the sweet songs of the pufferbirds, enough to ease some of the weighing doubts on my mind.

After what was probably an hour, I reached the edge of the mountain. Curiously, but cautiously, I lay on my stomach and poked my head over the edge. It was just as they described; a sheer cliff face that plummeted thousands of feet to the bottom of the mountain. There was a very slight slope, and a few ledges and plateaus that jutted out, but it was otherwise simply a drop that went straight down.

I knew the Order had built a staircase into the side of the mountain. It took me some time to find it, and when I did I was surprised by how bare it was. The stairs were just planks of wood jutting out of the side of the mountain. I regarded them from a distance, judging how safe they were, then decided to make my way down on them. When I pressed my weight down on the first plank, I was surprised that it did not feel any less solid as the ground I had been walking on. There was nothing but air underneath these steps, but they did not bend or flinch at all once I was standing on them. There was a slightly uncomfortable gap between each plank, and I had to make long strides with each step to reach them. Clutching to the rock wall with one hand was hardly effective but I did it anyway to steady myself against the wind and my nerves. Eventually, I reached a point on the stairs where to my right was just a big grey rocky wall, and to my left was a breathtaking view of the tapering mountains, rising above the forested valleys.

The staircase wrapped around the mountain like a giant coil, and eventually led me to a wide plateau in the mountain where I could continue my way down walking on solid earth. This place was different from the level the Sanctuary was built upon. Here, the trees and nature were denser. The treetops shadowed the land, the grass brushed against my thighs, and I heard new kinds of croaking and squawking; the sounds of certain wildlife I was only hearing for the first time. It was beginning to occur to me how silly I was to expect I was ready for ordainment. I had never even heard the sounds made by animals living below the Sanctuary. *What kind of enlightened master has never heard a sparrow?*

Continuing through became harder as I had to squeeze past shrubs and trees and mind my footing on the rough, uneven ground. I received a few cuts and grazes from some of the less friendly bushes, even a small rip in my trousers from an especially claw-like branch. At one point, I felt a weight moving on my arm, and discovered a tremendous ebony thornspider clinging to my sleeve. I must have displaced the creature from their home when I was squeezing through trees. So, naturally, I had to set some time aside to find the thornspider a new tree. It wouldn't be right to just throw him to the ground, so I searched for a suitable new tree and ushered him gently onto the wood, said goodbye, then continued.

By the time I reached another mountain-side staircase, the sun was slinking down to the horizon. Ribbons of orange, red, and purple scattered across the sky like paint on a canvas, and from the east, a cold blue night was creeping forward.

A hunger that had been growing angrier for hours now finally persuaded me to sit down and eat. I was still walking on the staircase when I made that decision, and with no sign of a plateau in sight, I simply sat down on the step. I was confident it could hold me. It seemed they were fused into the mountain using divination and could hold a weight a lot larger than mine. There, on that step, with my legs dangling over a deadly fall, I sat and ate some apples and bread, savouring the tastes and the spectacular view of the sun setting on the mountains. It was beautiful, and I felt grateful for the chance to experience it, grateful to be alive.

When I finally reached the bottom of the mountain, night had already fallen. It had taken me the rest of the day to get here, and now I needed to find the cabin the Order had built for the Sanctuary's retrievers. The songs of nature here were different at night. Birds were quiet, and instead, the humming and buzzing of insects filled the night air. It was strange in comparison to birds, but I still liked them.

After stumbling through the dark, I found the cottage. With the white walls and blue-tiled roof, it looked like the Sanctuary's little brother. The door was unlocked, and I entered.

Inside it was simply one room. It had a bed, a table, a stool, and a chest, all laden with darkness and dust. I placed down my things near the chest, disrobed, then slipped into the bed. It was strange to sleep in a bed that didn't belong to me, but it didn't matter. I was tired enough that after settling in, I quickly fell asleep, thinking to myself *Maybe this journey wouldn't be so bad.*

The next morning, I woke up to the sound of a scream.

I opened my eyes and saw the ceiling. Once I realised what I had heard, I flung myself to my feet, spilling the sheets to the floor, and went to the window. I peered through it, searching for anyone in the trees. I saw nothing.

Then it happened again. A scream. It was distant, but brimming with terror.

Someone was in danger.

As quickly as I could, I threw on my robes, gathered my staff and satchel, and sprinted out the door.

'*Hello!?*' I yelled out as I ran.

Once I was in the forest, I couldn't see or hear anyone.

Dark trees. Leaves and grass swaying in the breeze. That was all.

I slowed my breathing and stood still.

Birds. Wind. Leaves rustling.

Then a scream.

I spun around to face the direction it came from, and I bolted towards it. I was running as fast as I could, leaping over roots, ducking under branches, charging through shrubs. I didn't even have the time to consider if this was a good idea.

And then I saw them, and I froze.

Ahead of me, standing in a small clearing, a group of three men in black cloaks surrounded a woman in a hooded mantle. All of them were holding weapons; the men gripped big, crude daggers and the woman a long, thin sword with steel that shimmered in a ray of sunlight. She was clutching the side of her stomach with her free hand. Blood seeped through her fingers.

'Get back!' she barked at them with a shaky voice.

'Easy there, love.' A deep, cold voice replied. It was edged with sinister intentions. 'If you play nice, we'll make it quick.'

'I said *get back!* Or I'll kill you!'

A cruel snickering came from the man closest to her. 'That's fine. I like to play rough anyway.'

He made a lunge at her with his dagger, which she repelled with a quick swipe of her blade. It knocked his hand away. She moved back, bumping into a tree. The men surrounded her.

My heart was thumping hard against my chest. It occurred to me that I didn't have to be here. I could run for help. Or I could just carry on with my journey.

But I knew I couldn't do that.

I had to intervene.

'Excuse me,' I called out.

All four of them swung their heads around and stared at me.

Silence.

I did not know what to say, so I said nothing.

A man with rough stubble and a scarred, olive face spoke. 'You shouldn't be here.' His voice was cold and black. He was the one who spoke before.

I cleared my throat and asked them what they were doing here. None of them responded.

One of the men, who had a pale, gaunt face and flecks of blond hair under his hood, pointed at my robes and muttered to his companions '*He's one of the mountain people.*'

The man with the scar, the ringleader, glared at me with a look of fire in his eyes. 'Get out of here, boy,' he said with a low voice. 'Say nothing of this to no one. Go home, now.'

I didn't move. I thought about using the ring, but I was terrified of what would happen if I couldn't control it. Despite years of training, and knowing better, I did not believe in myself in that moment. I could not risk a fatal hesitance.

'From what I can see, you are trying to hurt this person.' My heart pounding, I slung my staff free from my shoulder and gripped it tightly in my trembling hands. If it came to violence, I felt better using something I trusted. 'For the sake of everyone, please put your knives away and go in peace.'

The ringleader sighed. 'Couldn't even have *one* day without some nosy prick.' He grumbled, sniffed, and tossed his knife into the air with one hand, catching it with the other. He moved towards me. 'I warned you.' His nostrils flared, and with a voice hot with fury he roared, 'I WARNED YOU!'

With a sudden and vicious speed, the man rushed towards me with his dagger gripped tightly in his hand. I remembered the lessons of Obadi.

When your opponent is like fire,
Be like water.

His knife hand flew for my heart. I struck it with the staff, knocking the knife from his grip, then swung it into his ribs. The staff collided with a sickening *crack* that startled me. The man yelped, then I jabbed at his chest. He gasped, and I swept out his legs with the staff, knocking him off his feet. He crashed to the ground with a deep grunt.

There was a pause as everyone stared at the ringleader on the ground. I didn't even have a chance to think before the other two men left the woman and sprang towards me. Instead of running, she dropped her stance and slid to the ground against the tree, clutching her wound.

The two men attacked me as a duo. Even if they were alone, both of

15

them were bigger than me. I dodged and countered, blocking attacks and redirecting their strikes away from me. I hit back a few times, sending precise jabs into pressure points and joints along their body. I was trying to disengage them without hurting them too greatly. I drove the staff into their diaphragm, their jaw, and their feet. The more I hurt them, the angrier they became. Eventually, one of the men threw his dagger at my face, missing, then charged me, intending to tackle me with his whole body. With the staff, I guided his attack into the earth behind me, and he crashed into a limp heap on the ground. The other hesitated, then spoke.

'Where'd you learn all that?'

I said nothing, keeping my focus on him.

'I've never seen anyone fight like you before.'

I noticed his knife hand was slowly arching back.

'It's just strange because where I'm from people aren't always so—'

He threw the knife at me.

I intercepted its path with my staff, striking it mid-air. I heard it clatter and thump to the right.

'Simple tricks will not work so easily,' I told him.

The man smirked. 'Are you sure about that?'

Dread ran down my back like icy water. I realised, in that moment, that he wasn't trying to kill me.

He was trying to distract me.

A thick arm wrapped around my neck from behind, and a big palm pushed against the back of my head. I was yanked backwards and my toes lifted from the earth. The staff fumbled from my grip. I started to choke.

My attacker's breath reeked of something foul, and his voice erupted in my ear. 'Got ya, ya bald little bastard.'

His hold on me was like iron. I knew how to escape it, but before I could, his companion sprinted towards me. Without hesitation, he hurled heavy punches into my stomach, ribs, and face.

Pain wracked my body as my consciousness began to ripple and shimmer. I gulped for air that I could not reach. Before long I was out of breath. I didn't even have the chance to use the ring to save myself.

My senses dimmed. My sight dissolved into mushes of colour and motion. My hearing faded. Darkness swam from the corners of my vision, and nothingness swallowed me.

I was on the ground with my face pressed against wet blades of grass. I couldn't remember how I got there.

Slowly, my senses returned to me.

I was in a forest. I was being attacked. Someone needed my help.

I stirred, and rolled, and rose to my knees. Waves of screeching pain tried to force me down but I endured it and stood. The effort made me nauseous and I couldn't stand for long before I lost my balance and stumbled over. I sat up but didn't push myself further.

My eyes focused and I saw a confrontation ahead of me; men wearing armour, wielding clubs, beating the men in cloaks on the ground. They were guards, enforcers of the law. I remembered reading about them.

One of the men, a guard, squatted by me. He slapped my face lightly. 'Are you alright, boy?' he asked me.

'I'm hurt,' I mumbled, wiping the blood from my nose and mouth.

'Were you attacked by these men?'

I squinted as I focused my vision on the cloaked men. 'Yes.'

He looked my body up and down. 'Can you stand?'

'I think so.'

'On your feet, boy.' He offered a hand and I took it. The edge of a cry hissed through my teeth as the guard lifted me to my feet. He slung my arm over his shoulder and, slowly, he walked us towards a cart tethered to large animals.

'Is this yours, lad?' he asked, handing me my staff.

Relief washed over me. 'Yes it is,' I said, then took it from his hand. 'Thank you very much.'

'You're welcome,' he said with a smile.

I looked up at where he was taking me. 'Is that a carriage?' I asked him.

The smile on his face drooped. He seemed confused by my question. 'Yes… yes, it is,' he answered.

When I got closer I realised the animals were horses. They looked much different from the sketches in the texts, so I hadn't recognised them.

'Those are horses, yes?' I said. 'They are bigger than I thought.'

The man raised an eyebrow, then laughed awkwardly. 'Yes. They're beautiful creatures. Stupid, but beautiful.'

Behind us, I heard chains swinging and clinking. I turned around to see the three cloaked men walking in a line behind a guard. Iron shackles were fastened tightly around their wrists, binding them together. Chains linked the three men together behind the guard leading them, who gripped the end of the chains tightly in a gloved fist.

The man leading them, who had a bushy moustache and the air of a leader, looked down on me as he approached. 'You there, what were you doing here? Are you one of the mountain worshippers?'

'I am a disciple of the Order of Light,' I clarified. 'I descended the Gentle Mountains to journey across the world.'

The guard studied me silently, confused and annoyed. I got the impression he was not fond of me. 'Right. And how did you get involved in all of *this?*' He waved his hand at the beaten men.

A voice came from behind us. 'I can answer that.'

The woman hobbled up to us alongside the third guard, her arm slung over his shoulder and her other hand clutching bandages wrapped around her waist. 'These cowards ambushed me at the gates to Cobble, hoping to part me from my purse and my life, and chased me to the forest.' I noticed she spoke with an accent that was different from that of the guards. Her voice was as clear and smooth as glass, and every word she said was refined and deliberate. 'One of the rodents managed to wound me. I fought them back with my own blade, but I would have eventually bled enough of my strength for them to gain the advantage.' She looked to me with ice blue eyes. 'The mountain man intervened, and saved my life.'

The leader guard set his gaze on me. He studied my appearance with a kind of distaste. 'What's your name, mountain man?'

'I am Kiro,' I said.

He leaned closer and said firmly, 'Listen... *Kiro*... the next time you come across trouble it's best you stay out of it. You call for us, you understand? Otherwise, you're going to get yourself and others killed.'

I didn't know what to say to that.

The guard moved along, dragging the captured thieves behind him. He hooked the end of the chains to the back of the cart.

The friendly guard nudged my shoulder and gestured me to take a seat in the back of the cart, before heading up to the front to join the leader.

I hopped onto the back, joined by the third guard and the woman.

The friendly guard grabbed hold of the reins then, with a flick of the leads and a commanding shout the length of a syllable, the horses set off. A chorus of clip-clops and the churning of the sturdy wooden wheels filled the air, and we were moving out of the grove.

I looked to the thieves, wondering why they were not sitting with us, and that was when I saw them being dragged along by the horse cart. The pace of the horses was hard for them to keep up with, and they stumbled along behind us; the choice to walk at their own pace stolen from them.

'Sir,' I said to the guard, remembering the polite manner of address. 'Why are those men not sitting with us?'

The guard and the woman both looked to me with a blend of shock and confusion.

'What?' he said as if I had insulted him. 'You want these killers to sit with you?'

His reaction immediately cut down my courage. I knew I wasn't wrong to feel concern, but I still felt like an idiot. 'I just thought they'd sit with us, because they're people, like us,' I said quietly. 'They're not dangerous anymore now that they're captured.'

'Those brutes are not like us,' the woman objected. 'They are murderous animals subject to their lowest instincts.' She pointed at their chains. 'This is a *merciful* punishment.'

My cheeks were burning hot. 'They are not animals, they are just misguided people. If we treat them without kindness and mercy, they will live without kindness and mercy. All life is precious, and—'

This time, the guard interrupted me. 'I know you mountain folk are all living that peace and harmony nonsense up there, but here in the real world it's a little more complicated than that,' he said flatly. 'If we hadn't come to save you two, those men would have killed you. They wouldn't have shown you any mercy or kindness. They are dangerous and will stay where they are.'

Shame dropped my gaze to my feet. He was right. The woman and I were lucky to be alive. I had not expected people to be so violent. I thought my training in the Order would have prepared me for any danger I might face, but already, I had nearly lost my life.

I had trained in the techniques of Obadi for thirteen years. How could I have lost control of the situation so quickly? The trauma in my body and mind left by the violence fed the doubts and disappointments churning in my heart. I thought I would have been better than this. I *should* have been better. I hadn't even left the Gentle Mountains yet, and already I almost failed. *Am I actually ready for this journey? Am I even worthy of being a master?*

These doubts weighed on my mind as we left the shade of the trees and entered the open green plains at the bottom of the mountain. I had never seen this grass up close before, only from the Sanctuary. I imagined it soft and lush, but it was actually rougher than I thought. The sound of the horses' steps changed as we moved onto a yellow dirt road. Dirt and pebbles crunched under the wheels of the cart. I looked back at the prisoners.

The dirt and dust lifted from the ground by the cart blew at the prisoners in thin mists that plastered against their cloaks and sheening, dejected faces. One of the men tripped and the rest were nearly pulled off balance by him. I felt sorry for them. I noticed the guard had seen me watching the prisoners. When we met eyes, he shook his head as if to tell me not to do or say anything.

We arrived at the town gates after a short trip. Cobble, I was told, was quite a small settlement, but it was larger than the entirety of the Sanctuary. The town was surrounded by stone walls made of individual bricks stacked atop one another, which rose just above the height of the buildings and houses inside. I was amazed by the size of the place; the lively movement, the ceaseless noise, and the potent smell. People I had never met, of all shapes and sizes, wearing clothes I had never seen before, and doing work I had only read about in texts. A lot of them were armed with crude swords on their hips and scowls on their faces. A group of boys who were chasing each other with sticks in the streets were stunned by the sight of me, and laughed as they pointed at my head. I didn't see how I could be funny, but it was nice to bring laughter to the world.

The friendly guard pulled gently at the reins and spoke a few simple commands to the horses to have them stop outside a tall building built of logs and stone, which I later learned was a station where the guards operated. The guards hopped off the front of the cart and collected the exhausted prisoners. The one sitting with the woman and I asked us to come inside and explain the story to their scribe.

The scribe was an old, bony man with thin grey hair, wrapped in brown and grey robes. He sat at a desk in a dusty, dimly lit room inside the station. On the table, stacks of paper and scrolls were strewn about in an order visible only to him. The woman, who introduced herself as Friss Crow, sat across from him first, and told her story. As he listened to her, he wrote on a fresh scroll with a fluffy quill he dipped in a small pot of ink. It was oddly pleasant to listen to it scratching against the paper as he transcribed her story.

Numerous times, he had to pause and ask her to repeat herself, followed by apologies and a remark about his declining hearing. Friss was understanding but grew more and more frustrated as he continued to stop her.

According to her, she had been returning to Cobble following a trip outside the town on matters of the local Count. When she returned to the town, she found the men waiting outside the walls. When they saw her, they approached her supposedly to ask for help. Once they got close, each of the men brandished a knife and demanded she give them all of her money. When she refused, they tried to stab her. She narrowly avoided the attack but was unable to escape unscathed and was slashed on her waist. She ran to escape them, leading her to the forest where she was forced to fight them off before the guards and I intervened.

The scribe thanked her, and she bid him goodbye before leaving. When I sat down to tell him my story, I found myself hesitating and losing focus as I recalled the violence in the forest. The strength would leave my voice and I would dwindle into mumbling until the scribe asked me to speak up. When we were finished, I apologised for being quiet then left, feeling tense and restless and full of dread for the long road ahead.

We had arrived at Cobble towards the end of the day. By the time I had left the station, the sun was hanging over the west, and the brilliant colours of the sunset were bursting across the sky. I admired them as I stepped outside, hoping to soothe myself. Outside the station, I noticed Friss waiting for me. She saw me, then approached.

'Pardon me,' she said politely, extending her hand towards me. 'I wanted to take the time to personally thank you for your bravery today. If it had not been for your timely intervention, it surely would have been my end.'

I hadn't properly noted her appearance until now. She was a slender

21

young woman who stood taller than me, with a perfect, upright posture that exuded great dignity. She had a long nose, thin lips, and sharp, ice blue eyes that seemed to emanate intelligence and a certain sense of superiority. She wore a dim blue hooded mantle around her shoulders that fell down her back, and a grey headscarf beneath her hood that concealed her hair. Under the mantle, she was dressed in well-fitting clothes; a buttoned waistcoat, black gloves that reached her elbows, and slim breeches with leather boots that rose up her shins. Attached to a leather belt on her hip was a long thin sword resting in a sheath. The hilt of it was exquisite; it was made of gold, or at least seemed to be, and the metal of the wrist guard was bent and shaped skilfully into elegant, curving lines that resembled the gentle strokes of an ink brush. At the top of it, embedded in the pommel, was a small red gem, shaped like a tear. Even for a weapon, it was beautiful.

I bowed my head. 'I am just glad I could help.'

After a few seconds, she frowned and her eyes sharpened into something cold and unfriendly. Abruptly, she withdrew her hand.

I noticed the change in her. 'Did I do something wrong, sir?'

Friss went to speak but closed her mouth. After a brief pause, she muttered, 'I suppose, since you're one of the men on the mountain, you are not familiar with the world's customs, are you?'

'Not really,' I admitted.

'When you meet someone, it is polite to shake their hand.'

My eyes widened. 'Really?' This had never been mentioned in the texts.

'Yes. It is a way of greeting a person with respect,' she explained. Then, after a short pause, she added, 'And I am not a sir. I am a lady. You call women "madam", not "sir".'

Heat lifted in the skin of my cheeks. 'Oh, I'm sorry. I didn't know that.'

'Don't fret over it.' She gestured to me. 'Tell me your name again, if you will.'

'I am Kiro,' I said. 'Your name is Friss Crow, yes?'

She hesitated, then glanced around us. From the look on her face, she seemed nervous. She made a decision in her mind, then moved close to me and spoke quietly.

'Friss Crow is the name I use, but it is *not* my true identity,' she whispered. 'My real name is Viella Vanclaude.'

Chapter Four

Viella Vanclaude

Over these many dreadful years, I have come to enjoy taverns like this, even if they are beneath me. I have observed that commoners have some unique wit to them in a raw, instinctive sense, given their disposition to compose such comfortable scenes with simple elements. Fresh bread, roasted meat, and sweet mead coupled with the warmth of a hearth and the good company of friends, and a decent tavern makes for a pleasant place of rest.

The bald boy in white sitting across me was hardly a friend, but after his service, my company and a meal were the least I could offer him.

'How are your wounds?' Kiro asked me. 'Do they still hurt?'

'The pain is faint now,' I said. 'Thank you for your concern, and your intervention. If not for you, it would doubtlessly be much worse.'

'It is my honour to have served you.'

'And mine to repay the debt.' I indicated the meal I bought him, which he had been shy to enjoy. 'Eat, please. Nourish yourself.'

His gaze fell on his food, but his hands remained folded on his lap. 'I… I don't feel hungry.'

'You will if you don't eat.'

He picked up a piece of bread and nibbled at it.

'You seem troubled,' I pointed out to him.

His eyes were fixed on the bread, but he was seeing something else. 'The violence in the forest, it... I had never seen such a thing before. It has shaken me.'

He truly did seem unsettled. 'Don't dwell on the memory, young man. It's over now, and we're alive. That's what matters,' I told him. 'How old are you?'

'Yesterday marked me seventeen.'

I raised an eyebrow. 'Quite an entrance into adulthood. And you've never witnessed a fight before?'

He took another tiny bite of his bread. 'I grew up sparring with my fellow disciples. I have been trained to fight but... death was never a possibility.'

I peered down into my cup of mead. 'Yes, the real world is like that.'

'Why do you call yourself Friss Crow?'

He said it too loud for my comfort. I almost lunged over the table as I leaned over to him. 'Keep your voice *down*,' I hushed him.

He recognised the urgency in my voice. 'Oh, I'm sorry,' he said quietly, his head receding into his shoulders. '*Why do you call yourself Friss Crow?*' he whispered.

'I hide my true name because...' Years of suppressed anger balled my hands into fists. 'I have no other choice. I *have* to live as Friss Crow.'

He leaned forward, concerned. 'Why don't you have a choice?'

I knew I shouldn't have told him. I knew it was a mistake. It just seemed iniquitous to deceive him, the boy who had risked his life for me, a stranger. And perhaps, it had simply been too long since I'd been able to introduce myself with my true name. I just needed someone to know me for who I truly was.

I sat back in my seat and brought the cup of mead to my lips. 'I can't tell you here. Please, if we are going to talk, I much prefer to talk about something else.'

He blinked curiously at me, then nodded his head slowly. 'Very well, madam.' He picked up the mutton and took a bite out of it. While chewing, he looked around. 'Many people are looking at me. Do they know me?'

I surveyed the room with a sweep of my eyes, searching for any suspicious faces. I did notice a few sidelong glances, but not at me. I cut a piece of mutton for myself. 'No. You just look strange to them.'

'Strange?'

I finished chewing before I replied to him. It occurred to me that I was going to have to explain many simple concepts to him. 'Yes. Have you not noticed that you look different to everyone around you?'

'I never gave my appearance much thought.'

'Perhaps you should try.'

'You think so?'

'Of course!' I said. *How was this not obvious?* 'Your appearance is not to be taken lightly. It is how the world perceives you.'

'True self is beyond the physical,' Kiro said, his tone shifting to something stronger, more assured. His words sounded practised and formal, as if he had rehearsed them for hours. 'The depths of our soul reach far deeper than our appearance would suggest. Visage is secondary to the true self.'

I smirked, stifling my amusement at his naivety, and took a sip of my mead. Nothing he just said sounded like words he had thought of himself. 'Yes, but again, how you look is how the world sees you. If you want to be respected, you must dress and behave in a way that commands respect.'

And so I took a moment to note his bizarre appearance. A word with the boy would be unnecessary to determine his distant origins. Kiro was shorter than me and had a completely bald head, as smooth as an egg. The only hair on his body I could see were his eyebrows. He had wide, curious brown eyes, a gentle resting smile, and a proportionate, modest face. When he spoke, his voice was soft and gentle like a spring breeze. He was dressed in simple white robes fastened at his waist by a white sash, with loose sleeves that ran down the length of his arms to his wrists. He wore leather sandals on his feet, and puffy, airy trousers that tucked into linen straps wrapped tightly around his shins. His clothes were completely white and plain, except for a small symbol that rested over his left breast; a simple black circle, split in half horizontally by a line, with the lower half divided by another line down the middle. It resembled an O with a T inside it. Though they had been in pristine condition, the incident in the forest had left some faint green, brown, and crimson streaks that stained his clothes. And despite his obvious predilection for a plain wardrobe, on his right hand he wore a rather nice silver ring, boasting a splendid sky-blue jewel. I found it to be a peculiar detail, especially for a commoner who so proudly flaunted his humility.

I had some curiosities about him. 'So why were you in the forest?'

Kiro sipped at his mead. 'I was descending the Gentle Mountains to begin a journey to the end of the world.'

I squinted at him. 'Forgive me – the end of the world?' I couldn't discern if he was serious or not, then I remembered he was one of those mountain people and the answer seemed less ridiculous.

'Yes, madam.'

'Why?' I could only ask.

'To find the ultimate truth, so I can become enlightened, and then ordained as a master,' he explained casually. 'Have you ever been to the end of the world, madam?'

I thought this wretched little village *was* the end of the world. 'What do you mean by that? Advenia is a continent, it has ends all around it.'

He stroked his chin. 'My master told me to travel east. I assume the east eventually ends at some place?'

I realised what he may mean. 'You may be thinking of the Edge. Yes, there is a cliff face to the far east of the country that one could call "the end of the world". They say the skies and seas meet as one there.'

His face lit up and he sat up straight. 'That must be it!' he said, louder than I was comfortable with. 'Do you know what's there?'

'I have never been there before, Kiro,' I said flatly. 'Supposedly, it has a remarkable view and some ruins nearby, but nothing else.'

He stroked his chin. 'Master said I would find the ultimate truth there. Maybe there's something there I need to see or collect.'

I shrugged. *A journey to the end of the world to find the ultimate truth* sounded utterly absurd to me. But even though he was evidently naïve, he had a good heart, and I had to afford him my respect.

And my concern. 'Are you so certain you want to travel there?'

'Without a doubt, yes.'

'Are you aware of how long this journey will take you? You will die if you try to walk that distance, especially alone.'

'I know it will be difficult,' he said, his eyes falling to the food on his plate, 'but it is important to me. I have dreamed of becoming a master since I was a child, so I can pass on the knowledge of the Order to a new generation. I will do what I must to achieve that dream.'

I leaned back in my seat, the old wood creaking with the movement. 'Since you were a child? How long have you lived up in the mountains?'

'All my life.'

I was surprised. I thought only old lonely men climbed the mountain to join the monks. 'Really? So you were born into the clan?'

'We're not a clan. We're an ancient order,' he corrected me. 'And, not exactly. I was found on the steps to the Sanctuary as a baby, and my masters took me in and raised me.'

I studied his face. 'Have you ever come down the mountain before?'

'No.'

Disbelief stole my wit from me for a moment and I gawked at him. 'So you've been sent to fend for yourself in a world you know nothing about?'

He shook his head. 'I have studied Advenia's history and cultures in our texts. I've seen maps. I do know some things.'

His youthful ignorance invoked an urge in me to protect him. I wondered if some mad drivel he heard up on that mountain had manipulated him to risk his life on this absurd quest. I felt it necessary to warn him. 'With respect to your bravery today,' I began delicately, careful not to suggest ingratitude, 'I cannot agree with you. There is still much you do not know, and where ignorance leads, death awaits. You didn't even know to shake hands with me when we met. You must agree with me, yes?'

He nodded shamelessly. 'There are gaps in our knowledge,' he admitted openly, folding his hands on top of the table. 'This is a natural consequence of our history, but I will learn much in my travels.'

I was not convinced. I leaned forward. 'Please understand that I appreciate what you did for me today, Kiro, but without the guards, we both would have died. Are you certain you can take care of yourself on your journey?'

His gaze dipped. 'Am I certain? No,' he said after a pause. 'But every failure is an opportunity to learn, and I have learned from today. I will be better next time.'

I sat back in my seat. 'But you have been trained to fight, yes?'

He thought on it. 'Yes. In a way. We use a practice called Obadi to discipline and train the body and mind. Obadi teaches us to redirect our opponent's energy away from ourselves. To evade, and disengage. We use it to protect ourselves and our opponent. Humans are not our enemy, so fighting is not the first purpose of Obadi. We use it primarily to unify the mind and body, to train them both and keep them healthy.'

I scoffed inwardly. What an absurd idea; training to fight with the expectation it will never be necessary. 'Why would you want to protect your enemy?' I asked him. Briefly, I imagined where I would be if I spared even a thought to all those who had tried to do me harm. 'If a man is trying to kill you, why would you care what happens to him in a fight to the death?'

My question seemed as preposterous to him as his answer did to me.

'All life is precious, madam,' he touted that phrase once more. 'It is not the way of the Order to bring death. We live to protect the beauty of life while we can. Life is a beautiful gift, but a fragile one, all too easily shattered in the wild whims of anger and hate.'

'And what if you *must* kill?' I was not satisfied with his answer. 'What if this man will stop at nothing to see you die? What if the only way to save yourself and others was to end your enemy's life?'

Kiro looked at me for a moment, and without an ounce of doubt in his voice, he said, 'There is always another way.'

I almost did not want to shatter his perception of the world. Truth be told, I found him to be a fascinating specimen; a boy who had grown up in a world entirely separate to reality. In a quiet home high up in the mountains, high above the grim truths of the real world. I almost envied the simplicity of such a life, and as my fingertips danced atop the hilt of Rosethorn, I wondered what it would be like to live without any greater destiny beyond. 'Do you know who your parents are?' I asked him.

'Sorry?' Kiro looked up from his food. 'I didn't hear what you said, madam.'

I looked into his eyes. 'Do you know who your parents are?'

'No.' He returned his attention to his plate.

I was taken aback; by the brusqueness in his manners and complete disinterest in his family. 'Don't you care to find them?'

He shrugged. 'The Masters did not see anyone when they found me, so there are no clues to follow. I am not interested in finding them anyway, madam. They did not want to, or could not, raise me. I am not concerned with who they are. The people who raised me are my family.'

His reasoning was understandable, if a little apathetic. 'Well then. I am surprised you are not at least curious.'

'If I knew who they were, I wouldn't say no to the opportunity to meet them.' He upturned his palms. 'But, I don't. So, I can't. It doesn't bother me.'

I admired his sensible perspective, but wondered if it was perhaps a shield for deeper wounds. I decided not to press him. 'Fair enough.'

'May I ask you a question, madam?' He put his fork down, then spoke quietly. 'You speak differently to the other people here. Why is that?'

I took a moment to again survey my surroundings.

No one was listening. A group of men across the room were howling with laughter, exchanging jokes over their beers. The tavern's owner was sweeping the floor. No one was looking in our direction.

I looked back to Kiro and studied his face.

I decided I would trust him.

I leaned over the table and gestured for him to do the same. As he did, I whispered, 'I hail from across the continent, from the city of Azale. I came here to Cobble because my life was in danger. I needed to hide.'

'Why are you in danger?' he asked under a breath.

I leaned back into my seat. 'I cannot say. At least, not here. Cobble is not safe for me anymore.'

And as the words left my lips, the heavy realisation fell on me and I became silent.

I have nowhere left to run.

I am cornered by enemies I cannot see.

I felt alone, and cold, and terrified.

Kiro sensed the change in me. 'Are you well, madam?'

I steeled myself. 'I am fine.'

He thought for a moment. 'Why are you in Cobble if it is not safe for you?'

'It *was* safe,' I told him, keeping my voice low. 'For a time. But as you already know...' I laid a hand over the bandages wrapped around the wound on my waist. 'They even managed to find me here. I was here for six years as "Friss Crow". I even found work as a clerk for the local Count. And now I will have to leave. Perhaps even devise a new name.'

'*They?*' Kiro cocked his head as he pieced the clues together. 'You lied to the scribe,' he deduced. 'Those men weren't thieves, were they?'

I shook my head. 'They were assassins,' I whispered.

He looked scared for me. 'Where will you go?'

'Somewhere far.'

'Azale?'

I scoffed. 'Into the den of my enemies?' I shook my head. 'Of course not.'

He pressed his lips. 'Azale is your home, yes?'

'It was.'

'Will you ever return there?'

'I will return, eventually. When I am ready.' My hand gripped the hilt of my family's blade resting in its sheath against the table. 'I have studied and practised the art of the sword since I was a child. Even after I fled Azale, I have continued honing my ability according to the techniques of my family. I have been training myself for the long journey home.'

Kiro stroked his chin. 'Since you were a child?'

'Indeed. I am doubtlessly quite skilled now, but... still imperfect.'

He hummed then asked, 'When will you be ready?'

My eyes dropped to Rosethorn. My fingers tapped on the pommel as I dwelled on the thought. 'I do not know,' I conceded. 'A few more years.'

'But for now, you will continue to run?'

'I have no other choice.'

Kiro was silent for a moment, then said, 'Madam, if I may, I would like to offer you some advice.'

I looked in his eyes. 'Proceed.'

'I don't think that's a wise decision. Forgive me, but if you continue to run, you will never find peace. Your problems will follow you everywhere you go until you finally face them.'

I sharpened my words. 'Are you calling me a coward, boy?'

'No,' he said softly. 'I believe you are simply misguided, and I want to help you by sharing my advice.'

Misguided. As if this mountain boy could understand even a smattering what I had endured. 'And what advice is that?' I questioned him, daring an answer.

'You talk about your home as if it is something you can never see. I can tell it brings you great sadness. I see the pain in your eyes when you talk about pretending to be someone you're not. To fill this longing in your heart, you must not run further away. You must embrace your true identity, and return to your home.'

My gaze fell to the floor and I sighed. 'If only matters were that simple.'

'So you will never go back?'

'No, I will. Just not yet. I am not yet prepared. The journey is a long and perilous one, and I am still not quite ready.'

Kiro smiled. 'We are never ready for the journey of our lifetime, madam. Not until the day we take the first step. And that is how a journey is walked; one step at a time.'

I contemplated his words as my gaze settled on my empty plate. They were simple and few, but resounding.

I decided he was right. What profit did I stand to gain by waiting any longer? Until I began my journey, the promise of revenge I whispered to myself was nothing more than a desperate delusion.

It became clear to me, and when it did, shame weighed down heavily upon me; *I am ready, but I have fed myself lies, because I am afraid.* That was the truth of why I had hidden for so long. *A few more years*, I would tell myself, *and then I will be ready.* How many years does one need to understand a sword?

No. I would not disgrace myself any further. I would not be made a fool by cowering away in the corners of the world under the name of a commoner. I would not be denied my home, my birthright. I would not allow the deceit of my enemies to corrupt the city I was destined to lead.

'You are right,' I told him, a new resolve turning my hands into fists. 'I am not going to hide any longer. On the morrow, I will begin my journey home.'

He smiled. 'May good fortune await you, madam.'

Even with this newfound determination, the path ahead was daunting. To cross such distance, a woman alone, I hoped that I should have the strength to spare for when I arrived at Azale. And though I was most certainly capable, I was ultimately but one.

Then an idea struck me.

'I have a proposal for you,' I said to Kiro. 'Come with me.'

He blinked curiously. 'To where? Azale?'

'Yes. I will head for it tomorrow at dawn, but the journey alone will be challenging and dangerous. Together, we are stronger.' For reasons that eluded precise wordings, the prospect of him travelling all alone troubled me. I had an inexplicable urge to protect him, so I persisted for both of our sakes. 'Our destinies are aligned for now, Kiro. It is safer to travel together, but I will not impose a decision on you.' I leaned back. 'How do you reply?'

He thought on it, then a warm smile surfaced on his lips. 'I say I would be honoured to travel with you, madam.'

'Glorious. Then it is agreed.' I extended my hand.

This time, he shook it firmly.

Chapter Five

Light of Dawn

Viella took me to her home to stay for the night. We agreed to begin the journey at dawn tomorrow. Her home was a small cottage shadowed by trees near the outskirts of town, tucked away around a corner and down a hill. It had a flourishing garden behind a fence, a pen for a few chickens, and was neighboured by only two other cottages.

She had two beds but lived alone. Her house was quiet and tidy, and smelled of dried ink and old books. She had many books and scrolls. There were rows of them on a small shelf and neat stacks of them in the corner on the floor. She told me reading was a necessary measure to keep the mind sharp, and I agreed with her. I asked if I could read one of her books. She said no.

Once we were inside, Viella took off her mantle and headscarf, and I saw her hair was an icy blonde colour so pure it was like snow, tied back into a bun. I was fascinated - I had never seen long white hair on a young person before, and she said it was a famous trait of her family, hence why she wears the cloak — to hide it.

I awoke before Viella, and slowly, delicately, made my way outside. I was careful not to disrupt her sleep. I meditated in the morning light until

Viella emerged from the house and told me to prepare myself.

The plan was to travel off the roads. Viella said the road north to the city of Ceren would be rife with bandits and anyone who may recognise her. Instead, for safety, we would travel directly east through forests and wildlands, then resupply at a small village near the southern coast before proceeding around a desert. My original plan was to travel on the roads, but I was happy enough to go through more natural landscapes even if they are not as convenient. We set out shortly after, walking out of Cobble through a gate that led to the farmland I had seen from the Sanctuary. We passed by some farmers, who had already begun their day of hard work. I waved at them, but most did not notice me. The two men who did put down their tools for a second as they stared at me from a distance, as if they were trying to figure out what I was. We kept walking.

Eventually, we arrived at the beginning of a forest. This one was darker than the forests in the Gentle Mountains. There were a lot more trees, and they were a lot closer together. They seemed older, sturdier, and were much darker than the colourful ones I had grown up amongst. Only a few beams of sunlight managed to penetrate through the treetops and reach the forest floor. I turned around to look back at where we had come from and was surprised to see that it was still bright in the world. Not only that, but for the first time in my life, I saw the Gentle Mountains from a new perspective. They were beautiful, and bigger than I could have imagined. They looked like colossal stone towers; steep, narrow columns of grey and white rock, adorned with clusters of flourishing forests, rising high up into the sky, high above Cobble and the world. Waterfalls poured from some of them into the misty, colourful valleys beneath them. I also understood, better than ever, why they were named the Gentle Mountains. They were massive, but at the same time so still, so serene. I squinted, and could barely make out the blue tiles of the Sanctuary's rooftops, just slightly noticeable through the gaps in the trees.

I stared at it for a moment. That tiny gap in the trees had once been my entire world. I couldn't believe how small it was.

As I gazed at the mountains, I wondered if Master Shien was watching over me at this very moment, as he had all my life. When I turned and entered the forest, following behind Viella, I realised this was the point where, if he was, he would not be able to see me anymore.

The deeper we ventured into the forest, the more I checked behind us to make sure Cobble and the Gentle Mountains were still there, just beyond the trees. Each time I looked, I saw less and less of the world outside through the winding corridors of old oak, until eventually, I saw nothing behind me but a forest of dark, rising trees.

Chapter Six

The Trees of a Thousand Colours

Traversing through the dark forest took Viella and I the whole day. When night fell, we found a relatively flat place to rest. I gathered some sticks and wood and made a fire for us while we ate from our supplies – berries, bread, and turnips. The buzz and hum of insects were here in this forest, too, and even louder than in the mountains, but now it was joined by the crackle of the fire, and Viella's advice about Advenia and how I should behave. Much of it was useful and good to know. Some of it seemed to be superficial and unnecessary. It seemed to me that she held little trust in people.

We slept, very uncomfortably, clutching to our blankets on the ground. We had built a simple shelter out of branches and sticks, but it didn't do anything beyond covering our heads and shoulders. We woke up the next day, aching and tired, continuing on with unsatisfying sleep. I was hoping we would come across a town soon, but even if we did, I wondered if Viella would feel safe enough to stay there.

An hour or so after we began the day, we had travelled so deep into the woodlands it began to feel like we were on a different world. The trees were huge, ancient, and dense. Unseen animals whistled, chirped, and hummed almost melodically. The ground became lumpy and slanted as massive roots thick with moss twisted through the soil. The sky became just a few patches of blue here and there that managed to pierce the dark green veil of the treetops. From them, askew beams of sunlight speared through to the forest floor. Eventually, the trees we came across began to change. While the leaves and wood had simply been green and brown, they became vibrant with other colours – leaves of red, blue, indigo, amber, pink, orange.

Then we went down a slope and entered a forest of trees with milk white trunks that stretched up, tall and thin, up into lush treetops where there was a leaf of every colour swaying in the wind. Beneath them, the forest floor was vast and flat, and rich with flowers of every type I knew, then some more I didn't recognise. Poppies, roses, daisies, tulips, daffodils, all stretching out as far as I could see, like an endless lake of colours.

A breath escaped me. 'What is this place?'

'The Trees of a Thousand Colours,' Viella called them. 'Not many know of this place, so the nature is undisturbed. I remember travelling through here years ago. It is a pleasure to see it again.'

I knelt to smell a blue flower. The scent and colour reminded me of home. 'It's beautiful.'

'Indeed,' Viella said, 'but don't get distracted.'

Viella continued ahead, not looking behind her. She seemed determined to stay on course, and the idea of appreciating the natural beauty around us never seemed to cross her mind. I stood up and followed her.

'Madam,' I said.

'Yes, Kiro?'

'Are you able to tell me now why you are in danger?'

'Well…' Viella sighed, then pulled the hood and scarf off her head, revealing her white hair tied into a neat bun. 'I suppose we are safe enough now. There is no reason why anyone else would be this far out here.'

I caught up to her side. 'Who were those men who attacked you?'

'They were just assassins sent for my life,' she said. 'I didn't know them personally, and they were not the first.' She looked at me. 'You may have noticed that I walk and speak in a way that is comparatively unusual to the people of Cobble. The reason why is because I am royalty.'

The word sounded vaguely familiar but I wasn't sure of it. 'What is royalty?' I asked her.

We came across a running stream that snaked through the forest. The water was so clear it was hard to tell it was there at all. Viella and I stopped here to refill our canteens while she answered my question.

'The royalty are people of the highest noble bloodlines,' she explained as she held her canteen in the stream. 'There are four royal families in Advenia, and each rule over a city and region in the country. I am of the House Vanclaude, from Azale. I was the heir to my father's regency. That meant after my father died, I would accede his position and become Regent of Azale.' She sounded wistful in her explanation, a sort of longing in her voice. 'The Regents rule their respective regions, which consist of their city and nearby land. The King, who is chosen by the Regents, rules over the whole country. As Regent, I would be charged with the duty of ruling Azale, and advising the 33rd King on important matters. It is a position that comes with heavy responsibility, but also great status and power.'

'Are there thirty-three kings?' I asked. I wondered if I had underestimated how large Advenia was.

'No, there is only one and can only ever be one,' she said as if this was obvious. She stood up and carried on, and I followed behind her. 'He is the thirty-third King in history.'

'So there have *been* thirty-three kings.'

'Yes, but never mind the King for now, he's not important. What's important is I was heir to a position of great power.' She glanced back at me from over her shoulder. 'Are you following so far, mountain boy?'

I tripped over a wayward root, and after regaining my balance, answered, 'I believe so.'

'Glorious.' Then as she spoke, her words became a darker colour; heavy and grey. 'When I was fifteen, my father... my father became gravely ill. Everyone knew his time was soon, and suddenly people were paying a lot more attention to me. My father's advisors took care of me, made strides to correct my posture, speech, and demeanour. We all knew that inevitably I would have to step up to take my father's place. It was something I had been prepared for my entire life.'

Then, she paused, and for a long time, was silent. Her pace slowed

39

until she was standing still, her eyes staring off into a place that wasn't here.

'Are you well, madam?' I asked when I became concerned for her.

She blinked, and her focus returned to me and the forest. 'Yes,' she said softly. 'Eventually... my father's time came. A few days before I was to be officiated and become regent... a cabal of traitors conspired to kill me. Someone who I... who I thought dearly of... saw a phantom entitlement to my rightful role and wanted it for herself. A servant, Gerard, overheard her plans and...' She drew in a slow, deep breath. 'He smuggled me out of the palace, and out of the city. He saved me. That was eight years ago... and every day since has been one of fear and hiding.'

Telling her story seemed to open old wounds in her, and she became forlorn.

'What happened to Gerard?' I asked. 'Where is he now?'

There was an ever so slight wince in Viella's blue eyes, then she looked ahead, a new expression of resolve on her face. 'We need to keep moving,' she said quietly, marching away.

I knew immediately she was in pain. I wanted to help her, but I had no idea how. As I followed behind her, thinking of what words I could offer to ease her pain, she stopped suddenly.

'Is something wrong?' I asked.

When I caught up to her, I looked up at her face. Her eyes were darting around, and she seemed tense. She dragged her hood over her head.

'Stay calm,' she said, grabbing the hilt of her sword. 'I think someone is here.'

We were standing in a sunlit clearing in the forest. We were surrounded by an audience of colourful, vivid flowers, all swaying silently beneath the towering columns of rainbow trees. After seeing Viella's face, and hearing the seriousness in her voice, the forest's beauty began to feel ominous.

I slowed my breathing and listened carefully, searching through the trees for any sign of another person.

From somewhere behind us, somebody coughed.

Viella and I spun around, her sword drawn and my staff in my hands. '*Show yourself, coward!*' Viella bellowed at a tree.

From behind the tree, a man's voice swore quietly.

Then from behind another tree to our right, another man groaned.

'*Nice going, Nell!*' he grumbled before revealing himself. The man was skinny and pale, and had messy brown hair and a patchy beard. He was garbed in black leather armour and held a sword in his hand.

The man hiding in the tree in front of us, Nell, stepped out. He was beefy and balding, and also dressed in leather armour. A large axe in his hands dragged against the ground as he showed himself. 'Sorry, lads,' he said sheepishly. 'That was my bad.'

Viella and I turned so both of them were in our sight. 'Of all the assassins sent for me,' Viella said, 'you two are, without doubt, the most incompetent.'

A third voice spoke from somewhere behind us. '*I don't disagree.*'

The voice belonged to a tall man standing several feet behind us. The man had striking green eyes and long blond hair that fell just past his jaw. He wore a handsome smile, and a dark green coat that hung loosely on the broad frame of his shoulders. The sleeves were limp and empty, and his arms were instead propping his hands onto his hips. Under his coat, he wore a ruffled white shirt under a vest of boiled leather. His shirt tucked into charcoal black trousers that ran down to knee-high boots of the same colour. Linked to his belt was a sword in a leather scabbard, and something else that was in a smaller sheath. He looked like a friendly and dependable man, making it hard to believe the real reason he was here.

'Hey there, dummies,' he greeted us with an out of place friendliness. His voice was deep yet smooth, rich with confidence and charm. His accent was strange, too. He and the other two men sounded completely different to everyone I had met so far. 'How ya doin'?'

Neither of us responded. I didn't know what that question meant.

The man cocked his head. 'No response?' He sounded disappointed. 'I would've thought some pompous kingling like yourself would have lots to say.' He smiled then pointed at Viella's head. 'By the way, Miss Vanclaude, you can go ahead and take off your hood. We already know who you are.'

Viella's face hardened with contempt as she ripped the hood off. I was worried his friendliness was another distraction, so I made sure to keep my eyes on the other two men, ready for anything they might try.

The leader looked at me and pressed his lips. 'But I don't know you. What's your name, baldy?'

'My name is Kiro,' I said, my eyes switching between the three of them. 'Who are you?'

'Hey, why are you bald?'

The question didn't seem relevant, but I thought if we kept talking, maybe we could end this peacefully. '…We shave our heads in the Sanctuary.'

His eyes creased into slits. 'Uhh, what?' He made a confused laugh. 'Sanctuary? What are you talking about? Are you one of those religious guys?'

'What is… a guy?'

He widened his eyes. 'Yikes, you're a character.'

'Enough games,' Viella spoke up. 'What do you want?'

'Oh, don't you know who I am?' The man seemed surprised. 'Most people do, snowball.'

'I am not most people. Lowlife criminals like you do not merit my attention.'

'This criminal certainly should.' He winked. 'The name's Synn.'

I saw a flicker of surprise flash across Viella's face for a brief second before she restored her composure.

Synn seemed to notice it, too. 'I can see you've heard of me. So you are like most people after all.' I made note of his keen eye.

'I do know of you,' Viella said. 'Zephelia must be getting desperate to resort to mercenaries.'

'I haven't the slightest idea who you're—' Synn stopped himself mid-sentence, then asked, 'Wait, what do you mean *desperate?*'

'Hiring you to kill me,' Viella said. 'I never imagined she could sink so low as to hiring the likes of you.'

Synn chuckled. 'Ooh, hurtful. That's probably going to be the closest you get to wounding me today, Vanclaude. I mean, look at you. You're hardly the sword-swinger type. You look like a boy who just found a cool stick.'

Viella pointed her blade at him. 'Come a little closer, and I will demonstrate precisely how lethal I can be.'

Synn grinned, excitement lighting his eyes. 'That's the spirit! Let's get this started.'

He clapped twice.

For a moment, Synn stood there, hands on his hips, a smile dangling from the corner of his mouth as he stared at us. His friends looked between him and each other. Viella and I kept our focus on them. A second passed without a word or movement. Then another. And another. Synn's smile melted and he squinted at his friends.

'What are you doing, you idiots?' He swung his hands up. 'Why are you standing there?'

'Oh.' Nell sucked in his lips and looked embarrassed. 'We thought you wanted us to wait for your call before we jumped them.'

'I *did* give you the call! I clapped, dumbass!' He jabbed a finger at us. '*Get them!*'

'Shit, sorry.'

The two men sprinted towards us. I braced myself, putting aside my fears and lesser instincts. I steadied my breath and heart. I would not fail as I did before.

I focused.

The first to reach me was the man with the axe, Nell. He roared as he charged at me, his axe raised high above him.

Before he had the chance to bring it down, I jabbed the staff into his chest, robbing him of breath. He sputtered and gasped, and stepped off balance. He brought the axe down, cleaving through air as I stepped to the side. That was my opening. With a broad swing of the staff, I swept him off his feet. He crashed to the ground with a ragged whimper.

Viella engaged the swordsman. With one arm tucked behind her back, she stepped forward, sword raised at him, and countered his attacks. Though her sword was thinner than her opponent's, it was much more resilient. The swordsman stabbed, reeled back, and slashed at her, again and again. Viella parried his attacks effortlessly, like she was swatting away a fly, then made a lunge with her blade, opening a wound across her opponent's nose and cheek. He yelped and flung himself backwards.

'My God.' Synn's voice came from a little way behind us. 'Are you losing to a *woman*, Corron?'

I didn't want to use the ring, but if we couldn't end this peacefully then I wouldn't have a choice. 'Everyone, please! Stop this!' I pleaded with them all. 'We do not need to fight! Let's talk about this!'

'Shut up!' Nell belted. He raised the massive weapon behind his shoulder, then swung it down onto me.

I met the axe with the end of my staff and carried its momentum to the ground. It cleaved into the dirt and flowers and lodged itself in the soil. The man grumbled as he tried to pull it free, then roared as he let go of the axe and sprung towards me. I flung the end of the staff up, uppercutting his jaw. He hissed and stepped back, gripping his chin.

Again, Synn called out from afar. 'Nell! What are you doing!?'

Nell's hands curled into fists and his face twisted with rage. He plucked out a dagger from his belt.

I glanced over to check on Viella; she was much faster, much more skilled, than the swordsman Corron. She was hardly exerting herself, yet Corron's chest was heaving and his breathing loud and heavy. He was bleeding from his face and right arm.

'You don't have to do this.' I looked back to Nell. 'None of us have to fight. Please, let's sit down and talk.'

'Oh, give it a rest, kid,' Nell huffed. 'Don't make this harder than it has to be.'

I slung my staff around my back, an offer of peace despite all my fear. 'I don't want to fight you.'

Nell smirked, revealing yellow, crooked teeth. 'Makes it easy for me.' He lunged forward, the knife on course for my stomach.

As he got close, I stepped to the side and let my hands redirect him into the earth. His knife couldn't get close. He tumbled into a ball on the ground.

Suddenly he shrieked.

'Are you alright?' I asked him. I wasn't trying to hurt him that badly.

His breaths became rapid and shallow. He shrieked again as he slowly pulled himself up.

His knife was stuck into his thigh.

I gasped.

'You jank son of a bitch!' he blurted out in rage and pain. He grabbed hold of the knife.

'No, stop!' I shouted. 'It's in your artery, don't—'

With a roar, he ripped the knife out. A jet of hot blood spurted from the wound and splattered over the grass and some tulips. His eyes and mouth gaped in horror and he fell back over.

My knees wobbled and I covered my mouth. A sickness swirled in the pit of my stomach and clambered up my throat.

He rolled around, crushing flowers under his flailing, suffering as he bled to certain death. I ran to help him, but when I got close he shoved me away and off my feet. I heard another pained yell to my left. Viella had disarmed Corron and was holding the tip of her sword at his throat, forcing him to raise his hands and sink to his knees.

Synn groaned behind me. He sounded annoyed.

'Guess I gotta do everything myself,' he muttered.

I heard a click, and that's when I felt it.

A familiar energy, rising in the air.

I froze. 'Is that…?'

Ka-THUM!

A flash of blue light stung my eyes, and an ear-splitting explosion erupted behind me. Something blindingly fast ripped through the air. All of this shared in a single second. I flinched and shut my eyes.

The world fell silent.

When I opened my eyes, Nell had stopped moving. Smoke was rising from a smouldering hole in his chest. He was silent and completely, utterly still. My heart stopped.

He was dead.

I spun around to see Synn pointing a strange object at Nell's body. It was a weapon, but unlike anything I had ever seen. It had a grip and a long, bone white barrel about the length of my forearm. Tiny, intricate etchings in the barrel were alight with a heavenly blue glow. Smoke wavered and slithered from the end of the barrel and faded as it lifted into the air. Synn's face, cold and unfeeling, relaxed into something warm and gleeful.

'God, I *love* that sound.' He grinned. He pointed the weapon at Viella, who was frozen and staring agape. 'Out of the way, lady.'

Viella did not hesitate. She leapt out of the way of the swordsman.

From the barrel, a bolt of blue light exploded forth with an eruptive *bang* that rang in my ears and echoed through the forest. In a blink of an eye, the bolt of blue light pierced Corron's head, killing him instantly.

I shrieked and fell to my knees. That time, I felt the energy burst through the air and I knew for certain that what was happening was real.

'You know, I was pretty mad with how worthless those guys turned out to be,' Synn said, admiring the weapon. 'But whenever I get to use this bad boy, I feel a lot better. And now, I'm in a *great* mood.'

I was fixated on the weapon's glow. *How could this be possible?*

'What in God's name is that thing?' Viella asked with a shaky yell.

Synn chuckled. '*This*... this is a gun. This is the only one of its kind in the world.' He spun it on a finger and stuffed it into a pouch attached to his belt.

I was horrified. My hands were trembling but I could not steady them. The strength left my body and I knelt there, trembling and voiceless.

Synn pulled out some rope from his coat. 'But more importantly, snowball, I'll be needing you to put this on for me.' He tossed it onto the ground in front of him.

Viella scoffed. 'What kind of weakling do you take me for? I will not surrender to common scum like you.' With a single flick, she rid her blade of Corron's blood and pointed the tip towards Synn.

Please, I wanted to cry out. *Please stop.* But the words came out as a choked whimper. My whole body froze up as I stared at the dead men lying still in pools of blood-stained flowers.

Synn smirked. 'C'mon, girl. You're smarter than that. Put that fancy stick away and let me tie you up.'

'Take out that weapon of yours, swine. It's the only chance you have to survive me.'

'Nah.' Synn rolled his shoulders and craned his neck from side to side. 'I won't need it.'

Then he drew his own sword.

Viella growled and dashed forward.

Despite Synn's considerable size, he moved quickly. He was confident, but Viella was very skilled, and he did not expect that. She barraged him with a flurry of quick, precise attacks that forced him back. With a skilful weave of her blade, she cut his hand and disarmed him.

The smugness vanished from his face.

Viella pressed the attack, forcing Synn to dodge and retreat. But then she made a lunge that Synn sidestepped. He swept out her legs with a kick, sending her to the ground.

Seeing Viella on the ground snapped me out of my shock. My heart pounding, I sprung to action, sprinting towards Synn. He had his back turned to me. I fixed my gaze onto the gun on his belt. If I could steal that from him, I could force him to surrender. I wouldn't have to use the ring.

But as I ran towards him, he heard me coming and spun around to face me, swinging a fist into my ribs faster than I expected. The first blow stole my breath. The next smashed into my jaw and threw me dazed to the ground. I crashed into the dirt hard. Pain rocked my skull and chest.

Synn stood over me, reared his foot back, and kicked me hard in the groin.

Crippling pain shot up my body like I was being impaled by a lance. I screamed. I had never been hit there so hard before. This man did not fight as we did back home. There was no honour, no grace.

As Synn went to stomp on me, his eyes darted to his right just in time to see Viella's sword sailing for his face. He threw himself stumbling back, and the sword just barely left a cut on his cheek. He tripped and fell and rolled away.

Viella advanced forward, stepping over me. Synn scurried to his feet. She leapt close to him, driving the sword forward, but he surprised her by throwing his coat at her. She slashed at it, but it wrapped around her and she stumbled briefly before ripping it off and throwing it away.

There was another tremendous *bang*, and a flash of blue light.

Silence held the air. No one moved.

Until, slowly, Viella stepped back and gently placed her sword down on the ground.

She raised her hands into the air.

'You know,' Synn said through heavy breaths, holding the gun up at her. Blood trickled from the cut on his cheek. 'I was having fun… until you went for the face.'

Viella just kept breathing hard, saying nothing. Synn kept the gun pointed at her. A cool gust of wind rustled the trees and flowers around us.

'Now… you're coming with me, Miss Vanclaude.' He looked at me. 'And you…'

He began walking towards me.

'You're going to die here.'

'Wait,' Viella called out, her hands still raised. 'How much are you being paid?'

'None of your concern.'

'May I propose a counter offer?'

'I don't give a—'

'Triple.'

Synn stopped. He was standing over me. I could see on his face; she had his attention.

He glanced over his shoulder. 'Go on.'

Viella gestured to her sword on the ground. 'That sword is worth a fortune. Do you recognise it?'

Synn did not say anything.

'It is named *Rosethorn*,' Viella said, slowly approaching, her hands still raised. 'It is a family heirloom of the Vanclaudes, passed on from generation to generation. It dates back to the Last War and was used by the Rose Knight himself. The steel is unbreakable. It's the greatest sword ever forged.'

'Is that your offer?'

'Spare us both, and it's yours.'

Synn took in a breath as he considered it. He clicked his tongue.

'Not bad. Not bad...' he muttered to himself.

We waited for him to reach a conclusion.

Then suddenly he swung a fist blindly into Viella's face, sending her to the ground. Just as quickly, he aimed the gun at me.

'I'll pass.'

I took in a sharp breath and braced myself.

The gun clicked.

Nothing happened. No light. No sound.

Synn looked confused and tried again.

Another empty click.

He took a closer look at the weapon. 'Is this thing empty?' he asked himself. Suddenly he was chuckling. 'That's embarrassing. I forgot to re-load.'

I simply lay there, speechless. I couldn't believe what was happening. I could hardly grasp my senses.

He snapped open the gun's barrel, revealing six small, empty chambers.

'Sorry about that, baldy,' Synn said, smiling as if we were friends. Despite everything he had just done, he still had an air of charm around him. He reached into his pockets and pulled out some small metal pieces to put in the gun. 'This won't take long.'

'What... happened?' I asked, my voice barely a whisper.

'I ran out of damn bullets,' Synn muttered, shaking his head as he focused on inserting the pieces into a mechanism of the weapon. 'Super unprofessional of me.'

'So, the gun shoots out... those little "bullets".'

'Yup.' He inserted the last bullet into the gun, then snapped the mechanism back into the barrel. 'Thanks for waiting, by the way.'

'Wait...' I raised my hands, trying to summon the power in the ring.

But nothing responded to me. My fears were proven true.

I was too weak.

Synn pointed the gun at my head, closing one eye and smirking.

I squeezed my eyes shut.

There was a deep, hard-sounding *smack*.

I was still alive. I opened my eyes just in time to watch Synn's unconscious body fall over on top of me like a rag doll. I coughed as his weight punched the air out of my lungs. I rolled him off me.

'You repugnant *wretch*,' Viella spat, her words inflamed with hatred and fury. 'Who are you to lay your filthy hands on me, you *commoner scum!*'

She kicked him hard in the ribs. His body bounced but he did not make a sound. As Viella calmed down, her face twisted in pain. She shook her right hand then gripped it with the other, soothing her knuckles with her thumb. She looked to me. 'Are you well?' she asked.

'No.'

She offered a gloved hand. I took it in my own and she pulled me up. I gritted my teeth through the pain.

'What happened to him?' I asked her.

'I punched him in the back of the head.'

'Oh.'

We looked over him. Viella flipped his body over with her foot so that he was facing up. His eyes were shut and his mouth hung open loosely. He was unconscious. Viella went to retrieve her sword.

I could not believe myself. I had failed *again*, and the pains that wracked my body were a loud, blunt reminder of that. Why was I so scared to use the ring? If I had just given up on diplomacy, and immediately used divination, then Viella and I wouldn't have come so close to death. I might have even been able to save those two men. *They were dead because of me.*

But maybe I could redeem myself. Maybe the man lying at my feet could be saved.

I held onto my ribs as I lowered myself slowly to Synn, pain clenching my jaw tight.

'What are you doing?' Viella asked, confused.

'I'm... I'm checking if he's alive.'

'Why do we care? If I hadn't intervened, he would have killed you.'

I felt with two fingers for a pulse. I hovered my ear over his face and listened for breaths. 'He's alive,' I reported.

Viella scoffed. She leaned the tip of her blade against his throat.

'Allow me to remedy that.'

I acted fast.

'Stop!'

I gripped the sword and wrenched it away. Pain tore through my hand as the steel bit into my flesh, but I resisted the urge to cry out.

'Kiro, what are you doing!?' Viella shouted at me in shock.

I looked up at her, up into her eyes. 'Don't kill him!'

She looked back down on me, almost scared. 'What?! He was—'

'I'm sorry, madam, but I'm not going to let anyone else die today.'

There was a pause. Viella's eyes burned with anger.

'Who are you to give *me* orders?' she snarled. 'Release my sword, you imbecile!'

A cry slipped from me as I held the blade against her force, away from the man. Blood seeped between my fingers.

Viella's face morphed from anger to disbelief and bewilderment. She relented, and I let go of the blade. A sharp, stinging pain prickled from a bleeding slash in my hand.

'You baffle me, Kiro,' Viella muttered, her brow furrowed. 'To spill your own blood in shielding an enemy.'

'He is not... an enemy,' I said. 'He is a life, and all life is precious. Ours, and his.'

Viella shook her head and flicked her sword clean of my blood before sheathing it. She walked away, over towards Synn's coat on the ground, and searched through it. She plucked out a pouch, a knife, and a folded parchment. She opened it and began to read it.

I gazed at the forest around me, its beauty tarnished and stained by blood and death. I felt sick with pain and fear. I wanted to go home. I wanted to burst into tears right there and then. But I needed to take care of myself.

I reached into my satchel and pulled out the pouch of pomegen berries. I considered eating one. The aches and pains in my body were quite persuasive, and I was very tempted to take one. But I decided against it. My body was hurt, but I could heal it without using the pomegens. I couldn't risk wasting them.

So instead I pulled out the canteen, the knife, and the blanket. I cut a cloth from the blanket to use as a bandage, then cleansed the wound in my hand with some water. Once it was clean, I wrapped the cloth around it tightly.

Viella frowned as she read the paper. After a short while, she growled. '*I knew it.*'

'What is it?'

'It's a letter,' she said. She turned the paper so I could read it, then tapped a part of the writing. 'Look! This wretch was paid to kill me! Ten thousand prences!'

'Is... is that a lot?'

'It's a fortune,' she said. 'Read the bottom, what does it say?'

I squinted. 'It just says "Z".'

'*Precisely*, Kiro!' Viella exclaimed. 'This is Zephelia's doing! All of this! She is still trying to kill me after all these years, and now I have the evidence to prove it.' She started pacing around the clearing.

I frowned. 'Who is Zephelia?'

Viella stopped, then looked down on me. Suddenly her fervour was gone. 'Zephelia is my younger sister,' she said softly. 'She is the one who usurped my regency, the one who tried to have me killed.'

My eyes widened. 'That's your *sister?*'

She returned to pacing around. 'Zephelia is currently the Regent of Azale.' She waved the letter in the air. 'With *this*, I can topple her.'

I was still trying to imagine any reason why a girl would want to kill her own sibling. 'Why is your sister trying to kill you?'

She stopped and folded the letter, slipping it into a pocket in her trousers. 'Because as long as my heart beats, her rule is fraudulent. If I return to Azale alive, her crimes will be made apparent and she'll lose the regency.'

I had many questions for her, but my mind was frantic, and we had other problems to solve first. I took in a deep, shuddering breath to centre myself. 'What should we do?' I asked her, hoping an answer would clarify my own buzzing mind.

'You tell me, boy,' Viella said. 'Since you insist on keeping this scum alive, then I will let you decide.'

'I am not sure,' I admitted.

'Then allow me to kill him.'

'Madam.'

'He is dangerous, Kiro. Far too dangerous to keep alive.'

I thought about it, then looked around, searching for the gun. I found it on the ground near his hand, and, carefully, picked it up.

'Is this weapon common in Advenia?' I asked, holding it in my palms.

'No,' Viella said, staring at it. 'I haven't even a notion of what that is. I have never seen anything like it before.'

Strange, even Viella didn't know what it was. I had just assumed it was another thing that came about after the Order's archives ended.

'Without this, he… he isn't dangerous,' I pointed out. I thought of a solution. 'We'll take him with us to Azale.'

Viella's jaw dropped. 'What? Are you mad? He will try to kill us!'

'You said he was a criminal, yes?' I asked to be sure. 'Who is he?'

She glared at his unconscious body. 'He is a notorious mercenary, infamous for a legacy of extravagant crimes for which he has escaped justice.'

I peered at the ropes. 'If he has broken the law, then… I would feel obligated to ensure he meets justice and reforms to be a better man.'

Viella considered it, her face shifting and twisting as she pondered on it. Then her expression settled into begrudging acceptance. 'Fine. If you insist on keeping him alive, I suppose taking him with us to Azale is our only option.'

'I'm glad you agree.'

'And there *is* a generous reward for his capture. You can have it once he's been taken.'

I narrowed my eyes. 'People are given rewards for turning in criminals?'

'Only the worst of them.' She tossed the rope to me, and I managed to catch it despite some fumbling. 'Can you tie a good knot?'

'Oh, um, yes.'

'Marvellous. Bind his wrists.'

Chapter Seven

Synn

This wasn't the first time I had woken up with a killer headache, but still, I probably would've preferred to not have woken up at all over feeling *this* bad.

I was barely able to think straight, but I was conscious enough to ask myself *What the hell happened? Where are those two meatheads? Did those idiots betray me?* The idea those two scum-suckers had the audacity to backstab *me* was enough to piss me off, and before I remembered that I already killed them, I started imagining beating the two of them to a bloody paste. Then I got sad. And lonely. *Why is it that everyone I meet sucks?* It's so lonely being at the top – nobody can keep up with me. I miss Harox. Maybe I shouldn't have sold him out. Although, those Merasian whores were worth the price. What a night.

Then I realised I was moving. Which was weird – I couldn't even feel my legs yet, let alone anything else besides this damn pain in my head. How was I moving? Where the hell was I?

I opened those beautiful eyes of mine.

Blurs of green and brown. Not a great start.

Alright, time to retrace my steps, I decided.

I was in some weird, colourful forest. With the idiots, yes. We were looking for some wannabe royal bitch.

That's when I remembered; I had, somehow, lost a fight.

Slowly, as I came to, I got the vague sense of being carried by someone. I didn't think much about it. I just wanted to move.

I rolled to my side and immediately fell off something, hitting the ground hard.

'Don't move, swine,' said a snobby voice.

To be honest, I was more concerned with how much that hurt. I was not expecting that. My ribs didn't feel right.

Something sharp was poking into my throat.

My eyes finally did their job and focused. I saw a sword.

I followed the steel to the hilt, to a gloved hand, then up to some smug jank woman's face.

'Oh shit,' I grumbled.

I was on the ground in some forest with normal colours, with the woman we were hunting down standing over me, holding a fancy sword at my throat.

Something that looked like a huge egg popped into view.

'Are you alright?' The talking egg was actually a boy. He was bald, for some reason.

'No,' I groaned. 'G-gimme a second. Just trying to figure out what the hell's going on…'

The woman opened her mouth. 'You made a pitiful attempt on my life, you insolent swine.'

I forgot she was a talkative one.

'But you were effortlessly outclassed, like the—' Blah, blah, blah.

I was not in the mood for gutter talk. In that moment, I just wanted the gun.

I made a quick reach for it, but my left hand went along with the motions of my right and swung me off balance. I fell over and planted my face in the grass.

It was at that point when I realised they had tied up my wrists.

The woman started laughing that snobby *Oh-ho-ho I'm better than you* kind of laugh, complete with a little snort. The kid was just staring at me.

Oh boy, did I get pissed off.

'Would you shut your damn mouth?' I snapped. 'You're going to

54

regret tying me up, you dumb whore.'

And then I took a boot to the jaw. She could kick pretty hard for a woman, enough to rattle my senses as I hit the ground. The taste of dirt and blood filled my mouth.

The woman stomped her boot on the side of my head and weighed it down. 'Be silent, dog,' she sneered. 'You will not insult me.'

I spat out the dirt in my mouth. 'Oh yeah?' I smiled. I had a good one ready. 'You're stupid.'

She stomped on my head. It hurt and rang my ears, but I didn't give a damn.

'Eat shit and die, cow.'

Another stomp. More pain.

'Kingling whore!'

Another stomp.

'Get the *hell* off me!'

Screw the code, I thought. *I'm going to kill this arrogant bitch.*

The kid stepped forward. 'Madam, please, that's enough.' Gently, he pulled the woman off me and stood between us. She looked furious.

'Stay out of this, Kiro.' She tried to get over to me, but the kid held her back.

'Stop this, madam. Violence won't solve anything.'

'Unhand me!'

He was holding her back well. An idea came to mind and I couldn't help but grin.

'What's wrong?' I flashed her a smile. 'All tuckered out?'

'Hold your tongue, bastard!' she snarled.

I sat up and shuffled backwards as I kept it up. 'Dumb whore.'

She didn't like that one. 'Shut your mouth, you commoner rat!' She tried again to push past the kid, but he didn't give up.

'Madam!'

I shuffled back some more, my hands searching for a weapon on me. 'Look at you, you think you're so high and mighty, talking with fancy words. You're nothing but some arrogant little bitch.'

'Impudent cur!'

'Viella, stop!' the boy pleaded with her.

'My God, you're pretty desperate to get over to me, huh? Sorry but I'm not interested, sweetheart. I'm not really into *tavern wenches.*'

That was it for her.

She elbowed the kid in the face, then lunged for me, her sword ready to plunge into my throat.

I couldn't help but laugh. I wasn't expecting her to hit her own guy.

The sword came inches away from my face, then it pulled back.

The kid had got her in a hug from behind and threw the both of them backwards onto the ground.

I started laughing harder.

She completely lost it. 'Kiro! Let go! I'm going to—'

'Viella, please! Stop this!'

'Unhand me!'

'Don't let him provoke you!'

'He doesn't deserve to live!'

I started clapping as best as I could. 'Oh my God, this is hilarious!'

'Control yourself, Viella!'

'I said unhand me!'

'Not until you calm down!'

'Who are you to command me!?'

I copied her in a dumb voice. "'*wHo aRe yoU tO cOmMAnd mE!?*'"

'WRETCHED SWINE!' she screeched. She kept struggling and thrashing in the kid's grip but she couldn't get out of it. I was surprised because I had busted the kid up pretty badly. His nose was bleeding from the bitch's elbow, too. He was tough, I had to give him that.

The bitch's struggle continued for a while. I just sat there and watched her with a little smirk on my face. Occasionally I blew kisses her way. It was all I really needed to do to piss her off. Eventually though, she got tired and stopped. The two of them just sat there, staring at me, and panting.

After a long silence, I asked, 'We all calmed down now?'

Her face didn't change. She just kept staring angrily at me, like she was trying to kill me with the sheer force of her feelings.

Then, abruptly, she took a deep breath and her dagger eyes melted away. Suddenly she was calm.

'Kiro,' she said, her voice steady and cool. 'Would you unhand me now?'

'Are you going to try and kill Synn?'

'No. We had an agreement, remember? And I am not one to fall back on my word.'

The kid hesitated, then let her go. I was expecting her to immediately lunge at me, but instead, she stood up and brushed herself off, straightened her clothes, then walked away from us, towards a little cluster of trees and bushes.

Baldy looked at me silently. He wiped the blood from his nose.

I winked. 'Name's Synn. You are?'

'...My name is Kiro.'

'Nice to meet ya.'

'We have already introduced ourselves.'

'Did we?' I shrugged. 'Yeah, I don't pay much attention to dead people's names so apologies in advance if I forget yours again.'

'But... I'm not dead.'

'Oh, but you are,' I informed him. 'You guys killed yourselves the second you tied me up.'

He realised I was threatening him and offered nothing in response.

'Nothing?' I prodded him, looking for a reaction. 'You're boring.'

Still nothing.

'That's okay. I'll have you begging for your life by... I don't know, give me five minutes. Ten, tops.'

He stood up. Wow, he was short. 'You do not intimidate me.'

I chuckled. 'Well, aren't you a big, brave ten-year-old?'

'I am seventeen years old.'

'Seventeen? I don't believe you. Look at you, you surely can't be finished growing, right? You're tiny!'

He reached into a satchel slung over his shoulder and rummaged through it. He pulled out the gun.

I hid my eagerness to get that back behind a cool grin. 'Oh, you found the gun. I must have dropped it. Thanks, buddy.'

'Where did you get this weapon?' he asked me firmly.

Uh oh. Mister Serious.

'I made it myself,' I lied.

He went bug-eyed. 'Really?' He was honestly amazed. He actually believed me.

I went along with it. 'Sure did. I'm the only one in the world smart enough to have made such a thing.'

'How did you acquire its power?'

'Ha! Nice try, but I won't be revealing any trade secrets to you, you sly dog,' I laughed. 'But seriously, let's just cut to the point.'

Baldy seemed unsatisfied, as if he had many more questions to ask, but still he shut his mouth and nodded.

'I'm getting really annoyed sitting here with my hands tied together, so let's talk about what your plan is. Because if you dummies are going to kill me, I'd rather you get that done now instead of dicking around and wasting my time.'

The woman chimed in from over where she was standing. 'Oh ho, if you're waiting for death I'm afraid you'll have to adjust your expectations for a fate *far* worse,' she said with a pleased little smirk on her face. I'd be more irritated if I hadn't just realised she was actually pretty hot.

'So...' I smirked back. 'What have you got in mind then?'

For a second, she just smiled smugly at me, relishing the moment she got to drop whatever reveal she had in store. 'I know you are wanted in Azale, Synn,' she said, 'and I know there is an attractive reward for your capture.'

Honestly, I was expecting something way worse. 'You're going for that, huh? Here I was thinking I had finally met some smart people with morals and all that stuff.'

The bald ten-year-old got all agitated. 'We intend to deliver you to Azale, to answer for the crimes you have committed,' he said. 'The money isn't important.'

'Whatever you say, pal.' I shrugged. 'I wish the both of you good luck though, 'cos you're gonna need it.'

The two of them frowned. The woman squinted at me. 'What do you mean by that?'

'Well, as you already know, I'm pretty famous,' I said with my notorious smile. 'And even when I'm doing the best I can to stay subtle, this handsome face of mine can't help but draw some attention.'

'Enough,' the woman snapped. 'Cut to the point.'

'What I'm saying is there's probably some folks following me, also keen to get a slice of this,' I said, technically truthfully even though I hadn't seen anyone. 'And if they're following me, they're going to find you, *Miss Vanclaude.*'

Though she tried hard not to show it, I could see a glimmer of fear in her eyes, and in her tightly pressed mouth.

'Kiro,' she barked his name as she gathered her stuff. 'Change of plans. We will stay off the roads for a little longer.'

'Are you sure, madam?' the kid asked her. He looked nervous. 'We're going to run out of food soon, and we're getting close to that town.'

'We have no choice,' she said, glaring at me. 'Thanks to your little friend here.'

I gave her a wink and a smile. 'There's nothing little about me, snowball.'

She rolled her eyes. 'Keep an eye on your pet pig,' she grumbled as she walked off.

The kid turned to me. 'Will you walk with me, Synn?'

'What happens if I don't?' I asked, testing the waters.

'I can carry you if you can't walk.'

There was a sincerity in his voice I was not expecting. I had kicked this guy in the balls as hard as I could and still, he was offering to carry me. I was twice his size. It was a little surprising, and not much surprised me anymore.

I stood up, towering over him. 'Do you honestly think you can carry me?'

'Yes,' he said straight up. 'How do you think you got here?'

'I...' I stopped talking because he had a point. There's no way that skinny bitch could lift my ass. And something about the honest, straightforward way he said that made me think he wasn't bragging, or lying. 'You really carried me?'

'Yes.'

'After I kicked your ass?'

He paused.

'*Ass?*' He repeated the word.

'Yeah... have you...' I squinted at him. '...*not* heard that word before?'

'No.'

What a weirdo.

But I had to give it to him, he had spirit. And a humility that was hard to come by.

Maybe I'll play along for now, I thought. *At least until I can get my hands free.*

'Whatever,' I said. 'I'll just walk.'

'As you wish.' He bowed.

Yes, he actually bowed. What a guy.

I smirked. 'What was your name again?'

'Kiro.'

'I like you, Kiro. You're interesting.'

Vanclaude was getting impatient. 'What keeps you two delayed?' she called out from the top of a mound. She had already started walking off, as if she had assumed we were following right behind her.

'Sorry, honey!' I called back. 'Perhaps you hadn't realised, but the world doesn't revolve around you!'

'Just make haste!'

'mAke hASte!'

Her face scrunched up then she whipped around and carried on. Maybe she would finally figure out I wasn't going to listen to her.

'Kiro!' she barked, 'don't let him out of your sight!'

'Very well, madam,' he called back. Then he looked at me.

And I looked at him.

'After you.' I smiled.

'I must insist you go ahead,' he said politely.

Whatever. I shrugged and went along. 'So, baldy...' I looked down at him as I began walking. 'What's your two coppers?'

'What do you mean by "two coppers"?' he asked softly.

I was starting to think he had to be playing dumb. 'That means your story. You look weird,' I pointed out for him. I checked out the staff on his back, and imagined how long it would take him to use it if I attacked. 'You didn't know what "ass" meant. Or "guy", if I'm remembering right. Do you live under a rock?'

'I come from the Gentle Mountains,' he explained. 'I am a disciple of the Order of Light, and the reason we look strange to you is because we cut our hair and dress all in white to relinquish our vanity. It is a symbolic gesture.'

'That sounds stupid.'

'You are welcome to think that.'

I laughed. 'So, did you live on top of a mountain your whole life?' I asked as I tested the boundaries of my restraints. Damn knot was pretty tight.

'Not on the top, but yes. That is why I am here.' He explained something about travelling across the world but I wasn't really listening.

I was weighing my options of running away or waiting for another opportunity. I could handle two on one, especially these amateurs, but not while they had my gun and my hands tied up. I'd have to wait for them to sleep, or for a chance to snatch it.

'Synn,' the kid said, grabbing my attention.

'Yeah?'

'Why do you speak so strangely?'

I blinked at him. 'Wow, okay, asshole. I talk normally.'

'I don't mean to offend, but you sound different to Viella and the people in Cobble.'

'This is just how we talk where I'm from,' I told him. 'Kinglings like your girl up there like to sound all snobby cos they think they're better than us.'

'I see.' He was quiet for a while as he thought of another question. 'What is your profession?'

'I'm a bounty hunter, kiddo.'

'Oh, so what was it that Viella called you before? A mercenary?'

'Mercenary, bounty hunter, whatever. Some fool wants some other fool dead, they pay me to go and make it happen. That's what I do.'

He looked at me, disgusted. 'You are paid to kill people?'

What a little shit. 'Don't judge, baldy. I'm a professional, not a madman.'

'What's the difference?'

'Hey, I do it because I get paid, and paid well. A job's a job.'

'You should not be proud of that.'

'Who are you to judge?'

'I watched you murder two men without hesitation.'

'Oh please,' I groaned. 'They were dead anyway. Your sword bitch got my sword guy, and my axe guy was going to bleed to death. If anything, I was giving them mercy.'

'I could have saved them both.'

I scoffed. 'Get real, buddy.'

'You did not kill them because you were being merciful. You cut their lives short, robbed them of their futures, because you wanted to look strong. You did it to intimidate us.'

'Wow, you're a genius, aren't you?' I said, generously laying on the sarcasm. 'No one else could have figured that out. Good job.'

He looked baffled, as if he had no idea what sarcasm was. He didn't know what to say so he just shut up.

We kept walking for a long while, and for the time being, I kept my mouth shut. I wanted to observe them a little longer before I decided whether or not to kill them. I came up with a few ideas in my head on how exactly I would do it. It would be pretty easy, and after rehearsing it in my brain, I figured I had all angles covered.

Eventually, the trees started to dwindle and through them, I could, just barely, see a rocky grey surface sloping up. This bitch was leading us back into Dagger Peaks. That was mildly annoying. I had just gotten through these damn mountains looking for her.

We passed through the last of the trees, and now there was nothing between us and these pointlessly large rocks. Thank God, Vanclaude was at least smart enough to let us sit down for a second, give us the chance to catch our breath. Looking at them, I saw just how bad I had messed them up. Vanclaude's weird grandma-hair was all out of whack, nice clothes scuffled and dirty. There was a bruise from my fist on her pretty face. The kid was all bruised, especially his face, and his white robes had streaks of his blood stained on his chest. I noticed him watching me carefully.

I eyed his bag; I could see the outline of the gun bulging in it. I wanted it back, but these damn ropes would make it tricky to use.

The kid's voice interrupted my trail of thought. 'May I ask you something, Synn?'

I lifted my eyes to his face. 'Yeah, sure, whatever.'

He hovered a hand over the shape of the gun in the bag. 'Your weapon, it is imbued with a special power. How did you acquire it?'

'Shooting's nothing special, buddy,' I gave him a dry, bored answer. 'People have been doing it for ages.'

'But your weapon is not the same,' he pointed out the obvious, like some kind of genius. 'The light, the energy—'

'I'm a sucker for theatrics!' I gave him a chuckle, a smile, and a cute little shrug like I couldn't help it. 'But also, I wanted something practical. So, I fixed myself up something special, much better than a crossbow.'

He looked amazed, but sceptical. He wasn't buying it.

'If that is true, then explain how you devised it.'

Nosy smart ass.

'I mean, I *would*,' I said as I quickly cooked up an excuse. 'But the complexities would be lost on your slow little brain, and I don't want to make you feel any more inferior than you already do.'

'I don't believe you,' he said flat-out. 'You don't seem to understand your weapon.'

'What I don't understand, *buddy*...' I stood up, towering over the stumpy weirdo, '...is your ridiculous get up. What is it that you are again? A priest?'

'I am a disciple of the Order of Light,' he said meekly.

'So, insane?'

'No.'

'Why shave your head? And wear only one colour?' I launched the questions at him before he had the chance to reply, mounting the pressure. 'Do colours offend your God or something?'

'It is a symbolic gesture of our—'

'Hold on,' I cut him off. Made him wait, then said, 'I don't care.'

I could see a twinge of frustration in the corners of his mouth and in the lines on his brow. He kept his cool though and kept talking. 'I do not ask for disrespect, only some answers about—'

'Oh I'm sorry, was I not *respectful* enough for you?' I laughed and sat back down, shaking my head. 'Baldy, you have no idea.'

Then the woman opened her mouth. 'You will mock him no more, criminal,' she said with that annoying, pompous accent of hers. 'Be quiet.'

She must have forgotten how the world worked. I decided to remind her. 'And what are *you* going to do about it, woman?' I challenged her. 'Ramble some flowery bullshit at me until I keel over dead?'

'There are other means I can see that done,' was her weak comeback.

I was starting to feel embarrassed for her. 'Look, I know you're going for that whole *hard-ass noble lady* thing but let me tell you now, honey; it ain't working.'

'Much is the lost on the slow of mind,' she said with a smirk, as if that wasn't sad.

I squeezed my lips shut to hold back laughter. I let it slip a bit, just to let her know how ridiculous she was. 'I'm sorry, it's just—' I paused to snicker. 'It's just you're really not that intimidating. Being a woman, and all.'

Her hand squeezed the grip of her sword, like she was actually going

63

to use it. She didn't say anything, but I could tell on her pouty little face she really wanted to say something back.

Then it hit me, and I snapped my fingers. 'Hey wait a second,' I looked over to baldy. 'Do you have women up in your temple?'

He blinked. 'It is called the Sanctuary,' he corrected me like I could give a shit. 'And no, there aren't any female descendants at the moment.'

I pointed at Vanclaude. 'So this is the first woman you've laid eyes on?'

He seemed confused. 'I... well, yes.'

My God. I could not imagine anything worse than living up on some mountain with a bunch of old guys and no women around. But this did open up a new avenue for me, in terms of weak spots.

I leaned over to him and whispered, 'I bet you're curious to see what she looks like under all those clothes, aren't you?'

He was caught off guard. 'No, not at all.'

'Oh look at those red cheeks.' I grinned. 'Have you ever seen a naked woman? Do you want to?'

'Please stop talking about this,' he stammered at me. His cheeks really were going red, he had no idea how to handle himself. This was too easy.

'Hey, don't worry, buddy.' I laid a hand on his shoulder. 'Let me see what I can do for you.' I nodded up at Vanclaude. 'Hey, Your Highness, have you shown little Kiro here how it all works?'

She glared at me, not sure of what I meant but knowing it couldn't be good. 'What are you blabbering about?'

'Synn, stop.' Kiro shot up to his feet. 'You're being cruel.'

'Well, the kid here hasn't been with a woman before. He wanted me to ask you if you could be his first time.'

Her eyes fluttered for a second, and she looked taken aback. The kid's face went white. 'No I didn't!' he said frantically. 'I did not say that!'

Quickly, Vanclaude put her Big Tough Girl mask back on and said, 'I will *not* tolerate your disgusting words any longer, you foul cur.' She stood up, her hand wrapped around the hilt of her sword. 'Hold. Your. Tongue.'

I copied her tone. *'You're. Not. Intimidating.'*

Her eye twitched and her jaw clenched tight. She stepped forward. 'This is your final warning.'

I wasn't backing down.

I looked to baldy, who seemed mortified. 'Sorry pal, I guess her red flower is blooming. I mean, you'd probably have a better time bedding a cow than her anyway, to be honest. At least the cow wouldn't—'

Pain exploded from the side of my jaw and my head slammed into the ground. She kicked me into the dirt. I won't lie, that hurt quite a lot. She was quicker than I thought, which surprised me. I made sure to remember that.

The kid came to my side after a few seconds and helped me up. I grunted and rubbed at my jaw. 'Nice kick,' I said, making sure not to sound any less badass from before. 'But I hope we don't make a habit of going for the face.'

She clenched her jaw. Her fists were shaking. Her face twisted like she was trying really hard not to cry, and she stormed off.

Baldy actually looked pissed off. 'That was horrible of you to say, Synn,' he said after a long pause. 'Why would you say things like that?'

I looked down on him. 'Why should I do anything different?'

'Kindness begets kindness,' he preached, looking up at me. 'If you treat people better, you can make them better people, and make the world a better place. You aren't going to make many friends by treating people so poorly.'

I rolled my eyes. 'They're not friends I need.' I laid a hand on his shoulder. 'Life advice for you, kiddo, for the price of your attention; the only friends you need in this world are gold and steel.'

He shook his bald little head. 'I completely disagree.'

I took my hand back. 'Whatever, man.'

Vanclaude picked up her stuff, flipped some hair out of her face and mumbled to the kid 'Gather some wood. We will need to make a fire later.'

He went to work. 'Okay.'

'What, are we moving already?' I asked. 'I had just gotten comfortable, too.'

Watching the kid walk, I could see just how injured he was. Even though he was watching me carefully, I figured I could take him out quicker than either of them would have the chance to respond. I looked ahead to check on the woman, and like an idiot, she had created a massive gap between us. She had walked well ahead, because she didn't want to wait for us, I guess. Neither of them were as smart as they thought they were. There was an opportunity here.

I glanced at the kid. Even tied up, I could knock him out. He was way too beat up to even stand a chance. Even though he says he has no vanity the little bastard was cockier than he thought. Then once I had the gun back, no amount of fancy swordplay was going to save that snobby kingling.

But then I had a thought,

What if I just… didn't do that?

Of course, I could just kill these two nobodies and get paid. But that would just be same old, same old. Nothing changes. I'd still have that empty feeling inside. I'd still be searching the world for that spark.

But I wondered where teaming up with a kid monk and an angry wannabe royal could take me. I didn't realise how curious I was to see where this was going to take me. Not being in charge for once was actually kind of interesting.

I think this might be what I was looking for.

I decided I'd play along. For now, at least. I really wasn't too concerned. If I wanted out, there wasn't much these two janks could do to stop me. And if, by some stupidly bad luck, I bit off more than I could chew? Oh well.

Whatever happens, happens.

Chapter Eight

Dagger Peaks

The forest rested at the bottom of a chain of mountains Viella called Dagger Peaks. The reason for the grim name was obvious once we approached the end of the woods. We could see them looming in the distance through the treetops. The mountains were dark and grey, and speared up into a gloomy sky, crooked and narrow, like many colossal stone fangs. There was no snow, no trees, no greenery on them. They were just sharp, rocky daggers jutting out of the ground to pierce the dark blue belly of the sky.

By the time we passed through the last of the forest, the daylight was fading. Viella seemed uneasy, and when I asked her why, she said there were many superstitions about Dagger Peaks. When I asked her to elaborate, she snapped at me to just stay focused. She seemed upset with me, and I knew it was because I refused to let her kill Synn. I could not lie to myself – I was having doubts if I could help him reform. It was difficult to show him patience after all that he's said and done, but if the Order's teachings were worth anything, then I had to try, even if it wasn't easy. If I was truly worthy of ordainment, then I could guide this man down a better path.

Synn bumped my shoulder with his elbow to grab my attention. 'It's because people think this place is cursed,' he said, answering my question. 'Lots of stories of death, madness, evil sorcery, shit like that.'

The mention of sorcery piqued my interest. 'Do you believe the stories?' I asked him.

He scoffed. 'Curses aren't real.'

The ground became steep and rocky. Synn struggled to keep up in his restraints, so I would help him up whenever I needed to, for which he thanked me. He complained that this venture seemed pointless and stupid, but to me, Viella seemed to be leading us somewhere specific, and I trusted in her. When we finally reached the top, I never expected to see what we did.

We were standing on a cliff overlooking a vast grey sea of fog in the valley between two of many enormous, narrow mountains. Just ahead of us, stretching through the valley, there was a bridge of dark rock that had apparently been formed naturally. The bridge was long and flat like a road, perfect for walking across, and was supported by pillars of stone that rose from the impenetrable mist beneath it. Throughout the valley, sharp spires of rock speared upwards through the billowing fog, reaching up to the sky like they were the hands of people drowning.

I was awestruck, but struggling to understand how this could be possible without human planning. There were hints of purpose in the natural design of the world, but never have I seen, or even read of, lands with such obvious intentions like bridges and roads. It's possible this place was shaped by people wielding godstones. But if so, then the Order of Light would have known about it. It was hard to believe something like this could be created without at least some mention in the texts.

As we stepped onto the bridge and walked it, I felt uneasy. I had lived in the mountains my whole life, but now I was nervous. There was something ominous in the unnatural perfection of the bridge, and its continuous, perfectly straight path into darkness. We walked for a long time, long enough that when I glanced back over my shoulder, I couldn't see where we started from. And in all the distance we had covered so far, I had yet to see any colour of life. There was no movement, no sound. Even the wind was dead and still. Occasionally there would be a low coo of a slow, cold gust, but nothing more than that. It felt like we shouldn't be here, like nothing living should ever be here.

'How much further does this go?' I asked Viella carefully, worried that the question might anger her again.

'At least another day of walking. I'm not precisely certain,' she replied, not looking back. 'I haven't travelled through here before.'

'Then why are we walking through it?' Synn asked her bitterly. I tensed as the air turned sour again.

'Because no one will follow us through here.'

'And why do you think that is?'

Viella smothered an urge to snap at him and kept moving.

Night fell quickly. And as it did, the vision of the bridge ahead became shorter and shorter. Abruptly, the wind began to quicken, wearing us down with whips of cold air that moaned like ghosts through the dark, lifeless lands. I could endure the cold because I was used to it, but I worried for Viella and Synn, who were visibly struggling.

Then, something strange and remarkable happened. As the full moon rose further up into the starry sky, its pale light seeped into the jagged rock of the mountains looming over our sides and began to flow through the stone like blood through glowing white veins. The milk-white light curled and traced through the rock all around us in elaborate patterns and paths, even coursing down the mountain faces, illuminating the parts hidden by the fog. Eventually, when the lines seemed complete, there was a harmonious pulse like a single heartbeat, and all the unfurling lines glowed dimly under a sea of glimmering stars, illuminating the mountains. The sight was breathtaking, and the three of us paused to admire it.

The lines and patterns reminded me of the marks left by divination, and I realised then that, somehow, this place had most likely been created by very powerful people. I went to share this knowledge with Viella and Synn before it occurred to me the existence of divination may overwhelm them. I worried they may turn against me, so I kept quiet.

'Wow,' Synn said as he drank in the view. 'Not bad.'

'Come now.' Viella continued ahead. 'Let's carry on.'

'Just a question, Your Highness,' Synn said, not moving. 'When are we going to sleep?'

Viella stopped, sighed, and then swivelled around on her heel. 'It is said the bridge connects with mountains and travels through caves. We will sleep when we find one of those caves.'

'Okay, and how long will that be?'

'I don't know,' she grumbled, moving on, 'but it will be faster if you shut up.'

Because of the light, we were able to see further ahead. Slightly further. The night was still dark and cold, and there didn't appear to be any end to the bridge in sight. I was growing all the more tired and anxious, and I dreaded having to sleep here.

And then, Viella and Synn slowed to a stop.

'What's wrong?' I asked.

I poked out my head to look past Synn.

The bridge, which had been just wide enough for the three of us to walk comfortably, was starting to narrow. Further up, the bridge became so drastically thin it was like the edge of a knife.

'Welp.' Synn tossed his bound hands up into the air. 'I guess this means we gotta turn back.'

'This changes nothing,' Viella said. 'Just mind your footing.'

'Are you kidding me?' Synn cocked his head and stared at her. 'Do you know how painful it's gonna be when you fall off that and die?'

Viella scowled and pointed ahead. 'Look ahead, you imbecile.'

On the other side of the bridge was a tower of rock. It was one of many that speared up through the fog, but this one was much taller and thicker, almost like a building. Where the bridge connected to it, there was a dark corridor that continued through the tower and breached the other side.

'That's one of the caves,' said Viella. 'We'll proceed across the bridge one at a time, and rest in there.'

'You're insane.'

'Just don't stagger about like a drunkard, and you'll be fine.'

'If you're so confident, you go first.'

'I intend to, dog.'

Synn snickered and watched on. Viella took a deep breath in, then proceeded carefully. Every step she made was deliberate and precise. Not once did she make a motion that wasn't calculated. Her balance never wavered, even as she delicately placed one foot in front of the other at the thinnest part of the bridge. She never looked down. Watching her cross the bridge made my palms sweaty. It was too easy to imagine her slipping and screaming as she fell to her death. I was more nervous watching her than anticipating my own turn.

Finally, she reached the other side, and spun around to face us.

'Now you, criminal,' she called out.

Synn hesitated, quietly mumbling a mocking impersonation of Viella's words to himself, then started making his way across. For a second, he looked down over the long fall below him and immediately regretted it, jerking his head back up. Even this far away, I could see how hard he was breathing. He paused when he reached the worst part, then crossed it quickly.

He reached the other side, where Viella waited for him with her sword drawn. Synn just ignored her completely and dropped to the ground, taking a deep breath.

'Ready, Kiro?' Viella called out.

I nodded, then made my way across. I knew how to maintain my balance, but carrying all these things was making it difficult. Holding onto all the sticks and wood forced me to keep my arms in an awkward position where I couldn't use them to balance my weight. It was fine, until I reached the scary part. The path was so thin that there was nothing under my nose but a long, deadly fall. There was a tiny wobble in my foot and my stomach dropped, as did a few sticks in my arms. I resisted the urge to panic and corrected my imbalance. Once I was ready, I focused on just placing my feet and my weight in the right spots, one step at a time, again and again, until I reached the other side.

Once I reached it, Viella grabbed my shoulder to steady me. 'Are you alright?' she asked.

'Better now,' I said.

We entered the cave and sat down. Viella and I amassed the sticks into a pile on the ground. After some effort in the dark, we gave life to a small fire, and its warmth became palpable. Orange light illuminated the cave.

'Well done, team.' Synn clapped as best he could with his wrists bound together, which wasn't very good at all. 'Look at those sparks.'

Viella sat down and laid her sword across her lap to polish the blade with a cloth. I sat down with my legs folded and my hands outstretched towards the fire. A long sigh escaped me as I was finally able to rest after such an exhausting day. The aches and pains throbbing in my body made me wonder if I was pushing myself too hard. *Maybe I should go back home. Is this journey worth risking my life?*

No. It was too late for that. If I went back to the Sanctuary, then that would be failure in the eyes of the masters. If this journey was my ordainment test, then failing it would mean I'd have to wait thirteen more years to try again. I couldn't disappoint them. I couldn't disappoint myself. I shook the idea from my mind.

I looked up to Viella. 'Madam, how were you able to stay so calm crossing over the narrow part of the bridge?'

She lifted her gaze to me for a moment, then returned her focus to her sword. 'Because I am certain of myself and my destiny, and when you are certain, you have no fear. Being a woman of my name and talents, it is obviously not God's will that I die here.'

Synn rolled his eyes.

I cocked my head. 'Who is God?'

She squinted at me, as if the question was nonsense. 'You don't know about God?'

'No. Please, tell me about them. What's their name?'

She sheathed her sword and placed it gently aside. 'God *is* his name,' she began. 'He is the creator of the world. He is the ultimate being, of almighty power, and decides the destiny of every living man, woman, and child. When you die, it is said you will be brought before God, who will either welcome you into heaven, an eternal paradise, or damn you to hell where you suffer forever.' As she talked about "hell", she shot a sidelong glare at Synn, who noticed it and poked his tongue out in response. Viella looked back to me. 'If you're good, you go to heaven. If you're evil, you go to hell. Understood?'

I took a moment to understand it. 'But what about people who are neither good nor evil?'

'There is no such distinction, Kiro,' Viella said, firm in that belief. 'If a person is not good, they are evil.'

'Well, that's not true,' I said. 'And neither is that story of God.'

Synn turned his head to me and smirked. Viella's eyes smouldered with contempt, as if I had just said something very arrogant and very stupid. 'Oh, isn't it? And what do you know?'

'I know the truth.'

Viella glared at me.

I realised the implications of my statement. 'I'm sorry, madam, I'm not trying to belittle you.' I tapped the image of the Totality on my chest. 'Do you recognise this symbol?'

She glimpsed at it. 'No.'

'This is the Totality,' I told her. 'It symbolises the three gods.'

'*Gods*,' she repeated, a sceptical smirk on her lips. 'You think there is more than one god?'

'Well yes, but what I think is not relevant. There have always been three gods and thinking otherwise does not change that.' I tapped a finger over the top half of the Totality. 'This part represents Yaru the Creator.' I lowered my finger over the two quarters below. 'And these represent the Twin Gods, Orisaea and Veinther.'

She hummed. 'I see. So this is what they teach you up in those mountains?'

'It is.' I gazed up at the glimmering stars. 'Deep in the library of the Sanctuary, we have ancient copies of scrolls which describe the beginning of the universe. The writings are transcribed from the words of the Lightbringer, a hero who became a vessel of divine power and saved early humanity from extinction.'

The two of them looked at me, unconvinced but interested.

'Before time, before creation … there was nothing,' I began. 'In that nothingness, the will to exist came to be. It chose the name Yaru, and the universe began. The first creation of Yaru was light and darkness. To do this, it split its divine soul in two, then one half into two quarters, creating the Twin Gods of Light and Dark, Orisaea and Veinther.' I indicated the Totality with a finger. 'Hence this symbol.'

Viella nodded slowly. Synn drummed his legs and looked around.

I continued. 'For ten hundred thousand years, the Creator and the Twin Gods sailed through the empty cosmos, crafting the stars you see above us.' I pointed to the sky. 'Then they created our world; Eteran. Yaru sculpted the lands, seas, and skies. Orisaea created life, the sun, and day. Veinther created death, the moon, and night. Orisaea's last creation was humanity; She crafted us in Her own image, and imparted unto us the divine gift of souls. With souls, we can learn, feel, and grow. We have our own free will. When their work was done, Yaru separated the heavens and earth, and forbid the gods from interfering with the world. But….Veinther…' I paused as my next words caught in my throat, afraid that by simply speaking them, it would revive the evils they described.

'Go on,' Viella encouraged me. She seemed genuinely interested now. So I continued. '…Veinther did not think it was right for mortal beings to possess souls. He came to resent humanity, and eventually, all living things. So, in spite and hate, He dropped a single black seed from the heavens, and what sprouted forth were the Unbeings; monsters that stalked the world with horrible, impossible bodies. They hunted not just man, but all creatures with beating hearts. To call them *animals* would not be right. They were alive, but not like we are. They hunted all that lived for centuries. Indiscriminate in their rampage, they killed people, plants, trees, animals. Their single, accursed purpose was to bring death to all that could die, to forever snuff out the light of life, and they very nearly succeeded.

'Until, one day, a man climbed the highest mountain in all of Advenia, the one place where the heavens could hear him. And there, he begged the goddess Orisaea for intervention. When She heard his cries, She defied Yaru, and descended the heavens. She infused the man with the strength of all Her divinity, and he became the Lightbringer. With Orisaea's power, the Lightbringer united the tribes of humanity, and together, they defeated the Unbeings.'

'Fascinating,' Viella said dryly. She propped up her chin with her fist. 'And where are your gods now?'

'That's not the end to the story,' I explained. 'After humanity's victory, Veinther learned of Orisaea's intervention, and He too, descended the heavens, intending to carry out His dark purpose Himself. Orisaea emerged from the Lightbringer, and stopped Him. The two of them clashed in the skies above Advenia, igniting a battle that threatened to tear apart the world itself. So, Yaru descended the heavens, and obliterated the Twin Gods, shattering them into billions of tiny pieces that rained across the lands. In grief, Yaru returned to the stars to sleep for eternity. And finally, after all this, humanity was safe. Led by the Lightbringer, these tribes went to a cliff by the sea and built the first city…'

'…Adven.' Viella finished my sentence.

I was surprised. 'You know of Adven?'

'Of course.' She watched the fire dance as she warmed her hands. She seemed unimpressed. 'It is a famous myth. Where do you think Advenia gets its name?'

I hesitated. 'Myth?'

Viella eyed me curiously. 'You don't actually believe in Adven, do you?'

'Of course, it's our history. Do you not?'

She looked at me like I was dribbling nonsense, and shook her head slowly. 'There is nowhere on the continent where such a city exists nor could have existed.'

I was baffled. 'If Adven did not exist, how do you think the Advenian Empire began? What was the first city to be built?'

'Azale was the first city,' she said.

Synn scoffed as he fiddled around with a pebble. 'Here we go again, kinglings saying they were the first ones here.'

Viella rolled her eyes and grumbled. 'I presume you're from Ceren, then.'

'Born and raised,' Synn confirmed, tossing the pebble away. 'Couldn't you tell from the accent?'

'All commoners speak our language equally as poorly. I do not pay heed to the uncouth variances,' Viella said, her gaze brimming with scorn. 'I will concede though, it should have been more obvious to me. After all, you are a criminal; Cerenian origins are befitting.'

'Hey, I don't do anything that breaks the law, lady.'

'If that is so, then tell me why you have a bounty over your head, Synn?'

'Because I'm too damn good at what I do.'

'Murdering innocents?'

'I don't usually do the killing. I have a code,' Synn explained, using his hands like puppets. 'I bring my targets to my clients, then let them kill them. It's my *thing*, you know? A way to challenge myself. Otherwise, it'd be too easy. That's what sets me apart from the amateurs, and that is why you're not dead at the moment.'

'Truly? Is that why you're my prisoner? Because you're not an amateur?' Viella almost laughed, but only allowed a small, amused grin.

Synn smiled thinly and shrugged. Despite his roped hands, there wasn't anything about him that suggested he was defeated and powerless. It was enough to worry me he could turn on us and probably win. I made sure not to underestimate him.

Viella looked back to me, and her smirk faded. She said, very seriously, 'You should be careful spouting blasphemy like that, Kiro, especially in Azale. I do, however, understand why you would believe such falsehoods.

75

You have lived far away from the world. The word of God was kept from you.'

Blasphemy? Falsehoods?

'They are not falsehoods. It's all the truth.'

'And by whose authority marks that true? The men in the mountains?' Viella shook her head and watched as the flames crunched and snapped the wood beneath, spitting out embers into the cave. 'There have been countless prophets of the so-called 'true god' or 'true gods'. They all come with stories as colourful as yours, and they all desperately profess to be messengers of the one, ultimate truth. Who are we to believe, Kiro?'

Ultimate truth. The way she said it seemed as if it wasn't one, distinguishable thing at the end of the world, but something that came in many different forms to many different people.

I believed I understood now. 'It seems in the many years that the Order has been gone, others have offered their own stories of how the world began.'

'Ours are not stories, they are the truth.'

Then abruptly, Synn sniffed and gagged. 'Do you guys smell that?' he asked. 'It reeks of...' He coughed and waved a limp hand in front of his nose. '... ugh, *hypocrisy.*'

Viella groaned and pinched the bridge of her nose. 'Oh, would you just be quiet?'

'How can you tell this guy he's wrong when you have no proof yourself?' he asked her. 'Anyone smart enough to think for themselves knows that your whole thing is made up for money anyway.'

'*Shut up*, Synn.'

'Now, don't get me wrong, I'm not hating on the church,' Synn said, raising his palms. 'I respect their hustle. It's a clever way to stack coin, right?'

'Enough of your—'

A scream.

The three of us turned our heads to the bridge, peering out into the darkness beyond the cave and the reach of our fire.

'What was that?' I asked.

Viella's fingers curled around the grip of her sword. 'Someone has found us.'

'No way,' Synn said quietly. 'That's not a person.'

Viella shushed us. 'Listen.'

We stared out beyond the bridge, at the dark and sinister contours of the mountains. The wind blew slow and cold. We waited for a long while, staying as still and quiet as we could.

Another scream, shrill and icy, echoed through the dark. It was only vaguely human, somehow wrong, somehow different. Viella and Synn bolted up to their feet, so I stood up as well.

Then we saw it – a pair of great black wings, cast against the full moon. It looked like an eagle of some kind, only many times larger. The creature was soaring through the sky, its sorrowful scream echoing through the lifeless mountains. It was gliding straight towards us.

With a flick of her arm, Viella unsheathed Rosethorn. 'Get behind me, idiot,' she ordered Synn.

'Not a problem,' Synn said as he moved back, eyes wide and fixed on the incoming creature.

'What do we do?' I asked, trying to stay calm.

It landed on the bridge outside the cave, its tremendous wings blowing fierce gusts at us that nearly swept the fire out of existence. I planted my feet, resisting the winds.

The sight of it was terrifying. The creature was huge, with vast wings as black as a raven's, but with a head that was like a twisted mimic of a human skull; bone white, with gaping black holes for eyes, and a long, sword-like beak for a mouth. It opened wide, revealing a long array of razor teeth, and a blue tongue like a whip. It screamed at us, the shrill sound an eerie copy of mournful keening.

I was in fear and awe. 'What is that!?'

Viella took a step back. 'That's a drackin,' she said, her voice firm but telling of her rising panic. 'Kiro, stand with me.'

I took a step forward, standing at Viella's side with my staff in my hands. 'Why does it want?' I asked them, trying to imagine a solution besides killing it.

'It wants to eat us, moron,' Synn said.

I glanced behind us, at the other side of the bridge that continued out of the cave and into the mountains. 'We should run.'

'*We can't*,' Viella said. 'If we flee the cave, it will fly around and catch us. We need to slay it here.'

I wanted to refuse resorting to that, but the drackin howled and made vicious stabs at us with its beak, forcing Viella and me to back off until we were beyond its reach. It was too large to fit in the cave, and after realising that, it seemed to calm down. The creature's wings folded back into its body, giving it a nightmarish appearance like an unnaturally tall and thin skeleton wrapped in pitch black robes. Scaly, yellow talons clutched into the rock beneath it with such force as to send cracks splintering through the stone. I shuddered, imagining what would happen if it gripped our heads with such force.

'Quick, cut me loose,' Synn urged us. 'You can't fight this thing without me.'

'No,' Viella said with a voice of iron. 'You cannot be trusted.'

A low, raspy moaning emanated from the creature as its head twitched rigidly, jerking its gaze from us, to the ground, to the ceiling. It seemed to be thinking of a way inside.

Then, abruptly, it began pecking away at the edges of the corridor, dislodging chunks of rock with each strike.

'It's breaking the cave,' I realised. 'It's trying to get inside.'

'It *will* get inside. C'mon, Viella,' Synn said, desperation swelling in his voice. 'Untie me, quickly.'

She ignored him, and while the drackin was focused on pecking the corners of the cave, she stepped forward, her eyes fixed on the creature's neck. She lunged her blade at its throat.

The sword pierced its neck, and the creature recoiled, flinging its head back and squealing. It was wounded, but not dead. It began stabbing at Viella, who stood her ground, dodging and deflecting its beak with her blade.

Synn turned to me. 'Kiro, Kiro, listen,' he said, staring into my eyes. 'Cut me free.'

Viella glimpsed over her shoulder. 'Do *not* let him out of those ropes, Kiro,' she commanded me.

Before I could reply, Synn grabbed my shoulder and forced my attention on him. 'Listen to me, kid, if you don't cut me loose now, we're all going to die.'

'I can't.'

The drackin lost interest in Viella and returned to feverishly pecking away at the cave. Chunks of rock began to rain all around us.

'You *need* to.'

Viella shielded her head with her arms as the falling rocks forced the three of us to the other end of the cave. I could feel the cold wind licking at the back of my neck. The drackin was approaching us, and we had nowhere left to run.

'Kiro, *listen to me!*' Synn grabbed my shoulders. He was yelling now. 'You can't do this without me!'

'*Do not do it, boy!*' Viella said firmly.

The fire was flickering out, smothered by falling rocks. The light in the cave was fading quickly, and the looming figure of the drackin was nearing us.

Synn squeezed my shoulder hard and yelled '*Kiro! Cut me loose! Now!*'

'*Don't do it!*'

'*Hurry! Cut me loose! Cut me loose!*'

I had to make a choice.

I dropped my staff and rummaged through my satchel until I found the knife, and pulled it out.

Synn held out his wrists. 'Quickly!'

'What are you doing?!' Viella's voice cracked.

I didn't respond. I couldn't hesitate. There was no time.

I grabbed his hands to hold him steady, then slipped the knife between his wrists and began cutting the rope.

'Kiro, *no!*'

'Hurry up, kid!'

I sliced at the ropes, grunting as I struggled to cut through. As the drackin's beak neared us, the ropes finally snapped with a sigh.

Immediately, Synn's hands dived into my satchel with such force he knocked me off balance. He pulled out the gun as I fell to the ground.

Six deafening *BANGS* erupted in the cave. The drackin wailed as bolts of blinding blue light penetrated its body. It tried to flee the cave, then let out a piercing death cry as its massive body tumbled from the bridge and plummeted lifelessly into the abyss, the echoes of its harrowing scream disappearing in the dark.

And then all was still.

My ears were ringing and my head was pounding. I rubbed at my eyes. Slowly, the world around me returned. First the wind, moaning as it swept through the barren mountains. Then the cold, the chill touch of the night air.

There was no screaming.

I sat up and pressed myself against the cave wall. I couldn't see anything, but I had a vague awareness of where we were.

'You guys still alive?' Synn's question penetrated the dark.

'I think so,' I replied.

There was a small click, and some metal things fell and clinked against the rocky ground. It sounded like someone had dropped little coins.

'Your Highness? You there?'

I could hear Viella's frightful breathing.

'I am alive,' she said.

I heard something click, as if placed into a slot, then a snap and a churning.

I realised what it was. Chills rippled up my arms.

Synn chuckled. 'Let's fix that.'

I would not hesitate again.

I shut my eyes, focused on the ring in my hand, and called upon the power it contained.

I felt it obey, and thin tendrils of energy wrap around my lower arm.

The gun cocked.

I threw my right hand out, fingers spread, and dispelled a shimmering beam of blue light forward through my palm.

A seventh *BANG* rang out with a flash of blue light.

The air in my chest was punched out of me as I felt an immense, heavy pressure rushing into my body.

'What in the…?' Synn's voice trailed off as he stared in disbelief.

I had caught it.

The bullet was floating in the air, suspended in an aura of heavenly blue energy. It was screeching and shaking violently as its momentum tried to launch itself forward against my will. I could feel echoes of its explosive power pushing furiously against my hand. It felt like I was holding back a bolt of lightning trying to burrow itself into my palm. I summoned every fibre of my being to call for its stillness.

The bullet was not even an inch away from Viella's shocked face.

I gritted my teeth as I imposed my will onto the bullet. A deep, guttural growl escaped me as I exerted every last thread of strength available to me to suppress its momentum and force it to stillness. Gradually, the bullet's pace slowed and its pressure on my body lifted until finally, it stopped.

I released, and the bullet dropped harmlessly to the ground.

Synn and Viella were speechless. They had no idea what to do, how to react.

I knew exactly what needed to be done.

I stood up and staggered over to Synn, then reached up and grabbed his forehead. *Sleep* was the command of my will. An azure glow lit up his face under my hand, and his bewildered eyes fell shut. His body fell limp and crashed to the ground, deep in sleep.

Chapter Nine

The Tyrant Sands

Kiro called it 'divination'.

According to him, it is the willpower of the universe, the lifeblood of all creation. It is, allegedly, the power used by the gods to create everything in existence, and what his order dedicates their lives in studying and practising. It sounded utterly ridiculous, something out of a tale for children.

But I had no other explanation for it.

There were many long, torturous hours before sleep finally graced me. My mantle and blanket were a woefully inadequate substitute for a bed. I was trembling, from the cold and from the terror I had experienced. All I could think about was when I stared death in the face – how I was saved from sorcery, by sorcery. The night was cold, and I curled up into myself like a pathetic child, clinging to whatever modicum of warmth I could afford. My ears were ringing and in pain from the sound of the weapon, and the screaming of that horrible creature echoed in my mind. Even after that worthless dog had betrayed us and immediately tried to kill me, Kiro still refused to let me toss him off the side of the mountain. I was too scared of him to argue, but I refused to show him that. Kiro assured me that whatever effect he had placed on Synn would keep him asleep for many hours. I still did not trust him. To sleep only a few feet away from the man who had just tried to kill me was madness.

When I awoke, the sun was peering over the top of the jagged peaks in the distance, and pouring light across the bridge and through the cave. Kiro was meditating, Synn was still unconscious. My body was aching from sharp pangs of hunger and my accumulating injuries. I felt degraded. I am royalty, sleeping on rocks beside a sorcerer and a mercenary in some cave high up in a mountain. This was not what I deserved. I deserved to be awaking in lavish chambers, in a warm silk bed with my husband beside me. I should be ambling over to a marble balcony to watch the sunrise over the city I governed, as servants downstairs prepared an exquisite breakfast. That was my destiny, the life that Zephelia stole from me.

But this boy tells me that God, and thus my destiny, is nothing more than a fable. The boy, who slings magic from his fingers and says that even an evil man like Synn can be saved, stood in defiance of everything I have known good and true. The Church would have called him a heretic and a sorcerer. And, of course, I would have agreed with them.

But there I was, for the first time in my life, unwilling to align with the Church's designations. There I was, scared of, but grateful for, a boy capable of things I never believed possible. The woman I was a year ago would never have tolerated this. Was this my mind slipping from me? Had this exile finally broken me?

Kiro and I ate sparingly, and mostly in silence. Though both of us were hungry, we had to be conservative with our supplies. After a silent breakfast, we continued our journey. Kiro persuaded me not to discard the gun, so I held onto it, while he carried Synn's limp body over his shoulders as the bridge descended deeper into the valley. I was still surprised by the boy's strength, but where I had admired it, I now feared him. He endeavoured a few times to spark a conversation, but I found it difficult to speak with him.

He noticed this. 'Is everything well with you, madam?'

After a pause, I muttered, 'Yes.'

'You seem nervous.'

'...I am,' I admitted. 'Can you find a reason why I shouldn't be?'

He hummed. 'I understand,' he said gently. 'That was... scary.'

'Why didn't you tell me sooner?' I asked him, unable to even look him in the eye. 'That you could... do that.'

He stopped walking. 'Let's rest, madam.'

Reluctantly, I slowed my pace to a halt, then sat down, eyes downcast. Kiro placed Synn's body down gently, then sat beside him. 'I'm sorry I didn't tell you,' he said sincerely. 'I wanted to avoid telling you because I was afraid it would scare you.'

I went to speak, but the words caught in my throat when I realised his fears were proven true.

After saving my life twice, and casting himself into danger for my benefit, I had the audacity to doubt his intentions.

I felt sick with guilt.

'It's not your fault,' I said quietly. 'It is wise to hide your powers, Kiro. To the world, magic like yours is... mythical. If people discover your abilities, it will terrify them, and lead to disaster.'

He nodded, bitter knowledge creasing his brow. 'I am well aware. The Order of Light lives high up in a mountain "sanctuary" for a reason.' He looked at his hand as he contemplated. 'So you know, Viella, I did try to save us from Synn in the forest with this power, but that decision came too late. Divination is not to be used carelessly. It is a sacred power, and one that human beings were never intended to wield. When we do use it in these times, it is only to protect human life, and only if there is no other way to do so... and it comes at a cost.'

He showed me his palm, revealing burns that scarred his flesh in strange, flourishing lines. They curled and danced through his palm like art, as if they had been carefully carved into his skin. The marks swirled and weaved from the ring on his finger, and reached past his wrist before fading away.

I veiled my lips with my hand. 'Oh, Kiro. What are those scars?'

He traced the lines with his finger. 'This is how divination courses naturally through mortal flesh.'

'Does it ail you?'

He withdrew his hand, cradling it tenderly. 'Not anymore. But my body will need to heal. If a person wields divination excessively or beyond their control, their body will splinter and break apart.'

I cast my gaze over the barren mountains, taking a moment to fully appreciate what Kiro had done to save my life. 'Thank you for what you did,' I said softly.

'Of course, madam.'

I turned my gaze back to him. 'Do you see now why we cannot trust him?'

A little frown appeared on Kiro's face. 'I'm sorry he did that.'

'You don't need to apologise for him,' I said firmly, anger returning some strength to my voice. 'I don't understand your obsession with keeping him alive. Scum like him will always be scum.'

Kiro winced at that. 'He can change, madam. All people can change for the better, even a man like him.'

Despite my gratitude, I could feel a resentment beginning to smoulder for Kiro's ridiculous commitment. I failed to see the worth in endangering ourselves in the hopes he could repair the virtue of a cutthroat. My frustrations surfaced in the slip of an exasperated sigh. 'Even after last night, even after everything he has said and done... you *still* believe that man is redeemable?'

'I do, madam,' he said doubtlessly. 'If a person is treated with kindness and compassion, shown patience when they make mistakes, they will reform. I will prove that to you.'

His confidence was persuasive. A small part of me yearned for him to be right, as if that alone would redeem all of mankind and I could let down my guard for the first time in nearly a decade.

But if this absurd trio was to continue, my limitations needed to be clear.

'Fine. I will give him *one* more chance,' I said to Kiro, standing up, prompting him to do the same. 'But listen well; if a breath of treachery ever comes from him, or if he *ever again* speaks of me in the manner he did yesterday...' I felt a rise of anger, and took a breath to compose myself for the boy's sake. '...I cannot tolerate risking our lives any longer, Kiro. I will not restrain myself if he threatens us again.'

Kiro frowned and his head receded into his shoulders. 'Madam, why are you so easily swayed to the idea of killing him?'

He seemed crestfallen. I pitied his naïve heart. 'Because, Kiro, if he's dead, he cannot lay harm on me, or any other person, ever again.'

'And he can't *help* anyone else ever again,' he said. 'He can't ever laugh, or dance, or smile, or bring smiles to others.'

I folded my arms. 'Does he do any of those things anyway?'

There was a pause, then Kiro asked me, 'Have you ever killed anyone, madam?'

The question was simple, but his tone revealed his ulterior hope for my answer to be no.

Sadly, I could not give him that answer. 'I have,' I said.

Kiro was silent. I had never seen anyone look at me the way he was looking at me now. It was like I had broken his heart. 'How many have you killed?'

'Two.'

He almost seemed to be holding back tears. 'Why?'

'Because there was no other choice,' I told him plainly. 'Because if I hadn't, then they would have killed me.'

He looked away, casting his gaze to his feet.

'You must understand this, Kiro,' I began this lesson gently, 'they were assassins who came for me years ago. I did not slay them merrily for sport like some sadistic fiend. I killed them to save myself. I fought back and survived. Some people cannot be reasoned with. Some people are like animals. Can you persuade a hungry wolf to spare a rabbit? No. There may be moments when you have no choice, and if you want to live, you must kill. Do you see?'

Kiro stared at his feet. 'I am beginning to understand that, yes,' he said with sadness in his voice. He raised his gaze to meet mine. 'I do not hold anything against you, madam. Your life has been hard, and I understand you have not always had a choice. But remember this, Viella. If you *do* have a choice, please… choose to be merciful.'

His eyes and voice were desperate, as if he was pleading with me to save myself. It reaped my courage from me, and I chose not to reply.

I glanced at the criminal. 'Wake him. He can carry himself now.'

Kiro hesitated, then knelt beside Synn. He woke him the same way he had rendered him asleep – by laying his palm over Synn's forehead. A blue light glowed from under Kiro's hand. I kept the gun visible in my grip, so Synn was aware his defiance would yield him nothing. He stirred awake, muttering some obscenities under his breath.

'Get up,' I ordered him. 'We're moving.'

'What happened?' he mumbled. He rubbed his head, pushing some blond hair from his face, and squinted at me. He seemed confused. 'Didn't I kill you?'

'You tried,' I said. 'And you failed.'

~

I came to understand why people would lose their minds travelling through here – the bridge seemed to go on endlessly through a grey, misty wasteland. We walked for hours, the entirety of which was unrelentingly tense. Synn was following behind me, and Kiro behind him, as I led the way. I relied on Synn's survival instincts outweighing any petty animosity towards me. At any point, he could likely push me off the bridge before Kiro could stop him.

Drackins were also a threat weighing on my mind. We never sighted any, but occasionally, we'd hear a distant, chilling cry that would first prompt one to imagine someone grieving a terrible loss, only to realise in the next second it's true, inhuman nature.

We marched on in silence. At sporadic moments, Synn would make a pathetic attempt at humour, or to insult me. I never paid him any heed, and even Kiro could not muster the strength to respond to him. Eventually, he seemed to abandon the effort.

After hours of walking the bridge and passing through the occasional cave, it eventually sloped down almost like a staircase to the floor of the valley hidden by the sea of mist. Here, in the vast and lifeless stone fields hidden under a low hanging canopy of fog, we decided to stop and rest. I nibbled on my last piece of cured meat, while Kiro ate sparingly and offered a generous portion of fruits to Synn, for which the criminal feigned gratitude. I did not approve of it, but I knew objecting would be pointless.

Hours more of gruelling marching eastbound through the foggy valley, then nightfall approached. We took refuge in a shallow cave while the sun slinked below the horizon. The eerie, whirling lights in the mountains did not reappear this night so we were submerged in darkness. We ate again, and to my dread, Kiro's generosity has led him to completely waste the last of his food by giving it to Synn. All that was left was a piece of bread, and I was not sharing it with a hired cutthroat. Cautious of drackins and Synn's murderous inclinations, Kiro and I agreed to keep watch in turns, but when I eventually fell asleep, I did not wake again until the morning – the boy had let me sleep. The noble fool.

We cleared through the last of the mist before the afternoon, revealing slanted mountains that loomed over our sides like colossal monuments of the crescent moon. In the distance, just beyond the last of the mountains, was a shimmering, amber desert. We were almost through.

Synn suddenly became concerned. 'Hold on, you can't be serious,' he muttered, worry blotching his tone. 'Are you really going to take us through the Tyrant Sands?'

'We have no other choice,' I said.

He planted his feet on the rocky valley floor and stopped moving. 'Yeah, we do.'

I sighed. '*No*, we do not.' I swivelled around as I stopped to deal with this. 'The desert stretches from Hauren Hill to the Jae Goh Isles.'

'We need to get to a town or something.' He pointed north. 'If we go north, we can get on the main roads.'

'The main roads are not safe. Any of Zephelia's puppets may recognise me, and any fool may recognise you.'

'But we have no food. Are you really gonna have us march through a desert on empty stomachs?'

'If we press on through the Tyrant Sands, we will get to Azale by tomorrow morning.'

'You really think we can last that long through the heat without any food or rest?'

Kiro spoke up, approaching my side. 'I think Synn raises some reasonable concerns, madam. Maybe we should find a village.'

I looked at Kiro, astonished and hurt that he would align with Synn against me. 'No. It's not safe, and we've come too far. If we try to get on the roads now, that's three or four more days of travel.'

'It's better taking that risk than starving to death in the desert,' Synn said.

I shot him a piercing glare. 'I will not have another word from you, fool. I will not be questioned by some two-faced murderer.'

'Oh, *I'm* the fool, am I?' he barked, prodding his chest. 'If you walk us through this, you will get us all killed. Trust me, I can show you a—'

'*Enough!*' I rose my voice to cut him off, the words echoing through the vast, dead mountains. 'You betrayed our trust once, and I will *never* give you the chance to do it again. We will march through the Sands and that will be the end of it. Now, hold your tongue or I will cut it out.'

'No, you won't.'

'Yes, I will.'

'*No*, you won't.' He smiled as if he was invincible. 'If you could kill me, you'd have done it by now. But here I am, still kickin'.' He threw his arms up to welcome a lethal blow. 'If you're gonna do it, do it.'

Kiro, seeing my next intentions in my eyes, stepped in between the two of us. 'Maybe we should all just take a moment to rest.'

I glared at Synn's smug face. Exasperation balled my hands into fists. The prospect of berating him with insults was enticing but I knew it would be fruitless.

'We have been walking through the mountains for hours now,' Kiro continued, a tepid grin on his face. 'Some time to replenish our strength would be good.'

He was not wrong. I swallowed my anger, pursed my lips, and then lowered myself to the ground to sit.

Kiro smiled and nodded, then sat on the ground with his legs folded. He gestured for Synn to do the same.

Synn sighed in relief as he plopped himself on the dirt. He drummed his legs. 'So, magic powers are real and you have them!' he said to Kiro. 'Just a question, why didn't you use them *wayyyy* earlier? Like in the forest when I was about to pop your head off?'

Kiro told him what he told me, and showed Synn the scars on his hand, which had healed slightly since yesterday. Synn was fascinated.

'What other things is this "divination" capable of doing?' he asked, scratching his dark stubble.

'Anything.'

Synn leaned forward, intrigued. 'Really?'

Kiro nodded. 'It is only limited by the strength of a person's focus and will.'

Synn hummed in interest. 'So, if I *really* wanted it, I could wave my hands and... create a beautiful woman out of the air?'

My eyes rolled skyward.

'Erm, I...' Kiro yawned as he considered it. 'I suppose it is possible, but you would need *a lot* of divination and willpower to create another living human.'

Synn clicked his tongue. 'So that's the catch.'

'Mortals were not supposed to be capable of controlling divination, but because we humans possess souls we can use small amounts to our own ends.' Kiro extended his right fist towards us and indicated the ring on his finger. 'Look. Do you see this small gem in my ring? This is called a godstone, and it contains a tiny fraction of divination. It is enough to allow me to influence the world. When the Twin Gods were destroyed, the fragments of their souls rained across the world and, over time, hardened into these gems. They used to be common, but they are now all but gone.'

'My, my...' Synn awed the ring with wide, twinkling eyes. 'So that must be worth a pretty fortune.'

'It is invaluable,' Kiro agreed.

Synn looked up at him. 'How does one use that power?'

'I have studied and trained all my life to reach where I am now,' he said. 'You must be in touch with your soul. Your mind must be focused, cleansed of doubt, with a purpose held firmly in your heart, and the will needed to bring the divination under your control.'

'And souls are actually real?'

Kiro nodded. 'Yes, sir. Every living human has one.'

'Could you teach me?' Synn pointed at the ring. 'How to use that?'

Kiro smirked. 'Maybe. If you promise to be nicer to everyone.'

Synn tutted, and swatted a hand. 'Nah. I'll pass.'

'If you change your mind, let me know.'

Despite Synn's annoying protests, we began travelling into the Tyrant Sands. I could still recall trudging through this very desert when I was younger, wrapped in rags to hide my hair, shielded from the sun by Gerard's arm.

The heat was just as I remembered it. Heavy, stifling, and dry. Our feet would sink into the sand with every step, and we had to expend more energy just to trudge through this torrid dominion. Every moment we spent here, we spent under an oppressive sun. The sand stretched on seemingly forever, and there was no shade anywhere in sight, no buildings or trees that we could use to escape the heat for even a second. We could do naught but endure it. The wind swept over the dunes, sculpting them into smooth hills, and carrying away hundreds of little sand grains that gave form to its gusts. Occasionally, and for reasons beyond my knowing, the sands would form large, perfect shapes; orbs, spires, pyramids, cubes, and obelisks, atop pedestals. The wind would give form to these random monuments for a brief moment before the sands slipped into the gusts and disappeared again. Kiro was mystified by them. He had a childlike curiosity for the world around him that I found endearing. A part of me envied him.

I had shed my waistcoat, but I would quite literally rather die than take off my blouse in front of Synn, so I kept it on. Even though it was sticking to my body and making matters uncomfortable and disgusting.

Synn began to speak. 'I know you're not going to listen to me, but—'

'Then why do you bother to open your mouth?' I asked him.

'It's worth a shot because... I'm way too handsome to die here,' he said through heavy breaths. 'This desert... isn't just hot... This place will... will play tricks on your mind.'

I was smart enough to know better. 'Delusions from the heat,' I dismissed him. 'It merely means you... you must drink more water.' I wiped at my brow and took a conservative sip of my flask. Its lightness was making me nervous.

'It's different than that...' Synn kept speaking. 'Haven't you heard the stories? Some... some say the sands can come to life...'

I made a sort of laughing sound, but I could not spare the energy to properly mock him. My focus was on pushing through this blistering heat. It was almost tangible, like the air itself was becoming a wall.

'I have travelled through here before...' I was breathing heavily as well now. I glanced back at them. Kiro was struggling but raised not even a whimper. Synn had draped his coat over his shoulder. His shirt, drenched in sweat, became transparent and clung to his muscular form. One would presume a man of such vigour would just endure the heat without complaint, but no. '...Those stories aren't true... the sands create those bizarre monuments, but they are harmless. I would have thought you worldly enough to see through such silly fantasies.'

'I am worldly, you dumb jank,' he jeered through panting. He had a desperate look in his eyes. 'That's why I'm telling you all this.'

I threw my arms up. 'What other choice do we have? Azale is on the other side of this desert. There's no other way! We cannot travel around this place!'

'We can!' Synn exclaimed. 'We can! And I know the way!'

I was reaching my limit. 'Why should we trust you?!' I yelled the question. 'The instant Kiro freed you... you tried to murder me!'

'Yes, but I killed the drackin first, and you want to know why?' He tapped his chest. 'Because I am motivated by my own self-interests... and it's in my interests... and yours.... to get us out of this godforsaken desert.'

I stood there, boiling in anger. The wind grew stronger, blowing lashes of searing heat and gold sand against our skin.

'Excuse me,' Kiro's voice said. He sounded far away. 'Madam, sir, there is someone here.'

I spun around, alert. The boy was on top of a dune behind us. He was gazing at something over the top of it. Synn and I scrambled up the dune until our heads were peering over the top.

Ahead of us, in the centre of a vast flat clearing, there was a figure standing motionless. It seemed to be a man wearing strange armour, nothing like what the protectors were equipped with back home. This man wore large rectangular bronze plates laced by cords, over his chest and arms. Both pauldrons were spiked, and two rising horns sprouted from the sides of his helmet. He was gripping a long spear topped with a curved metal blade, which he stood beside him. His entire appearance, down to his weapon, was coloured bronze. His image shimmered and wavered in the heat.

I grabbed Kiro's robes and pulled him down. 'Get down, boy.'

'Why?' he asked innocently.

'We do not know who that is,' I said. 'He may be dangerous.'

'Is that even a person?' Synn asked, his voice low. 'Looks like a statue.'

'Why would anyone build a statue out here?' I raised the question.

'Well, why would anyone wear armour like that out here?'

'Perhaps it's a mirage.'

'Is it a mirage if we can all see it?'

I glanced at Kiro. 'What was he doing when you saw him?'

'Nothing, madam,' he replied quietly. 'He was only standing there when I saw him.'

I observed the armour, and something about it seemed familiar.

'His armour... that is what ancient soldiers wore, is it not?'

'It... it *is*,' Kiro agreed. 'I have seen depictions of ancient imperial soldiers in our texts. I recognise the helmet.'

'Who cares?' Synn grumbled. 'If that guy is alive, he's going to die soon. Let's just keep moving.'

'Strange fool.' I looked to Synn. 'We will proceed east.'

'I say we go north.'

'Into a den of your allies?'

'To somewhere where we won't die from just walking through it,' he said, glaring at me.

I felt Kiro shuffling around beside me. When I looked at him, he was stripping off his trousers.

'What are you doing, boy?'

'I am taking off my pants,' he answered flatly, apparently unaware of how bizarre that was.

I averted my gaze. 'You do realise you can cool yourself more effectively by removing the top half first, yes?'

'I'm not taking them off because I'm hot. I felt something crawl up my leg.'

He stripped off his pants and that's when we sighted it. Clutching to his leg was a pale yellow bug about the size of my hand, with six legs and a long barbed tail.

I gasped in disgust and lunged back. 'What is that thing?'

'Shit, kid. That's a garicuda,' Synn said, suddenly serious. 'Don't move.'

Kiro was calm and even seemed confused. 'Why are you two so afraid?' he asked.

The creature had thorny, bony legs wrapped around Kiro's calf, and a long, needle-like stinger that swayed in the air. Six gleaming black eyes bulged at the front of its hideous, shelled body, between two hairy forelegs that prodded blindly around the area in front of it.

'Stay calm,' Synn instructed, reaching towards him. 'I'm going to get it off you, then you get the hell away from it.'

Kiro was completely unfazed. 'Is it dangerous?' he asked.

Then as quick as a blink, the stinger plunged deep into Kiro's leg. He screamed.

'Shit!' Synn rushed over to his side and grabbed the bug. He tried to pull it off, but the garicuda's legs clung tightly to Kiro's flesh. The boy's breathing turned rapid and shallow, and agony contorted his face.

'Damn it!' Synn yelled. 'It's buried the needle.'

'What does that mean?' I asked, staying calm.

'It means we can't get it off.'

'What? Is he going to die?'

'Unless I can get him to help...' Synn looked up at me. 'Yes.'

Kiro's eyes were welling with tears. 'It... hurts... so much,' he sputtered out through strained cries.

I glanced over at the figure.

It was looking right at us.

'Synn.' I drew his attention, and indicated the statue.

He raised his head to check. 'Shit. What does he want?'

'I don't know,' I said. 'Could he know how to save the boy?'

'Not a chance. We need to get him to my friend's place. It's north of here.'

I shook my head. 'We're not going north.'

'Viella!' he shouted. 'If we don't, he'll die!'

'There has to be another way.' I drew my sword. 'I'll sever its legs, then you can pull it off.'

'You can't cut it off,' he said. 'If you try, it'll shoot its venom into his leg and then he's *truly* screwed. You have to burn it off.'

My hands clenched into fists. 'Oh for... just... *damn* it all!' I roared. As I did, the winds around us quickened.

'Viella, shut up and calm down,' Synn ordered, raising his voice over the rising winds. He lifted a wailing Kiro in his arms. 'We have to go north. There's someone who can help him. It's our only chance.'

I hesitated.

'Viella!'

'Quiet! I'm thinking!'

'There's no time to think!' Synn belted out. 'We need to go or he'll die!'

My fists quaked. My whole body tensed up as two decisions tore my mind in twain.

Kiro's dry voice cracked as he screamed, and tears streamed down his red face. His eyes were glazed with fear and desperation. His hands clutched helplessly to his leg. I couldn't bear to see him like that.

I swallowed my pride and forced myself to shout, '*Fine!* Lead the way! Just don't let him die!'

Before we could move, the ground beneath us began to tremble and shake. The winds were roaring now, and moving so fast that my waistcoat flew from my shoulder and into the air. Kiro's pants and Synn's coat joined it as they spiralled up into the sky.

'What is—?' I went to speak, but a sudden shift in the ground interrupted me.

The dune we were standing on was falling apart.

'*Let's go!*' Synn shouted. He began running, and I followed him.

As we tried to flee, a flurry of sand carried by the fastest winds I had ever seen formed a wall in front of us. We stumbled to a stop, then turned and tried to run in a different direction. Again, the winds blocked our way. The air encircling us became so dense with sand that our surroundings faded away into a grainy darkness. I gazed up and saw the sand spiralling all the way up to the sky.

We were trapped.

'Viella!' Synn shouted for me.

He was staring into the whirling winds. I saw it too, the shadow of a figure moving towards us. It reached out and its hand breached through the winds, then its legs, then its body.

It was the soldier. He was not a statue nor a man.

He was made of sand.

I stepped forward and pushed Synn behind me with my free arm. I stood with Rosethorn, prepared to strike this faceless monster down.

Slowly, and silently, it reared its spear back, then thrust it towards me.

I stepped to the side and struck the weapon with my sword. My blade clashed against the sand as if it was steel. Without hesitance, I pushed forward and drove Rosethorn through the soldier's chest.

It plunged right through, but the soldier did not die. Without even glancing at my sword, it raised its spear and swung it at my neck. I let go of Rosethorn and ducked, a heavy *whoosh* flying over my head.

I bolted up, grabbing the hilt of Rosethorn and pulling it upwards with a roar. The blade dragged through the soldier's neck and head. Once its head was sliced asunder, its entire body lost its form and collapsed into a pile of harmless sand.

The wind was making it difficult to see and hear. I turned around and saw Synn facing the other side of the wind wall. Two more figures were moving towards us.

I rushed towards them. I was already exhausted. My entire body was aching and calling out to rest. The walk itself had been draining, but fighting in heat like this was unbearable.

As the soldiers came forward from the whirlwind, I refused them the chance to even attack. I yelled through the pain as I swung Rosethorn on a horizontal path through their heads, their bodies collapsing in the blade's wake.

My breathing turned rugged and heavy, and the heat withering my body was excruciating. My arms were wobbling, and even holding up Rosethorn was becoming a battle.

'Viella!' Synn called to me over the winds.

I felt his back press up against mine.

Three more soldiers moved in from the whirlwinds in front of me.

'Three ahead of me!' I shouted over my shoulder.

'Same here!' Synn shouted over his. 'You got the gun!?'

'Yes!'

He laid Kiro down on the ground, and stuck his open hand in front of me

I hesitated. It felt wrong, deeply wrong, to trust him. It felt like I was forcing myself to eat mud. But as he said before, our interests were aligned. After a pause, I reached into my bag and gave it to him.

'Their weakness is their head!' I yelled. 'Stay on guard!'

'You too!'

My three began to march slowly towards me, spears raised and ready to strike.

I swallowed a gulp of air and pushed my burning, stiffening body forward. I dashed to the side and, using my shoulder, pushed the spears away from me and into each other. Before they could move, I slashed at their heads. I only succeeded in killing two. The third was spared by distance, and without delay, it swung the spear. I could not avoid it. It plunged into my side, reopening the old wound on my waist and jolting my body with hot, screeching agony. I screamed, then pierced its face with the tip of my sword, destroying it.

Three explosive *BANGS* ripped through the air, and I saw Synn standing over three piles of sand. Kiro was flat on his back in the centre, the only part of him to move was his chest, rising up and down slowly. He was scarcely conscious.

I returned to the centre. I was nauseous and struggling to even stand. Synn returned and we stood back-to-back.

'You good!?' he asked over the winds.

I pressed a hand over the wound on my side. Blood seeped through the bandages and blouse. 'No,' I said, 'I'm bleeding.'

All around us, shadowy figures appeared in the whirlwinds. They were surrounding us. They pushed through the sands and showed themselves, forming a ring that trapped us.

A deep thunderous voice shook the ground.

'*PAAAAAAAYYYY THEEEEEEEEEEEEE TOLLLLLLLLL.*'

The whirlwind slowed, its roar diminished until it was nothing, and the sands obscuring the world fell to the ground.

A quiet wind cooed as it swept over hundreds of these soldiers, standing completely still and utterly silent, in every direction for a hundred yards around us. The dunes had reformed to become sloping walls that trapped us in a crater. We were completely surrounded.

My shoulders slumped, and my heart sank. There was no hope of surviving this.

I heard sand shifting and falling, and slowly, I turned my head to look.

In the dune walls, sand was pouring onto the ground, forming craters in the wall. Then, these craters shifted into two furious eyes and a frowning mouth.

With a voice as loud as thunder, the face bellowed '*PAAAAAAAYYY THEEEEEEEEEEEEE TOLLLLLLLLL.*'

Chapter Ten

The Toll

In all my years of roaming this world, stealing, killing, and scheming for prences, there wasn't any sum that could've convinced me to go into the middle of this hell.

Actually, no, there was a sum. A hundred thousand prences. I probably would have done it for a hundred thousand prences. There wasn't much I wouldn't do for a hundred thousand prences.

Still though, this was real bad.

But hey; whatever happens, happens, right Synn?

Yeah well, this was happening. That big face, that army of sand soldiers, they were all very real. At least it was something new.

'Any plans, Your Highness?' I asked Viella as I loaded more bullets into the gun.

'Survive,' she answered between breaths.

'Wow, that's very helpful.'

'Oh, and what are yours, then?'

'Get the hell out of here.'

'It's a tad late for that, don't you think?'

'Well, maybe we should—'

'*PAAAAYYYY THEEEE TOLLLL!*' The face in the sand roared.

All at once, the soldiers pointed their spears at us and widened their stance.

'Is he saying "pay the toll"?' I asked to be sure.

'I believe so.'

'HEY BIG GUY!' I shouted up to the face. 'HOW MUCH IS THE TOLL!?'

The face looked offended, then screamed, 'WHAT DID YOU CALL MEEEEE!?'

'Sorry! Sorry! Totally my bad!' I raised my hands. 'What is your name!?'

'I AM GARNUSHKANA, LORD OF THE SANDS!' the face boomed. 'YOU ARE TRESPASSING ON MY LAANNDSSS!'

'That's her fault!' I pointed at Viella. 'Personally, I never wanted to be here! In fact, we were just on our way out of here, uh… Mister Lord of the Sands, so—'

'ENOUGH WORDS!' the face roared. 'PAAAAYYY ORRRR DIEEEE!'

The soldiers began marching towards us.

'Vie, you good?' I asked her.

'I can't… endure this forever,' she said, still puffing.

The soldiers were getting closer.

'Keep the kid safe,' I stepped forward and cocked the gun. 'I'll clean up.'

It's a good thing these sand guys were slow, it meant shooting them in the head was easy. Not that I needed it to be. These bastards could've been bouncing around and I still would've hit them where I wanted to hit them. The only problem was I only had six shots at a time, and about ten bullets left.

And there were at least a hundred of these sons of bitches.

I aimed. Boom. One went down. Did it again, that's two. Repeated this and then three, four, five, and six were all piles of sand. But it hardly made a dent in their numbers, and that was only for my side. Viella had her own share to worry about. When I checked on her, she hadn't even killed one yet. She was standing next to the kid, waiting for them to get closer. This wasn't going to work.

I ran over, swept down, and picked up the kid's staff. 'Can I borrow this? Thanks, bud.'

Kiro groaned and creased his eyes. He was conscious, barely. The thing on his leg was getting quite fat off his blood. He didn't have long.

The gun wasn't very helpful without bullets, and loading it will take too long, so I slipped it away in the holster, and put two hands on the stick. Never actually used one of these in a proper fight, but I didn't need to live on a mountain to figure out swing, swing, poke.

So I tried it; swing, swing, poke. It didn't do much until I hit these things in the head, but it was helpful for keeping the spears away. Whatever wood the stick was made of was good quality, though. Heartpine was my guess. Doing this all by myself was getting tricky though, and as I crushed seven, eight, and nine more heads, number ten managed to get close enough with his spear to stab my shoulder. It stung, but it wasn't deep. More of a sharp poke than a stab, and another cool scar to add to the collection. I called number ten a little bitch as I caved in his face with the stick.

I heard what sounded like Viella fighting, so I turned around to check up on her. She was finally picking up the slack, killing a few of the closer sandmen. It didn't matter much though, because all together they had already advanced enough that the space we had to move around in was getting pretty squishy.

'We can't kill 'em all,' I told her. 'Figure out a way to... charm the big guy.'

She was barely able to speak. 'I doubt he's... much for diplomacy...'

I wiped at my forehead and pushed off some hair sticking to my sweaty face. *I wish the sun would piss off for a second, goddamn. So hot.* 'Seems like he's... got a big ego,' I pointed out. 'I'm sure you're... used to that. Work with it.'

She gave me a look that said she could use a little more help than that. I shrugged, to say maybe she think for herself for a second while I do most of the work.

I turned back around just in time to see a spear go right through the space my chest was occupying half a second ago. Shit, that was close. I grabbed the shaft of it, then ripped it out of the sand man's grip. For a thing with no face, it looked surprised. Now I had a better weapon. I flipped it around then ran the pointy end into the soldier's head – boom, that was eleven dead. But the spear also collapsed into a useless pile of dust. It was a good idea at least.

But all this work in the sun was exhausting. I was breathing pretty hard at this point, and I could feel the veins behind my jaw throbbing. My heart was thumping against my chest. My muscles, as big as they were, were starting to ache, and swinging around a stick with a stab wound in my shoulder wasn't getting any easier.

But these goddamn sand men didn't stop coming.

'Life's easy when you're not made of flesh and blood, huh fellas?' I said, cracking a bad joke. None of them laughed. That's fine, I deserved it. I smacked away twelve's spear before caving his head in. Dodge, thrust, repeat. Pretty easy formula.

And then I got stabbed in the stomach.

I looked to my right and saw the culprit. Ol' Straight Faced Thirteen. I ripped the spear out then smashed his empty face in, then backed off and kept the kid's staff between me and the other soldiers.

Good heavens, that felt really bad. I took a look down and yep, I was bleeding all over my clothes. These were such nice pants, too.

Also, this wound was probably, most definitely going to bleed me to death. At least I couldn't feel the pain through this blood rush.

And of course, these bastards were still getting closer.

I was about to shout at Viella to do something, but then she flung her arms into the air and started yelling.

'O, great Lord of the Sands! I beg of thee, hear the pitiful cries of this pathetic soul!'

The big face, which for this whole time had just been glaring and frowning very angrily, softened a little.

The soldiers stopped moving. The tips of their spears were about five feet from us.

'SPEAK, PATHETIC ONE!'

I looked at Viella in disbelief. She glanced at me, with an expression that said *Wow, that worked?* I gave her a thumbs up to say *Keep going.*

Viella blinked a few times, then said, quite dramatically, 'We are unworthy to walk these sacred grounds.' She sketched a deep bow. 'O great and mighty Garnushkana, we beg thy divine majesty for pardon. We implore thee, bestow a shred of thy pity upon us, so that we may… pay the toll.'

The face was quiet as it thought about it. Very quickly it went back to being very loud. 'VERY WELL! YOU WILL BE SPARED… IF YOU

PAY THE TOLL!'

She sounded like an actor. 'Great Lord of the Sands, what price dost thou name?'

'FOR YOU THREE, YOU MUST PAY... THREE HUNDRED PRENCES!'

Wait, that's it?

'Tell him it's no trouble,' I said to Viella. 'I got three thousand in my pocket.'

She nodded then spoke grandiosely, arms flourishing. 'Allow us to humbly offer this fare to thy prodigious greatness.'

I dug my hands into my pockets.

They felt pretty shallow and empty. But there was no way I didn't have it. I wasn't the type to just lose money.

I kept digging around, patting my legs. I started getting nervous.

Then it hit me. 'Uh oh.'

'What is it?' Viella hissed under her breath as she held a dramatic pose.

I looked at her. 'The prences were in my coat.'

She glanced at me from the corner of her eye. 'So? Just—' Then it hit her, and her face dropped. 'Oh.'

'Yep. Flew right off my shoulder,' I said. 'You got any money on you?'

'No.'

'You're kidding me. Aren't you a royal?'

'I don't carry my family's wealth on my person!'

'Well.' While we had the chance, I took out the gun and loaded it. I gritted my teeth as the pain in my stomach really started to hit. 'If this is it, snowball, let's go out giving them hell.'

Viella let out a defeated little sigh, and then, after a few seconds, stood up straight and gave me a nod. 'Agreed.'

The face noticed us taking our time, and got angry again. 'THE LORD OF THE SANDS WAITS FOR NO ONE!' It bellowed. 'TRESPASSERS PAY WITH GOLD OR BLOOOOOOD!'

The soldiers, in unison, marched forward one step.

I didn't have many expectations of how I would leave this world, but this I would never have guessed.

Oh well. That's life.

Something grabbed my ankle and spooked me.

It was the kid.

'Yikes, baldy. You're still alive?'

He was barely conscious, but he made a tiny, dried rasp.

I think he tried to say something. 'What was that?'

'Gold,' his voice rattled. 'I have…'

With one hand, he lazily pulled out a handful of gold and silver coins from his satchel.

'Holy shit, kid.' I was stunned. 'How the hell did you get this much money?'

He didn't try to speak. Instead, he focused his efforts on passing me the prences with a weak, pale hand. I took the handful and counted quickly in my head. This weird little hermit somehow picked up four hundred and fifty prences.

Whatever. I wasn't going to question this. 'Hey! Big—' I stopped myself and gestured to Viella. She took the lead.

'O great and powerful Garnushkana!' Her voice was starting to crack. The hot air was drying her throat out. 'We have thy toll in our grasp! Allow us to bestow it to thee!'

The face gritted its non-existent teeth and roared 'PAYYY OR DIEEE!'

She stuck her hand out in front of me, and I dropped three gold coins into it.

She held them up in the air; three hundred prences, just as asked. The face turned its big fat frown into a big fat smile.

'VERY GOOD!' It bellowed. 'PAY!'

The crater forming its mouth sunk further into the sand wall, becoming deeper and creating the opening to a dark pit. Viella aimed, then threw the coins.

They sailed through the air and landed in the face's mouth.

All at once, the soldiers stood straight and lifted their spears away from us. The pit sealed and the Lord of the Sands smiled.

'You have paid the toll!' It said, pleased. The winds began to fly fast and hard all around us, tossing sand everywhere. 'Go and never return!'

Our surroundings disappeared in a whirlwind of sand, and after trapping us for a few seconds, the winds settled and set us free.

Everything around us for miles was completely flat. The soldiers, the dune walls, they were all gone. It was like they had never been here.

The pain from my stab wounds were a reminder that they had, in fact, been real. I clutched my stomach with my hand, as if that was going to help, then dropped onto the ground next to Kiro.

'Nice going, snowball.' I slipped the rest of the coins into my pocket. 'How did you think of that?'

Viella dropped to the ground as well, sighing out a lot of tension. 'Growing up around nobles… I learned quickly that the arrogant fools who loudly boast to be the "some lord of someplace", yearn for one thing above all else… praise.'

I smirked, despite the heat and the pain. 'Good thinking.'

'I must commend you also, Synn…' she began. 'You were… effective in destroying them.'

I did a tiny bow with my hand and head. 'You're welcome.'

We sat there for a while, breathing hard and saying nothing, listening to the wind.

'We're still going to die here though, aren't we?' I asked, looking at all my blood in the sand.

Slowly, and rigidly, Viella pushed herself up to her feet. 'Unless we move now,' she said. She made it a whole three steps before collapsing to her knees then flat on her face. She didn't move.

I would have preferred being killed by those sand monsters, not something boring like bleeding to death.

Kiro moaned and shifted on the ground.

'Still kickin', kiddo?' I asked him weakly.

He nodded slowly.

For some reason, I felt proud of him.

He rummaged slowly through his satchel, searching for something with his fingers. Finally, his hand stopped, then pulled out a small, red pouch. He untied it and dipped a finger and a thumb inside, taking out a little blue berry and slipping it in his mouth.

He chewed on it for a few seconds.

Then his eyes came back to life.

He rose to his feet, limber and fresh, and grunted like he had just woken up from a good nap. Then, his face changed and he took in a sharp breath as he felt the pain of the garicuda stabbing into his leg. He winced but didn't scream.

My thirsty, dying self thought this was funny and I started giggling. I fell over backwards onto the sand. It felt warm.

Kiro came to my side and blocked out the sun with his bald little head. He opened my mouth and slipped a little blue berry in. Then he moved my jaw with his fingers to make me chew.

I felt the berry crush between my teeth.

The taste was like a bolt of lightning running through me. It was sweet and juicy, and when I swallowed it, my entire body jumped awake. It was like being splashed with icy cold water but if that was a good feeling.

The pain in my muscles and wounds turned into a fuzzy tingling and then into nothing. A bursting rush of energy and strength flowed through my whole body. I felt like I could run up and down a mountain.

I sat up and looked down on the wounds on my body; the bleeding had stopped, and the skin was visibly healing itself. I could see and feel layers of my flesh stitching itself back together until the stab wounds disappeared and left behind only a pair of faint, pink marks.

'Holy shit,' I said as I stood up without any trouble. 'Kid, what is this?'

'This is a pomegen berry,' he said. His voice and face looked clear, like really detailed. I hadn't noticed how my senses had eroded during this whole thing. Everything was clear now. Kiro winced, gritting his teeth, and put a berry in my hand. 'Please give this to Viella, it still hurts to walk.'

A part of me, the smart part, said this was the chance to ditch them. Another part, the dumb part, said that would be super mean. I sided with the dumb part. 'Why are these so... good?' I asked as I walked over to Viella.

'Pomegens heal the human vessel, rejuvenate the mind and body. We use them to recover after practising with divination, but sometimes for their medicinal value as—' He interrupted himself with a pained grunt.

'You good, bud?' I asked him as I stuffed the little fruit into Viella's mouth.

'Y-yes,' he stuttered. 'Pomegens... can cleanse pain, but... not for long... and this... is... intense.'

After a few seconds of forcing Viella to chew, she sprung back to life, flinging herself up and whipping me in the face with her hair. 'What happened?'

I grinned. 'We cheated death.'

Viella rubbed at her eyes then stopped as she noticed something. She lifted up the side of her blouse and pulled off a bloody bandage wrapped around her waist. Under it was a faint scar. 'My wounds are gone,' she marvelled, checking a few other spots on her body. 'What happened?'

'The kid had these little miracle berry things, isn't that right buddy?'

When I turned around to glance at him, he was flat on the ground.

Uh oh.

I rushed over to him, because I could actually do that now, then swept him up in my arms. 'It's alright, buddy, I gotcha,' I whispered.

His whole face scrunched up, and he took in quick, sharp breaths as he tried really hard not to cry. His eyes fluttered open for a second and he managed to look at me and say '*Thank you.*'

The way he said that hit me in a way that I didn't expect. For a second, I couldn't speak. It caught me off guard.

I checked out the garicuda clinging to his leg. The damn thing was quite engorged by this point, and its gross little body was pulsating and coloured a deep red.

'Alright, we need to go now, he's running out of time,' I told Viella. 'Get his stick. I'll carry him.'

Viella didn't hesitate, thank God. She grabbed the staff and followed me as I started trudging as fast as I could through this damned desert.

'You're going north,' she said.

'So?'

There was a pause.

'If you prove me wrong for trusting you,' she said as we ran. 'I vow to you that you will die for it.'

'Oh come on, even after all that?' I glanced at her over my shoulder. 'Still don't trust me?'

'As you said, our interests aligned for the moment.' She glared at me. 'Keep them aligned for your sake, Synn.'

'I'm not doing this for you,' I said. 'But a little gratitude would be nice.'

'I am thankful,' she said. 'And I am also wise enough not to pour my trust unto a mercenary.'

She had a point but still, man.

We ploughed through the desert for hours, until the sun was hanging low over the horizon and our flasks and stomachs were completely empty. Why the hell was this place so damn big, and why did this dumb kingling think she could just walk right through it and live?

And what the hell was that toll shit? How come no one knows about that? Why do garicudas even exist?

I hadn't felt that genuinely angry for a while. *Keep it cool, Synn. Not like you to get so riled up.*

Lucky for us, as it got darker, the desert became cooler. We had been walking around for so long that it got dark quicker than I thought, which was good. If we had to tough it out under that sun for much longer we probably wouldn't make it.

As we plodded through the Tyrant Sands in the dusk, the dunes became flatter, and the heat eased up, until finally, the sands met the edge of flat grassy land. Dark green plains awaited us, and where the ground met the sky, there was a familiar little cottage.

'That's it, up there,' I said to Viella, getting excited. 'We're almost through.'

I looked at her, but she didn't even crack a smile. She kept that determined expression as she kept pushing forward.

We were already exhausted again. The pomegens had taken us far but even those little miracle berries couldn't last on a trip like this. Now, all we had left to drive us forward was the sight of the cottage. As we got closer, it got bigger and bigger, and along with that, our hopes of surviving this. We kept pushing forward, not quite running, we didn't have the energy for that, but as fast we could manage.

And then we arrived.

I got to the door, laid Kiro down, then knocked on it. *C'mon, don't be dead, don't be dead.*

There were footsteps, then an old woman's voice called out from behind the door.

'What'd'ya want?'

'Ms Egree!' I called out. 'It's me, your pal.'

The door creaked open as the tiny figure of an old friend appeared. The smell of a fireplace, hot soup, and yarn wafted forward.

'Synn?' her weary little voice croaked. 'Is that you, you dumb, hot bastard?' She made an annoyed squawk and gestured to Viella and Kiro. 'Who are these jokers?'

'Ms Egree.' I smiled. 'You're everything I needed to see just now. I'd love to catch up, and I know how you feel about strangers, but my boy here is in bad shape. You think you can get this damn garicuda off him?'

Ms Egree saw his leg and gasped. 'Oh God, what the hell did you do to him?' She waved us in as she scurried off to the fireplace. 'Quick, get him in here.'

I picked him up and carried him in. 'Thanks, Ms Egree. You're a lifesaver.'

'Yeah, yeah, I know,' she said, then jerked her head towards the couch. 'Lay him down.'

I put him down gently, then tapped his face. 'You there, bud? Wake up. C'mon.'

He blinked slowly, drawing in raspy, weak breaths.

'Now, listen close, kids,' Ms Egree said from across the room, over at the fireplace. 'You're both going to have to hold him down, and once the garicuda lets go make sure it doesn't get near you, got it?'

I gripped the kid's arms. 'Got it.'

Viella hesitated then did so, holding his legs down. 'What are you going to do?'

'Alrighty, here it comes. Is the kid awake?'

I checked his face. 'Not really.'

'Well, he's gonna be.'

Ms Egree pressed the end of a red hot iron rod under the garicuda's stinger. Kiro's eyes flung open and he screamed like a banshee. He flailed about on the couch but we managed to hold him down.

The garicuda made a sort of screeching sound as it writhed and twitched at the touch of the heat. After a couple of seconds, it pulled its stinger out of Kiro's leg, then flung itself away and sprawled onto the floor. Baldy stopped screaming and sank into the couch, while Viella and I backed off from the parasite.

It was a fat and swollen thing now, and not as nimble as it used to be. It even struggled to get off its back, and its various legs and appendages flailed mindlessly in the air.

As it was about to get onto its feet, Ms Egree batted it with the rod, sending its bulging body skidding across the floorboards to the door. I jogged up, opened the door, and booted its ass out. I was going to stomp on it, but bursting that thing would've been messy.

Kiro lay there, clutching to the couch, taking short, quick breaths. At least he wasn't screaming anymore. His leg was looking pale and veiny though, and the hole the garicuda left was red and swollen.

Viella stared at him, slack-jawed and wide-eyed. We were both just kind of standing there, catching our breaths, coming to grips with the fact we actually made it out alive.

'Ms Egree, you're a champion. Thanks so much,' I said with a smile.

Ms Egree hobbled over to him with a sopping wet cloth, which she pressed over the kid's wound. 'It's what I do.'

I ambled over to Viella. 'So,' I said, cracking a grin. 'I guess this means that I…'

'Shut up.'

'…was right.'

Viella scrunched her face up. 'Enough, Synn. I haven't the energy to deal with your inanities.'

'Who are your new friends, kiddo?' Ms Egree asked, looking up at me. 'They don't look like they're in the business.'

Friends. Funny word.

'Right, of course. This fine young man is Kiro,' I told her. I gestured to Viella. 'And this is my new wife, Viella.'

Her mouth fell open, utterly aghast. 'I am *not* your wife.'

'Kiro here is our son.'

Viella punched my arm. 'Enough of your nonsense.'

Ms Egree punched my other arm. 'Oh, cut it out, would you?' she chuckled. 'It's been a long minute, stretch. What brings you here?'

'Well…' I took a knee in front of her, laying on the charm. 'We've been walking through the Tyrant Sands all day. We fought off some sand monsters, and I carried this little cutie here so, if it's all good with you, it would mean the world to me if we could stay here the night.'

'Oh for God's sakes,' she groaned. 'Suppose I can't really say no, huh?'

I nodded graciously. 'You're too kind for this world, my friend.'

'Yeah, yeah, shut your handsome mouth,' Ms Egree grumbled as she hobbled over to a steaming pot in the hearth. 'You know I hate it when you appeal to my humanity like that.'

'Sorry, ma'am,' I said with a smile.

'I was just finishing up my pottage stew when you came banging on my door. If your pals don't like it, you can tell them where to shove it.'

'Probably won't be the last time I come banging on your door.' I smiled.

'I certainly hope it is,' she squawked, 'so I can finally get some goddamn peace and quiet.'

Chapter Eleven

The Twisted Seas

When the garicuda latched onto me, I was in so much pain I thought I was going to die. The helplessness I felt as the stinger burrowed through my flesh, draining my blood, was horrifying. Even after the creature had been removed, I could still feel echoes of the harrowing sensation throbbing in my leg. I was foolish for being so careless when I saw it climbing on me. I owed my life to Viella and Synn, and his kind friend Ms Egree.

Ms Egree was a generous yet aloof old lady, and apparently the only person in the world who had Synn's respect. She gave us water and allowed us to stay in her home for the night. In many ways, she reminded me of Synn. She had the same accent and mannerisms, and was like a smaller, older, female incarnation of him. After realising that, I wondered if he had adopted many of his own characteristics from her.

Because Synn's clothes were bloody and ruined, and I had no pants, she offered us spare clothes that Synn had left behind from his earlier visits here. She gave him a beige linen tunic fastened at the waist with a thin leather belt. She was also going to return him a pair of loose brown trousers he had left years ago, but since I was obviously more in need of pants, she gave them to me instead. They were huge on me. I tightened the sash around my waist to secure them, then tucked the excess fabric into my shin wraps, but still looked silly enough that Ms Egree and Synn snickered at the sight of me. I couldn't blame them. I looked like I had chicken legs.

Each of us had a bowl of thick, tasty soup called pottage stew. It was hot and filling, and just what we needed after what we had been through. The four of us sat around the fire while we ate, Ms Egree on a chair, and the three of us on the floorboards, while Synn entertained Ms Egree with stories of varying truth about our journey. When he told her how long the garicuda had clung to me, she said she was surprised that I was still alive.

'Why is that surprising?' I asked.

'Garicudas suck you dry,' Synn explained as he chewed. 'They dig their sucker thing into your flesh until it reaches the bone. That's why we had to get it off quick, 'cos once it did, there's no getting it off until you've got no blood left.'

That must be why it was hard to stay awake. 'Why do they do that?' I asked. 'Why do they take so much that it's deadly?'

'They're parasites. That's how they survive.'

I stirred my spoon through the bowl as I thought. 'Why can't they just… take some of my blood, then move on?'

He swallowed a chunky spoonful of soup, then said, 'Because they don't care. They just want blood. They'll drain you of everything then move on until they find another poor animal.' He glanced at me from the corner of his eye. 'You get the point?'

I looked down on my leg. 'I do.'

Though the pain was subsiding, a stabbing ache continued to throb under the wound. When I had inspected the puncture, it was a swollen, red mess. The skin all around the wound was pale and veiny, and it seemed as if the leg itself was skinnier. I couldn't put weight on my leg without bolts of pain shooting through me, so I had no choice but to eat the last pomegen so I would be able to walk.

To call garicudas *precious* seemed wrong to me, but I was not sure why. All life is precious, I knew that, and that creature was a living being. So, it was precious and beautiful.

But how could something that could only survive by draining the life of other beings be called precious? Why would Orisaea, in all Her love and wisdom, create such a horrible creature?

I remembered the teachings of the Order. *Humanity cannot understand the perfect vision of the gods,* my masters would ruminate. *The world is a beautiful work of art that can only be understood by divinity. We are each a mere stroke of paint on this grand tapestry, our perspective is too limited to see its whole greatness.* It was a bittersweet lesson – the world is beautiful even if we cannot understand it. So, we must love and appreciate it anyway.

But after what I went through, that lesson did not sit well with me. If that is so, why must that creature bring so much pain to survive? Where is the beauty in pain? If anguish is beauty in the eyes of the gods, is divine beauty really to be loved and praised?

Why was this the only time in my life I had ever questioned that?

Ms Egree's voice plucked me from my conflicting thoughts. 'It's a good thing the three of you got here when you did. Why the hell were you going through the Tyrant Sands anyway? Did you have a death wish?'

'We are travelling to Azale, madam,' Viella replied, shifting around where she sat, still struggling to be comfortable on the floor. 'Passage through the sands was the swiftest option.'

'To die, maybe,' Ms Egree said, resting her cheek on her fist. 'You have smarter ways.'

Synn put his bowl down in front of him. 'Which brings me to this; I need to ask you a favour, Ms Egree.'

She groaned. 'Oh God, here we go.'

'We need to go through the Twisted Seas.'

Viella's icy blue eyes flickered. 'We *what?*'

Synn gave a lazy wave of his hand, as if to dissolve her worries with the gesture.

'So what you're really saying is you want another ride on the old Quickfeather, hmm?' Ms Egree smirked, sitting up straight. 'I knew you'd come back for more.'

'Can I be blamed? I hear the captain is a legend.'

Ms Egree chuckled, then the smile dropped from her face. 'Alright, cut the crap, Synn. What do I get outta this?'

'We can pay you,' he said.

'I don't need money anymore, kiddo. I didn't move out here to be reliant on merchants for anything.' Ms Egree folded her arms and leaned back in her chair. 'C'mon, make it spicy.'

Synn grumbled and thought for a moment. 'How about this; you take us through the seas, and we call it *even*.'

Ms Egree's eyebrows lifted. 'That right? We talking that favour I owe you from Gatchet?'

'We sure are.'

She leaned forward. 'Then we understand after this, I don't owe you jack, yeah?'

'We understand.'

Ms Egree clapped her hands together, a big toothy grin on her face. 'Great. Then tomorrow we're setting sail.'

'Thank you, ma'am. You're too kind,' Synn purred. 'I always knew I could depend on you.'

'Okay you can stop kissing my ass now. You look like a little bitch.'

Ms Egree then devised some makeshift bedding for us. She had enough blankets for two separate beds, one on a piece of furniture called a couch, and another on the floorboards. She grumbled about making such an effort for us 'janks' but admitted '*If I'm going to do it, might as well do it right.*' I offered Viella to take the couch while I took the blankets on the floor. It wasn't very comfortable, but it was warm, and I was in no shortage of weariness.

As I lay on the floor below the couch, listening to Ms Egree and Synn snoring in their bed across the room, I noticed Viella was still awake. Even though it was dark inside the cottage, I could make out in the moonlight seeping through a window that Viella's eyes were open. She was staring up at the ceiling, her hands woven together over her belly.

'Madam,' I whispered, careful not to wake Synn or Ms Egree, 'are you awake?'

'I am,' she murmured.

'Is something troubling you?'

She inhaled, then sighed softly. 'So many times of late, I have come so close to death, and I have been utterly powerless to save myself. It seems my life goes on only because destiny allows it.' She took another breath. 'And I wonder… if my destiny truly is the regency, or… if it is something else.'

I thought on it. 'I'm having my own doubts on my destiny, too,' I admitted.

I had come to a realisation that had been bothering me. The idea of a singular, *ultimate truth* that is found at the end of the world does not make any sense. None of the masters had been to the Edge, yet they were all judged to be 'enlightened' and then ordained. I didn't want to think of Shien as a liar, but I could not ignore my doubts. *Was there another, hidden purpose for this journey? Am I searching for something that even exists?*

'No matter how much we would like to, we cannot see the future, Viella,' I continued, drawing from what I knew to advise both of us. 'Only the present. Only what is now. Do not forget to live in the now, madam. You do have a destiny, and it is shaped by how you live in the present. Live now and live well.'

A tiny, sad laugh came from Viella. 'Such wisdom,' she remarked flatly, before rolling onto her side and clutching her blankets closer to her body.

The next morning, I checked my leg. It had completely recovered. There was a pink mark where the garicuda had punctured me, but the pain and the swelling were gone. It was worth using the last pomegen, but now that I was without them, we needed to be very careful for the rest of our travels.

Ms Egree took her time crafting a wonderful breakfast for us; beans, eggs, and rye bread, fashioned from ingredients she collected from her garden outside. She insisted we take our time to enjoy the food. Viella was prompt with her meal, but Synn and I savoured the food and its flavour. For all we knew, it might have been a while before we could eat like this again. While we broke our fast, I took the opportunity to ask about the Twisted Seas.

Ms Egree led us outside and pointed to the horizon beyond her home. Thundering in a gulf in the distance was a raging storm. Immediately, I noticed something extraordinary about it. Phenomena I could only describe as twisting blue pillars rose from the unseen seas below and up into the sky. The storm was situated in a gulf that cut into the land like an enormous monster had bitten into the continent and torn out a chunk of the country. She said the storm in the Twisted Seas had raged on since the beginning of time. The sky around it was perpetually darkened by gloomy clouds that preceded its wrath all the way up to where we were standing. Scattering streaks of lightning flashed rapidly, briefly lighting up the colossal, spinning columns for a split second at a time. According to Ms Egree, that is where we would be sailing through.

I was stunned. Nothing in our scrolls ever spoke of this place. *How is it that no one in our Order knew of this? How much knowledge is missing from our archives?*

Viella, with the utmost politeness, pardoned herself and asked if she could speak with Synn and myself in private. Ms Egree obliged her.

'Do you honestly expect us to go through *that?!*' Viella hissed quietly to Synn.

'Easy, sunshine,' Synn replied coolly. 'Ms Egree is the finest captain to ever grace those seas.'

She crossed her arms. 'You must be mad. Even the most experienced captains can't control a flying ship, much less a frail old woman who can hardly see past her own nose.'

Synn clicked his tongue. 'No need to be so mean, Vie. Do you think I'd be going anywhere near that goddamn place if I didn't trust Ms Egree to take us through it? We go way back, I trust her.'

'It's far too dangerous,' Viella said dismissively. 'We'd have better odds getting on the roads and fighting off bandits and assassins.'

'C'mon, snowball. *Trust me,*' Synn said, patting his chest. 'I had your back yesterday, right? You can trust me on this. A ship will save us days on foot.'

Viella pursed her lips and looked out over the horizon as she thought on it. Thunder rumbled in the distance while she pondered quietly. Her eyes switched to me. 'What do you think, Kiro?'

I rubbed my chin as I considered our options. 'Well as you said, madam, the roads will take us too long to travel on foot, and we don't have any supplies to last us until we get to the nearest town.' I didn't truly understand what the alternative was, but I was too embarrassed to show that. 'I think we should go with Synn's idea. I trust him.'

Synn's lips lifted into a smile. Viella was silent for a moment. She seemed unsatisfied with my answer, like she was hoping I would support her doubts. Eventually, she shook her head and muttered, 'Fine.'

Synn rubbed his hands together. 'Great. Let's get going then.'

Ms Egree hobbled along slowly with us towards the gulf. Along the way, she told us a story of how she and her husband, when they were young, threw a rotten tomato at a guard in Ceren then leapt across rooftops to escape them. She laughed as she recalled the struggle of the guards to keep up in their heavy sets of armour, and reminisced about how she and her husband spent their "retirement" days building the ship she owns now. Viella seemed to regard the story with a degree of contempt that you could only see in her eyes, but Synn was smiling and laughing along with her. I wasn't sure how to feel about it.

The shuddering cracks of thunder in the sky grew louder and louder as we approached the storm, as did the winds grow faster and stronger. We passed into a thin drizzle of rain that was like an intangible curtain surrounding the gulf. Now that we were closer, I could see the pillars were colossal spirals of black seawater, being sucked up into the sky and crashing back down on the seas as an endless volley of rain. There were near to fifty of these towering spirals that I could count, swirling up into the clouds. As I looked north, the mainland ended at a sheer cliff, and the seas below continued ever forward until they met the sky at the horizon. The water spirals, however, did not exceed the gulf. It was a striking sight, and the first time I had ever seen the ocean. I always knew it was vast, but even still, to see all that water was amazing.

Ahead of us, extending off the cliff face and hanging in the air, was a rickety bridge of old wooden planks soaked in seawater. Beside it, floating in the middle of the air, was Ms Egree's ship. The ship was cream coloured and held a slender shape. Two large beams rose from the centre and hoisted up a series of rippling white sails. A series of complicated ropes and pulleys strung from place to place. Attached to the ship underneath the hull were two massive metal structures that looked like giant bells. Inside them were large, flat blades, spinning slowly.

I was astonished. 'That's your ship?' I asked Ms Egree.

'Sure is, kiddo,' she said, a proud smile on her lips as she gazed adoringly at it. 'Her name is *Quickfeather*.'

Quickfeather was massive. It would have been heavier than a hundred men. And there it was, swaying in the air like a flower petal. 'But how is it floating?' I asked.

Curious, I rushed ahead of the group and peered over the cliff, to see how far down it went. The fall continued for miles, down further than I had ever seen a depth plunge. Far at the bottom, ferocious waves as big as large hills thrashed against the craggy rock walls of the land beneath us. In the centre, they surged up and down, smashing into each other as if locked in a perpetual struggle for domination, the entire sea rising and falling with the rhythm of a slow beating heart. As the waters neared the swirling pillars, the waves calmed as they were drawn into the spiral that led all the way up to the pitch black clouds above us. I was in complete awe and totally speechless. There was a raw, striking beauty to the overwhelming scale of its chaos.

Synn steadied my shoulder and pulled me back a step. 'Easy, buddy,' he said with a smile. 'One little slip, and you'll be falling long enough to pray to every god in the world.'

He was very much right. I stood back and watched Ms Egree walk across the buckling bridge and hop onto the ship with ease, as if this was just one of the hundreds of other times she had done this. Synn followed behind her and walked with just as much indifference. Viella and I were hesitant to go, as the planks were flapping precariously in the gusts. Synn looked over his shoulder at us.

'C'mon now!' He waved us over. 'Just walk! It's easy!'

Viella took a breath and walked forward carefully. She pressed a foot down on the first board and was surprised. Now that she was standing on it, it balanced and became relatively still. She tutted, then took another step. The next plank did the same, calming as it supported her weight.

'Fascinating,' she remarked.

I followed Viella. When I stepped on the boards, I felt them almost rise up to welcome my foot and properly support me. It felt as solid as earth. I was amazed by it, and thought about how any of this was possible. *Was there divination here?*

Viella and I hopped over the gap between the ship and the bridge and landed on the deck. 'It's a good thing there's four of us!' Ms Egree said from the back of the ship, holding onto the spokes of a wheel she stood behind. 'Means we can properly run the engines!'

'How does this ship work?' I asked over the rising winds. 'Aren't ships supposed to sail on water?'

'Boats sail on water.' Synn grinned. '*This* sails on air.'

'You mean to say,' I said slowly, my nerves wobbling my voice, 'that we're going to fly through the storm? Like birds?'

'That's right, pal!'

'But… how?' I was struggling to imagine how this could be possible.

'The wind does most of the work,' said Synn. 'We just control where we go.'

'Listen, kid.' Ms Egree came up to my side and pointed to one of two large, barrel-like contraptions on the sides of the deck. Both of them were fixed securely to the floor and had a protruding lever. 'Go take hold of the winder over there. We're going to need you to keep it churning.'

'O-Of course, madam.' I hurried my way across to the machine she pointed to, minding my balance on the swaying deck.

'And you, sunshine,' Ms Egree said to Viella. 'Take hold of the other one, to the left.'

Viella seemed displeased with the job assigned to her. Begrudgingly, she moved towards the contraption, her usually poised, dignified stride reduced to an awkward scramble by the rocking of the ship. She gripped the handle attached to the side of the machine. 'What are these?' she asked.

'Winders, for the propellers under the ship,' Ms Egree explained. 'Don't stop turning them, otherwise, the engine will go out and we'll get tossed around in the wind like a leaf.'

Viella's jaw dropped. '*What?!* Why am I doing this then? Shouldn't it be Synn?'

'I have a more important job,' Synn bragged. 'I'm the navigator.'

'Is that not what she does?' Viella gestured to Ms Egree.

'No, sweetheart,' Synn said with a grin. 'The Quickfeather is her ship, which means she gets to steer the ship. Her eyesight isn't too good anymore, so I tell her what's ahead.'

'If she can't see, then why is she flying this?'

'I literally just explained why.'

Ms Egree pulled out a pair of round, oversized spectacles bound in leather and strapped them over her eyes. 'Are we ready, crew?' she called out from the helm.

Synn wrapped an arm around the main mast in the centre, swung himself around to face her, and shouted 'Yes, Captain!'

'Fantastic. Winder monkeys!' she yelled, meaning Viella and I. 'Start *winding!*

With both arms, we began turning the levers with round, sweeping motions. A constant and rhythmic *whirring* noise came from inside the winders as we spun life into the mechanisms. Ms Egree gripped a lever beside her with a tiny hand and grunted as she cranked it forward. There was a *clunk* sound, then the propellers underneath began to spin faster, enough so that we now could hear them moving through the air.

She gripped another lever to the right, pushed it forward, and yelled *'HERE WE GO!'*

The ship's propellers roared to life as the Quickfeather jumped forth, launching into the air. A tremendous force slammed into me, and a scream slipped from my mouth in surprise. Howling, surging winds smashed into us as we lunged into the skies. I planted my feet firmly on the deck and gripped the winder tightly.

But abruptly, the ship began to lean to the left. Barrels on board slid across the slanting deck. My feet were very close to slipping.

'WINDER MONKEYS!' Ms Egree bellowed over the winds. I hadn't expected her to be able to shout so loudly. 'WE'RE DROPPING SPEED! WIND, DAMN YOU, WIND!'

Viella was sprawled over the ground. One of her hands was still gripping onto the winder. She scrambled to her feet and started spinning it frantically. I continued, churning as quickly as I could, the machine's *whirring* noise matching my tempo.

The ship leaned back to the right and found balance. I only just realised how hard my heart was pounding in my chest. I took the chance to fully realise what was happening.

We were soaring through the open air, with all the grace and freedom of an eagle. I could've never, in my wildest imaginations, conceived of what was actually happening in this moment. Once the ship was flying smoothly, a feeling of utter freedom rushed through me. Chills rippled down my arms and back. Ms Egree celebrated with a hearty cackle behind us. Synn cheered as he pumped his fist into the air, with a wide grin on his face. He let out a whoop of joy to the world, yelling out against the wind, and a booming crack of lightning and thunder replied to him. A huge grin spread across my face.

Something wet hit my forehead. A drop of rain. I felt another, then another. Soon enough, rain was falling on us like a barrage, battering down mercilessly on the ship. It soaked into my clothes, and already my body was drenched. There was so much of it that the world began to fade in a dim blue fog.

'Steady as she goes!' Synn bellowed. Even at his loudest, his voice against the wind and rain was only faint.

I flinched as a bolt of lightning crashed near the ship, and a deafening clash of thunder boomed in the sky above us. Its all-encompassing, ear-splitting sound was a reminder of how tiny we were in comparison to the storm and the seas.

'*Steady!*' Synn roared again.

My hands were slipping from the winder because of all the water. I squeezed the handle so hard my knuckles went white. I clenched my teeth as I endured the lashing of the cold wind assaulting my drenched, shivering body. So long as I kept winding the machine, I could build up some warmth.

I heard a new sound now, amongst the wailing winds and relentless rain. It was a heavy rumbling, reminding me of a waterfall pounding against rocks but deeper and louder. I looked to my right and I saw it; a spinning monolith of water. My mouth fell open. It was utterly colossal. It dwarfed the ship and every building I could think of, and I could see it now in stunning detail. The water coiled like the twisting winds of a tornado as it was sucked up into the sky. My eyes followed up the pillar, and where the water met the storm, the black clouds swirled around the connection. Thin streams of seawater continued in the sky, branching like veins along the all-encompassing tempest. Hundreds of little flashes of lightning crackled in them, and briefly lit up tiny fractions of the billowing, pulsating darkness that loomed over us.

'*TWISTER AHOY!*' Synn roared, urgency heightening his pitch. '*STEER CLEAR! STEER CLEAR!*'

I looked ahead of us. A different twister was weaving into our path. If we did not change directions, we would smash into it. I glanced back and up at Ms Egree, whose wrinkled face was in deep concentration. She really did seem like she was in her element, calm and unabated, and just like that I had complete faith in her. I kept churning, my arms now the warmest part of my body. Ms Egree spun the wheel to the right, hitting it again and again to spin it faster. The ship slowly manifested her direction as it leaned to the right, the heavy beams of wood creaking as it moved. I kept my feet firmly planted, and continued winding. The sound of the twister grew louder and louder as we approached it. This one was thinner than the others, and it was moving faster than any of them I had seen. Even the spiral weaved and twisted more extremely, like flames in a hearth. Lightning flashed around us. Thunder ruptured the skies over our heads. The entire world was slanted now, and it was becoming a great strain to maintain my balance. Some barrels dropped off the side of the deck, and I watched them fall to the ravenous sea far below.

We were now getting close enough to the twister that a spray of salty mist was swirling into us. The sounds of the wind and rain and Quickfeather's propellers were overpowered by the rising roar of the twister's rumble. Synn hugged the mast, clutching to the beam tightly. Ms Egree cackled madly as she steered the ship out of the way of the twister, narrowly escaping it.

Once we cleared it, she steered left and balanced the ship. I was beginning to feel ill from the rocking, a thick, bloating sickness now bubbling in my belly. I looked over to Viella to see how she was enduring and caught a glimpse of her bent over the rail and retching.

'*Synn! How much longer will this take!?*' I yelled over to him. He didn't respond, so I built up some power from my stomach and repeated the question.

He looked back at me, his chest heaving, and pointed behind us. '*See for yourself!*'

I glanced over my shoulder, and to my surprise, the edge of the gulf we had departed from was almost just a speck in the distance. We were crossing over stretches of land that would have taken us hours, maybe even days on foot.

Synn threw an arm out, gesturing widely to the ship and the world around us. '*IS THIS NOT HOW LIFE WAS SUPPOSED TO BE LIVED?!*' he roared, then let out a wild laughter, holding nothing back.

'*SYNN!*' Viella's voice triumphed over the gusts. She was pointing ahead. '*LOOK!*'

Synn turned back around to see.

Ahead of us, there were two more twisters, much wider and thicker than the last one. They were moving slowly, but closing in all the same, in front of us. The first was on our right, and the next was on our left. Steering away was not an option, we simply didn't have enough time.

Synn must have known this, too. He hopped off the mast and stepped towards Ms Egree. '*TWISTERS AHOY, EGREE!*' He bellowed with all his might. '*FULL SPEED!*'

Ms Egree gritted her teeth and yanked her neck from side to side. '*Hold on, folks!*' she yelled as she cranked the lever to her right all the way forward.

Quickfeather sped up, the gusts now whistling as they flew past us. A heavier pressure crashed into our bodies. I kept winding, the contraption's *whirring* now louder than my thoughts, but my arms were beginning to ache. I glanced at Viella, who had the same agonised expression on her face.

'*STEADY!*' Synn roared the command.

We were going to slip through the middle.

The roar of the twisters grew louder, shaking the ship and quaking our eardrums. I could feel the rumbling in my chest.

We were about to collide with the first one, on our right.

'*STEADY!*' Synn screamed.

I was putting everything I had into spinning this machine. My arms and chest were burning, but I refused to give up.

The entire ship buckled and shook violently as we sailed past the first twister, narrowly scraping by it. I looked to my right and saw the dark blue water merely a few feet from my face. Terror and awe shrieked in my heart.

The instant we cleared the first one, the next was only seconds away. I glanced at Viella and my looming fears were true. Her pace was slowing, and her arms wobbling.

I acted fast. I gathered as much strength as I could spare and screamed louder than I had ever before, '*SYNN!*'

He looked to me.

'*VIELLA!*'

He looked, then bolted towards her. He took hold of the winder and Viella stumbled backwards, her arms limp and quivering. He clenched his jaw as he kept it churning.

Ms Egree steered the ship to the right, tilting it away from the twister. Quickfeather began to lean right but it was too late. The entire ship quaked as the left flank skimmed against the twister, slashing it like a knife. An overwhelming wave of water spilled from the spiral and crashed like a flood onto the deck. I watched as Synn disappeared in the foam, and my only thought before the water hit me was Viella.

The water smashed into me, engulfing me in a mute and breathless world of bubbles and shimmering aqua. It took every fibre of strength in my body to hold fast against its force. The tang of saltwater prickled my tongue, and my nostrils burned as water filled them. I felt something crash into me.

It was Viella's body. She was about to be washed off the ship.

I let go of the winder and grabbed her ankle in the same second I would have missed it. Her momentum almost pulled me off the ship with her, but I dropped my body and let myself be dragged forwards, my back now scraping against the deck. My feet pushed up against the sides of the railing, and I gripped onto her ankle tightly with both hands, almost screaming as it felt like the force of the water would rip my arms from my body.

Then the water cleared off of me. The sounds of the world returned in ear-piercing clarity and I dropped heavily against the floorboards. I gasped deeply as I swallowed big gulps of air. But now that I had let go of the winder, one of the propellers was slowing down. The ship was about to start tilting, and Viella's body was still dangling overboard.

I screamed out for Synn. He swore, then his footsteps thumped across the deck. He grabbed hold of Viella's other leg. We both grunted as we pulled her up and over the rail, then laid her down. She was thoroughly drenched and completely limp.

'Viella!' I yelled at her face.

She was unconscious. I couldn't tell if she was breathing. Fear tightened my throat. 'Viella!' I shouted again.

'*Get back on the winder, kid!*' Synn yelled at me as he ran for the other one.

The ship started groaning and creaking. I could feel our momentum slowing. I had stopped winding for too long. We were about to lose control, but I couldn't get back on the machine yet. Viella was still unconscious.

With panic swelling in my heart, I flipped her over and hit her back with the heel of my palm. Water gurgled and sputtered from her mouth. I smacked her again, and more water splattered out, but she was still lifeless.

The world started to slant, and I felt gravity's push move onto my left side. Before we could fall, Ms Egree threw her little body against the winder and started spinning the handle. Quickfeather slowly, slowly, began to tilt back up.

With a burst of strength and desperation, I struck Viella one more time. A burst of water flew from her mouth. Viella coughed and hacked and wheezed, and tumbled in my arms. She was alive. Tears almost burst out of me in sheer relief. She had a harrowed expression, with wide frightened eyes that darted around. She raised a trembling hand and I sat her up against the railing.

'*Sit and rest!*' I yelled. Viella, shaking and sputtering, abided.

My saturated clothes squelched as I stood up to take over from Ms Egree, who moved her old body as quickly as she could back up to the wheel. I continued churning, but my strength was all but gone. I could not match the speed I had before.

The lever cranked, and the ship slowed its pace. It was still fast, but much more controlled now, and at a pace that was feasible for me. We were flying through a clearing in the storm, where there were no twisters. In the distance, the other side of the gulf was getting closer. There was a path that led into a dense forest, awaiting us at another floating bridge. It was only minutes away. I could gather the strength to push through the last of this trial.

'*Land ahoy!*' Synn shouted. His voice was high and bright. He started laughing. '*Land ahoy!*' he shouted again, laughing helplessly.

A smile spread across my face. We were nearly there, nearly through.

Synn's eyes found something in the distance, and his laughter dwindled into nothing. I watched the joy on his face drain away and dread take its place. His eyes were locked onto whatever he had seen. I gazed ahead.

Far off into the distance, amongst the chaos of the twisters, was the shape of another flying ship. It was enormous in comparison to our vessel. It had large, billowing black sails and was being lifted by four giant propellers at the bottom. Protruding from the front of it was what appeared to be a giant, hooked spear mounted on a massive crossbow. For a ship that massive it was moving quickly, weaving deftly through the twisters.

It was flying towards us.

Chapter Twelve

The Final Judgement

We never stood a chance.

Once they had fired the hook into Quickfeather, the sheer size of the damn thing was enough to practically rip her apart as it reeled us in. They swarmed us, the whole pack of them whooping and crowing as they leapt from their monster of a ship onto ours. Kiro was smart enough to follow my lead and put his hands up. I didn't have enough bullets for all of them even if I did land every shot. Our royal swordswoman was out of commission. The kid could hardly swing his arms. There were probably forty of them. There really was nothing we could do, except throw our hands up and let it be done quickly. They appreciated our common sense, and beat us only a little bit, before searching us and plucking every little valuable thing we had. At least they spared Ms Egree. Maybe they weren't so bad.

They dragged us onto their ship then let the shredded remains of Quickfeather drop into the seas like it was the carcass of a pig. Ms Egree was dead silent, which was worse than if she was screaming about how she was going to kill them all like how she used to be. Her lips trembled as she watched Quickfeather fall with red, teary eyes. I hated seeing her like that.

They tied the three of us to the mast like beaten dogs and sat Ms Egree on a stool behind us. One of their crew held a parasol over her head while she sat there, totally crushed. I noticed that and thanked them for it, and their reply was a knee to my face.

'Shut yer hole,' the ugly bastard spat. 'Ye don't git to speak.'

I decided that when I killed this man, I was going to stick the gun in his mouth and pop his head wide open. Seriously, if I got hit in the face again I was going to kill someone.

But the trick to these things is to never take them seriously. That gives them power. On my face, I showed them nothing but a little smirk.

'Do ye know where ye arr?' His breath reeked like the gutters back home. I managed not to gag. 'Yer on board the *Final Judgement*, boy. And judgement is what yer got comin' for ye.'

I didn't pay this wannabe tough guy any attention. This was bait to get me to speak so he could punch me again, so I said nothing.

Then he punched me hard across the jaw anyway, a wave of pain exploding from the hit. 'Yer'll answer when spoken to, boy!'

I shook the pain out of my face. 'Oh, my mistake, pal. I thought you didn't want me to talk.'

He hit me again, probably knocking some childhood memories out of my brain. 'Don't sass me, boy!' The crew around him began to snicker and titter like girls. He was just toying with me.

I spat, and a wad of blood smacked against the deck. I clenched my jaw, stayed cool, and kept up the gutter talk. 'Credit where it's due; you hit pretty good for a girl.'

He growled. That pissed him off. This time he kicked me hard in the ribs, knocking the air out of my chest. 'A girl, is it? Ye look like a woman with all that hair!'

'Oof, honey, you're taking my breath away!' I laughed at him. 'You sure know how to make a man feel good, don't you?'

'Shut it!' He reared his foot back and kicked me in the face, mashing my head against the mast and grinding his boot against my cheek. Hard, crushing pain pressed down on my whole skull.

'Not so smug now, are ye?' he mocked. I would've smacked back, but I would've sounded like an idiot with my mouth squashed, so I just focused on not letting out any kind of whimper. I clenched my jaw hard.

My body burned with pain and rage. I couldn't wait for the chance to beat the life out of this scum-sucking bastard.

'What do you want from us?' Kiro asked carefully.

The scum-sucker took his boot off my stinging, dirtied face, and looked over Kiro, sizing him up. 'We want what yer good for,' he said, sauntering over to him with a cocky attitude that was only there because we were tied up and outnumbered. 'Yer coins, yer loot…'

Then he kicked him hard in the face.

'And yer silence.'

Kiro cried from the hit then whimpered. Blood poured from his nose and down his lips. His eyes were welling up. *Oh God, he's going to start crying.*

'Why…' He sniffled, then spoke up with a shaky voice. 'Why are you doing this?!'

'Oh lad, are ye *crying?!*' The bastard started cackling. 'I think I *broke* him!' He and the crew howled with laughter. Kiro bowed his head and tried to stop himself from tearing up to little success. Watching this made me even angrier, which surprised me. Never thought I'd give this much of a damn about another person.

'You want what we're good for, yes?' Viella piped up, her voice steady and measured. I wished she'd just stay quiet for God's sakes. 'I would like to offer you a proposal.'

'Oooh,' the man's slimy voice rumbled. 'This one's a gem. Talks pretty. Looks pretty.' He crouched down and got real close to her face. 'I bet ye'd *feel* pretty, too.'

The crew howled like animals, shouting some gross comments. Viella kept her composure and ignored them. 'My name is Viella Vanclaude,' she said, clearly and loud enough for everyone to hear. 'If your men deliver us to Azale, untouched and unharmed, I swear to you, by the honour of my family name, I will reward you all for your service.'

The bastard squinted at her for a while without saying a word. 'I think I know of a reward ye can give to me,' he mused, licking his lips. I don't think he had any idea who the Vanclaudes were. 'But we don't much like Azale. Far away, and full of posh little janks like yerself who think they can get their papa to buy them outta any troubles.' He latched a filthy hand onto her cheeks and yanked her face forward. 'Listen well, ye uptight little wench, yer name doesn't mean nothin' out here. Only thing matters is what the Captain thinks of ye.' He paused, then stroked her chin with his thumb. 'But that doesn't mean we can't enjoy yer... *generous reward.*'

Viella said nothing, refusing to give him any kind of reaction.

Ahead of us, the door to the Captain's quarters burst open with a crash, and the crew, who had been rowdy and hollering, fell silent. The guy let go of Viella's face and stepped away.

There was a long pause before the Captain walked forward from the shadows. He was a giant of a man, bound in muscle, who stood head and shoulders above his crew. He wore a long crimson coat, a tattered black waistcoat over his bare chest, and long black breeches that tucked into dirty cuffed boots. He had a wiry black beard that fell to his collarbone, dark bulging eyes that had a wild look to them, and a wide hat under which long streaks of oily black hair fell from.

'Ahoy there, friends,' he said with a booming, gravelly voice. 'Me name is Deadeye, I'm the Captain of this fine vessel, the Final Judgement. I trust ye've met me crew, and me collarsnapper, Waylon.' He gestured to the bastard I was going to kill later. 'By now, he would've told ye what our intentions are.'

Waylon suddenly seemed nervous. 'Err, Captain,' he piped up. 'I hadn't the time to explain yet.'

Deadeye stared at the moron. His eyes were freaky. He hadn't blinked yet. 'Ye didn't tell 'em?'

'No.'

The Captain growled and clomped over to us. 'Fine then. I'll say it to 'em.' He squatted down to get closer to our faces. God, he smelled bad. 'The four of us are going to play a little game.'

Ah, fantastic, yet another one of these 'play-a-game' types.

'Listen close, now; I'm going to ask ye all a few questions. Ye get them all right, ye live to see another day.' He looked at me with his wide, unblinking eyes. 'Ye get three *wrong*, and I throw ye into a twister and let the seas feast on yer bones. Ye get all that?'

We just stared at him blankly.

I mean, he couldn't be serious. A game of questions?

Suddenly, Deadeye stomped his massive foot on the deck and screamed in our faces 'DO YE UNDERSTAND ME?!'

'Yikes, pal, yes,' I said.

Viella and Kiro stammered their responses. Deadeye, satisfied, stood up and laughed, his rage gone as quick as it came. 'Aye, ye do.' He swung his arms up and announced to his crew, 'It's time for another game of TRIVIA QUESTIONS!'

They cheered, but not as enthusiastically as they had for the collarsnapper. There was something about it that was rigid, a touch of staleness to their voices, as if they were not really on board with the whole trivia thing, but were too afraid of their Captain to say so. I looked over to Viella and Kiro, and the two of them were just as confused as I was.

'Hold on a minute, Cap,' I said. 'So all we need to do to live is get your questions right?'

'Aye,' Deadeye said. He cocked his head. 'Any other rules confuse ye?'

'N-no.' I was honestly not really sure what to say.

'Righto then, let's begin.' Deadeye whistled, and a lackey pulled up a rickety wooden chair and placed it behind him. Deadeye sat on it and rubbed his palms together. 'Before we get started, I want to know yer names.' He pointed at me. 'What's yours, man?'

'You can call me Synn,' I said.

'I think I've heard of ye, Synn. Yer a little famous, aren't ye?' Deadeye beamed. He looked to Kiro sitting next to me. 'What about ye, boy?'

Kiro looked up at him with sore, red eyes. 'I am Kiro,' he mumbled.

'Strange name, where are ye from, boy?' Deadeye asked, leaning forward. He seemed actually interested, or was at least polite enough to pretend he was.

'I hail from the Gentle Mountains,' Kiro sniffled. 'I am a disciple of the Order of Light.'

'Never heard of 'em,' Deadeye said flatly, before looking over to Viella and asking her name. While she was busy taking a thousand years to introduce herself, I tilted my head ever so slightly to Kiro and whispered in his ear.

'*Psst, Kiro.*'

He leaned his head over as well, but only a little, apparently learning the value in subtlety.

'*Why don't you pull some magic out of your ass and bust us outta here?*'

'*They took my ring when they captured us,*' he whispered back. '*I can't use divination without a source.*'

Shit.

'Vanclaude, Kiro, and Synn,' Deadeye said our names loudly. 'I'm going to ask ye all a question. Answer it if ye can.' He grinned, excited like a kid. 'First question; what was the former name of the 13th King?'

History was never my thing, but luckily Viella answered quickly. 'Epherio, son of Daldin.'

'Right, Vanclaude!' The Captain applauded her. The crew joined in, clapping with him.

This is so weird.

'Next question,' Deadeye continued. 'How many islands are there in the Jae Goh Isles?'

Viella opened her mouth, but paused and said nothing. 'It escapes me,' she mumbled.

'Thirteen,' I said. It had been a while since I'd been south-west, but I couldn't forget the Jae Goh Isles. Fun times.

'Right ye are, Synn.' Deadeye grinned and clapped. The crew clapped as well. When Deadeye grew tired of them, he raised a fist and just like that they were as silent as the grave. 'Who was the firstborn son of the famous explorer, Mercurio II?' he asked, his eyes leaping between the three of us.

Again, history. I was wondering where this hairy moron even learned any of this. I looked over to Viella, who was squinting as she tried to remember the answer. Finally, her head perked up and she answered, 'Grigori.'

'Yo ho! Right again, Vanclaude!' Deadeye cheered, pointing at her.

Waylon stepped forward, all of his cockiness missing. 'Uh, Captain,' he said, nervousness gripping his voice. 'She's wrong… his name was *Grigorio.*'

Deadeye turned his head and looked down on his puny collarsnapper like he was an annoying bug. 'It was close enough, Waylon,' Deadeye grumbled, his voice low and dark. He turned back around to us.

Waylon's beady eyes fluttered nervously. 'B-but, Captain—'

Deadeye's head snapped back to Waylon, and his jaws opened wide as he roared, 'Are ye questioning ME?!'

Waylon flinched and receded submissively, bowing his head. 'No, Captain. I'm sorry.'

Deadeye stared him down, and Waylon crumbled under his penetrating gaze. No one said a word. All you could hear was the wind, the thunder in the distance, and the ship's wood creaking as it swayed in the sky. The air reeked of fear.

Then, as quickly as sheathing a sword, Deadeye turned back to face us with a smile that stretched from ear-to-ear. 'Are ye ready for the next question?'

The three of us said yes.

'Good-o.' He cleared his throat. 'Elisane Loycott, the famous actress who drank real poison on stage and killed herself, died performing *what* play?'

'Oh, I know this, I know this one,' I said. And I really did, it was a famous story. The tragedy of something. 'Uh... the tragedy of...'

'*The Tragedy of the Moon Sisters*,' Viella answered.

Deadeye clapped and pointed at her. 'That's the answer! Three cheers for Vanclaude!'

The crew cheered obediently. *Hoo-ray! Hoo-ray! Hoo-ray!*

'Vanclaude, ye've earned yer life today,' Deadeye said gleefully, patting her on the head like she was a puppy. 'Ye need not answer anymore.'

She relaxed a little bit, but kept a frown on her face. I didn't like her, but to see her bruised and battered was not a pleasure. This stupid game wasn't going to make me forget how I was going to butcher these fools when I had the chance.

'Now, boys,' The Captain said, his eyes bouncing between Kiro and I. 'How many towers are on the outer wall of Ceren?'

I grew up in Ceren, so this was an easy question. Except, I couldn't remember off the top of my head how many there were. I wanted to say forty-four, but I wasn't sure. 'Four...tee...' I looked up to Deadeye, whose big black eyes looked back at mine, urging me to continue. 'Uhhh....' This was embarrassing. The number was in my brain somewhere.

Then Deadeye's eyes flicked downwards. He was hinting something. I looked down and saw his hand; he was sticking three fingers out but keeping it subtle. I wasn't sure if he was misleading me or helping me, because I couldn't understand the motive for why he would do either.

'Forty-three,' I said, wondering where the answer would take me.

Deadeye grinned. 'Yer right, Synn! Brilliant!'

There was some scattered applause. I noticed Waylon shake his head and scratch his neck with his pudgy fingers.

It looked like as long as we kept this guy entertained with this ridiculous game, we had a chance.

'What is the name of the man who said this famous quote?' Deadeye hacked, clearing his throat, then said dramatically, *'Today is a battle, and tomorrow goes to the victor.'*

I knew that one. 'Kier Zan, the Conqueror.'

Deadeye grinned and almost wiggled with excitement. 'Synn wins!' he celebrated.

The crew cheered but were much less passionate. They were getting bored of this. I had no sympathy for them. If they hated their captain, they could man up and replace him.

'And that leaves you, lad...' Deadeye smiled at Kiro.

Oh shit.

I had completely forgotten about Kiro.

He wasn't going to know anything.

'Ye've been quiet, it's always the quiet ones who are the smartest,' Deadeye said, his expectations already way too high. Kiro was staring at him, and I could tell even though he was trying his best to keep calm, he was getting scared.

'What is the message written under the sign that welcomes travellers into Raider's Rock?'

Kiro stared at him blankly. The entire ship was silent. Deadeye looked confused and leaned forward. 'Did ye hear me, lad?'

'Yes,' Kiro replied with a tiny voice. His lips quivered, then he admitted, 'I don't know the answer.'

Deadeye was surprised. He leaned back and stared at him, disappointed. 'It says "Welcome ye brave and foolish",' he said flatly.

There was an awkward silence, then Deadeye shook his head and asked another question. 'What is the nickname of the famous captain who built the Marauder's Fort?'

The same response. Kiro shamefully admitted he did not know. Deadeye took a breath. He asked Kiro if he was sure. Kiro confirmed that yes, he was sure he did not know. Deadeye looked at his feet, a kind of gloominess about him.

'Aye, an easy question, then.' The Captain thought for a second, scratching his beard, his eyes fixed to his boots. They flicked upwards, then he asked, 'Who is the Regent of Meras right now?'

Once again, Kiro said he did not know. Deadeye made the slightest whisper of the name '*Zafar*' and nodded at Kiro. The boy stared at him, confused, then after a few seconds, figured out to say 'Zafar?'

Deadeye practically leapt from his seat. 'Aye, that's it! Yer right!'

No one clapped. No one cheered. Waylon sighed and took a brave step forwards. 'Captain, ye told him the answer,' he said defiantly. 'That doesn't count! When are ye goin' to stop being so damn lenient, and—'

Before Waylon could finish speaking, Deadeye drew his cutlass and roared as he slashed open his collarsnapper's throat. A gush of hot blood squirted out and splattered across the deck and the bottom of Kiro's trousers. Kiro and Viella shrieked. Viella shut her eyes and turned away, while Kiro watched on, frozen stiff. A series of choked gurgles escaped Waylon as he struggled to speak and breathe. But he wasn't like that for long. Deadeye panted like a feral animal as he hacked and slashed, hacked and slashed, hacked and slashed, tearing off chunks of Waylon's flesh with each vicious swing. Even after Waylon stopped squirming on the ground and was clearly dead, Deadeye kept shredding the corpse with his sword, roaring like a beast all the while. Hack and slash. Hack and slash. Stab, stab, slash.

When he finally stopped, his fancy clothes and long beard were stained with blood and gore. A pool of crimson had formed under a gruesome and mutilated corpse. Chunks of meat had been scattered across the ship, along with fresh bloodstains that sprayed along the deck and crew. The body hardly looked human anymore. Kiro's face went white. He couldn't tear his eyes away. He just stared, his gaping mouth trembling, completely horrified. I understood now why Deadeye's crew were so damn scared of him. One of his men stumbled over to the edge of the ship and vomited over the side.

Deadeye huffed like a horse, his massive chest heaving up and down. A splash of red covered half of his wild face. His gaze snapped to Kiro. He still hadn't blinked yet. He clomped over to Kiro, knelt, and said, very slowly, 'It's true, lad... I have been more than... reasonable with ye... very patient...'

Kiro said nothing between his trembling, rapid breaths. Deadeye kept staring into his eyes as he ground his teeth. 'I'll ask ye one last question.' There was a long pause. Deadeye just kept gaping at him as if his mind had left him for a moment. Eventually, he asked him, 'What is the name of the bread that is sold on the streets of Raider's Rock?'

Kiro pressed his shaking self against the mast, vainly trying to get away from Deadeye. He said nothing between his shallow, panicked breaths. He shook his head.

Deadeye frowned, and his eyes fell shut. He stood up and wiped his face with his palm. He sighed.

'A shame,' he mumbled sadly.

I had to try.

'Listen, Captain, the kid here… he's a little weird, you know?' I tried to smile but couldn't quite make it. 'He actually, um, lived on a mountain all his life, so it's, uh, you know, not like he knows much about the world, and, uh—'

Deadeye walked off. He waved a hand to his crew. 'Get him up.'

Instantly, they obeyed him. Four men scurried over to us and loosened the ropes. They grabbed Kiro and hauled him up to his feet.

'Hold on a second, guys,' I spoke up. 'Just let me explain—'

Viella started up. 'Captain! Please spare him! I will reward your mercy, you have my word! Please!'

When the crew ignored us, Viella tried to stand. One of the pirates knocked her down and yelled at her to stay. She tried again, and they kicked her down harder.

'Vie, don't,' I told her.

She stayed down, defeat and pain on her face. They dragged the kid over to the railings, where they laid a long plank that led off the ship and hung over the massive plunge to the seas below.

'Rally, ho!' Deadeye bellowed the order, his voice like thunder. His crew scurried around the ship like rats, pulling ropes and waking up the ship. It shot forward with a resounding *kur-kung*, surging through the Twisted Seas and into the thick of the storm. Rain began to pound the ship. The thunder grew louder. The twisters got closer.

'*HALT!*' Deadeye roared. The ship slowed to a stop. There was a spray of mist floating in the air, and I could hear the roar of a twister growing louder. I looked over and that's when I saw it. It was just off the side of the ship, just ahead of the plank, towering over the ship like a huge, hungry monster.

The crew pushed Kiro onto the plank. He wobbled his arms as he tried to maintain his balance. Viella was begging now. '*Please! Don't do this!*'

Deadeye stomped over towards him.

134

I didn't resist the inevitable. There was no point.

Kiro gazed up at the twister in front of him.

The crew parted for Deadeye, who walked up to Kiro on the plank. The kid looked over his shoulder, back at us. There was a desperate look in his eye, a silent call for help. To my surprise, it made me feel a twinge in my chest. I went to say something, but my voice got caught in my throat.

Deadeye raised his leg, and kicked Kiro in the back, sending him hurtling off the plank and up into the twister.

Chapter Thirteen

The Ghost of a City

I was alive.

I felt my heart beating and cool air filling my chest.

I couldn't remember what happened after he kicked me off the ship. There was a surge of rushing water that enveloped my body and carried me up. My hearing vanished. The pressure. I remembered the pressure. It felt like I was being crushed in the hand of a giant. I must have fallen unconscious.

I was flat on the ground. It smelt like wet soil and stone. It was dark and cold, and I could hear a distant rumbling echoing like deep, muffled thunder. It sounded like I was in a massive cavern. I sat up and looked down at my body, to see if it was real. I could hardly see it through the darkness, but I noticed something strange; I was dry. My clothes had been drenched on the ship, but now, they were dry.

My eyes settled on a red stain that was sprayed along my trousers, and suddenly I was there in that moment again. Violence and rage and steel and blood. The Captain's roars as he gashed and slashed and cleaved a man into a pile of wet, red meat. A pile of meat that used to speak and walk and think. My heart started pounding. My breathing quickened until

I couldn't control it anymore. My stomach churned and a lumpy sickness crawled up my throat. I dropped my face into my hands and tried to calm myself. It felt like I had no control over my own body, and that I couldn't get enough air no matter how many breaths I took. All I could see, again and again, was Waylon's flesh being ripped apart by steel and rage.

A man sighed behind me.

I shrieked and stood and turned around.

There was no one there.

I was alone in a land completely drowned in darkness. It seemed to be contained in one enormous cavern that stretched on for miles. High above, there was a bleak, dark grey sky. There was something deeply wrong about it. There were no clouds. No stars. No sun. No moon. And, even stranger, the sky was billowing and fluid. Occasionally, there was a pulse of pale blue light that scattered across the looming grey in many thin, branching veins. Each flash dimly lit the land beneath for a brief instant. In these short moments, I saw the silhouette of a vast land in ruin. I could make out the shadowy, wretched shapes of destroyed buildings and toppled towers, scattered bricks and shattered stone. The ruins were countless and stretched over a vast, sweeping expanse of desolation, all buried under a crushing, absolute silence.

What is this place?

As I stepped forward cautiously, I noticed my feet made no sound where they tread. I tried stamping and jumping and no matter what effort I exerted, my feet could not make a sound. It was as if the ground itself was not real, or if this was soil I was never meant to walk. It was dizzying. It felt like a dream.

I wondered if I was really alive, or if this was an afterlife. A cold wind sighed as it swept very slowly over the forlorn land. It brushed past me, fluttering my robes ever so lightly. On the edge of the wind, I heard something strange.

A woman's voice.

With the strength of just a whisper, she called out, '*Vasidea, slow down!*'

I flinched and spun around. I searched for any movement in the darkness, any sign of another person. I called out a greeting into the shadows to invite anyone forward.

There was nothing. No movement. No sound. Just stillness and darkness.

But I had heard someone. I was sure of it. I had heard the voice of a woman with a strange accent.

Warily, I wandered forward.

As I walked, I heard quick, light footsteps, and the giggling of a child. I looked back and saw no one. But the footsteps continued, getting louder as they approached me. The laughter also grew louder, until I felt a presence move through me and continue ahead. A tiny voice, in the same accent, said, '*Look, mother! Look!*' The sounds of the child faded.

Then, the pale blue light in the sky pulsed again with a deep, rumbling *thum*. The laughter and the footsteps returned, from the same distance behind me. They sounded exactly the same as before; the same rhythm, the same giggles. I felt the same presence move through me again. Then, the voice repeated, '*Look, mother! Look!*' and faded as it ran away.

And then the pale blue light flashed again.

It seemed whatever this place was, it was condemned to repeat the same few moments over and over again. But even if it did, the land itself did not change. The crushed marble never moved as much as an inch. Even when the wind would occasionally sweep over it, nothing moved. When I tried to pick up even as much as a pebble, it did not rise with my hand. The ruins were perfectly still, like a shadow frozen in time.

I wandered through what appeared to be the ruins of a street. I was walking on a stone road, where deep cracks splintered like lightning. There were gaps and missing pieces in the road, revealing the dirt that laid beneath. I stepped over a crushed pillar. All around me, there were many houses, and all of them were destroyed. The only remains that stood were fragments of the walls and the foundations. I could not imagine what kind of force must have ripped this place apart. It was what I imagined the aftermath of a war to look like. I ventured inside a relatively intact home. It was small, and the door would have led into a modestly sized room. There were pieces of shattered glass and ceramic scattered chaotically along the ground. In the corner, there was a wooden bedframe. A man's voice murmured to himself.

'*What is that?*'

Thum. The flash.

I heard the man grunt as his invisible presence rose from the bed in the corner. I heard his footsteps carry him to the window, where he would have been standing in front of me. Even though there was nothing and no one around me, it felt as if I was standing behind a man a little taller than me. He gasped, then murmured, '*What is that?*'

Thum.

Scared by that, I left, returning to the street and gazing around at the devastated landscape. My eyes were slowly adjusting to the darkness, and I could see the ruins in better detail. This was indeed a settlement, a town of some sort where people may have once lived, except it was something many times larger. Unlike a simple village, it was sprawling and elaborate. *This must be what cities are like*, I thought. Curiously, the toppled marble pillars and broken homes seemed to have collapsed in the same direction. Everything was toppled away from the city, as if whatever force of destruction that laid waste to this place came from the inside, from the centre. I visited some other houses to test this theory, and I was confident I was right. Even fragments of furniture and people's belongings were thrown in one direction – away from the city's centre. Glass from obliterated windows facing the city scattered inside the house. When the destroyed windows were on the other side, facing outwards, the glass was outside on the ground.

I gazed towards the city, searching in the distance for anything that could explain this. I noticed, far ahead, a lofty building that may have once been a castle. It seemed to be in the direct centre of the city. Even as a ruin, its blackened rubble towered over every other building around it. I walked towards it.

I heard more whispers on the edge of the wind, the voices of people who might have once lived here. The words and voices would change depending on where I was, and I figured out they were bound to physical locations.

'*Wait… do you feel something?*'

'*No. What is it you speak of?*'

Thum.

They spoke with a strange accent that twirled and rolled their syllables. Their sentences flowed almost like music or poetry. But, more importantly, I noticed a pattern. Nearly all of the voices spoke of a light or sound, moments before the pulse in the sky.

'*By the Creator, what is that?*'

'*The palace, there's a light!*'

'*Quickly, Egero, sound the—*'

Thum.

These people spoke of the Creator. They followed the teachings of the Lightbringer, just as we did in the Order.

But when Viella and Synn saw the Totality, it was something completely new to them. Our story had been lost to the world, so how did these people know of the Creator? What was this place?

As I drifted slowly through the desolate streets, I took note of the buildings and their architecture. They seemed familiar to me, as if I had read descriptions in my studies that matched what I was seeing. The architecture, from what I could discern from the crumbled remains, was symmetrical, rational, and ordered. There were long columns, flat roofs, and many arches. Marble was a prominent material.

The names the voices spoke had an archaic quality to them. *Vasidea. Egero.* These were old names, similar to the ones I had seen in the literature I read for study.

These were vital hints, and my mind was buzzing with ideas.

And then, the realisation dawned on me.

The architecture, the names, the accents, the faith in the Creator. There was only one place this city could be.

This was Adven.

Somehow, I was wandering through its ruins. *But how? How did I get here? Where is this?*

I looked up at the strange sky. I watched it bend and billow. It was surreal to see it behave like this. The closest comparison I could make to its movement was that it resembled the motions of water.

It was like a sea.

Am I under the Twisted Seas?

I had to be. The twister, it must have taken me here when I was thrown into it. That would explain why the world had forgotten Adven, why they believed it never existed. Its remains are buried under the sea. But how is any of this possible? How can this place exist at all?

Maybe whatever effect that compelled the Twisted Seas to rise and rage so ferociously was the same that sustained the existence of this place, the same effect that caused the souls of the city's inhabitants to echo endlessly.

Maybe, while I was here, I could find out why.

The texts were terse in describing the fall of Adven, as no one knew what destroyed it. It was thought the high amount of divination interwoven in the city's structure was somehow involved.

If that's true, I thought, *I may be able to detect it.*

So I sat down in the street and closed my eyes. I took slow, deep breaths in. With meditation, I could leave my body and embrace my soul. I could see what happened.

Slowly, as my concentration deepened, I began to feel the divination in the air. There was more here than I had ever seen in my life. The energy flowed and whirled freely through the air, and washed against my soul like I was a rock jutting out in a river. I could see that all this power was surging from a physical source in the centre of the city, inside the building that the voices had called 'the palace'. With each pulse of the sky, a tremendous burst of blue energy exploded outward from the source, rushing in all directions. It reached the edge of the city and this strange dark world, pressing against the surrounding walls of black rock, then receded, returning to the centre; the palace. The divination compressed into a tiny orb, becoming blindingly bright even for my soul, then there was a pulse and it exploded outwards again, repeating the cycle. The entire process took about seven seconds.

I opened my eyes and returned to my mortal body in the street. Whatever happened to Adven, whatever destroyed it, divination must have been the source of the event.

I had to leave. I would not survive here, trapped in the grave of an ancient city. There was a cold feeling deep within me, spreading slowly like a rot. I feared to imagine what could happen if it consumed me wholly. I decided my best chance of escape was to go to the palace and find the heart of all this power.

So I walked towards it, passing ghostly whispers and pushing through lingering presences. The closer I got to the palace, the more elaborate the streets became. The ruins were larger and more difficult to surmount, leading me to believe these buildings would have been bigger and more intricately designed. There were many more whispers, from many different voices.

'Diormi, do you feel that?'

'Yes, it's—'

'Ah! What is that light?'

'I can't see!'

141

'What is happening?!'

Thum.

The palace was a looming, elaborate, and imposing building that had been raised high up into the sky like a beacon of order. I could only imagine how grand it may have once looked. Even as a ruined pile of stones, it was still remarkable. Sadly, the devastation here was the most severe. There had been high and mighty walls that surrounded the palace to protect it, but the stones had melted together and been violently blown away. The divination was so powerful as to have warped its very construct. All that remained of the wall was like a splash of water frozen and turned into stone. I squeezed through a gap and continued forward.

The entrance to the palace was a grand archway of marble that seemed to have been stretched out as it was blown away instead of simply shattering apart. There were voices here, too. It sounded like two men who I assumed were guards.

'Argh! What is that!?'

'My eyes!'

'I can't see! Jarus!'

'It's so hot! What is happening!?'

Then they both screamed, their echoes long and anguished.

Thum.

I pressed on, pushing through my fears. I had no other choice. The cold feeling inside was spreading, sapping the strength from my body, the speed from my pace. My limbs began to feel heavy and hard to move.

Inside the palace, I wandered through what I was sure would have been a magnificent hallway. Whatever happened in this place had warped the entire room into something strange and surreal. The pillars were stretched and bent into extreme formations that would never be possible for the marble to attain without collapsing. The stone floor was rippled, like the surface of a pond struck by a thrown pebble. The walls and ceiling were distorted, pulled and moulded as if it was clay. Such an unnatural sight was unsettling enough, but what was worse were the voices I heard here. They didn't say any words. They only screamed, and they too had been contorted. Their wails were stretched and boiling, twisted into a shrill, harrowing sound that accompanied a cacophony of frenzied, heavy footsteps, a crowd fleeing in terror. I felt the density of their bodies as they ran through me like a raging river, all rushing towards the doors I had just passed through.

Listening to the mangled echo of their screams turned my blood to ice. But somehow, amongst the whirlwind of twisted wailing, I managed to maintain my bearing and push on, wading through the invisible bodies, and enter a hallway even grander than the last.

Here, though, it was different.

The divination in the air was palpable. I did not need to meditate to sense it, I could feel it against my skin; a tingly sensation both hot and cold. And for the first time since I had woken up in this strange, forlorn world, I saw colour. A heavenly blue glow emanated from branching cracks that splintered along the ground and walls. Tiny, blue sparkles drifted through the air, floating like the embers of a blaze. The hairs on my arm stood, lifted by the energy in the air. For divination to become tangible, and visible, could only mean I was in the presence of overwhelming power. I must be approaching the source.

Though the ruins here were as twisted as the halls that preceded it, there was something at the far end of the hall that had been unaffected. Atop a wide, flat dais was a lonesome throne. Tall and imposing, it had been spared of distortion and was in perfect condition, a jarring contrast to the warped ruins around it. The glowing cracks in the hallway all came from this seat. I noticed something small and shiny resting on it.

Once I sighted it, my body froze. The muscles in my neck stiffened, and my eyes became fixed on it. I couldn't move. I couldn't look away. And as I stared, something filled me; divine energy flooding through my eyes and pouring into my soul. Immediately, I began to walk towards it. My feet moved with a rhythm and initiative that did not belong to me. I was just a spectator, watching my body march towards the throne, and despite any reason to, I was exceedingly happy to approach it.

As my body traversed the warped ruins and neared the throne, I realised the object resting on the seat was a crown. It was a simple thing; a gold band to rest on one's forehead. It was adorned with a single, glowing jewel of blue. A godstone. As I got closer, the godstone became brighter, and brighter, until its blue light was beginning to swallow my vision. I walked up the steps to the throne, no conscious will to object to this, and now I could feel the ancient power bleeding from it. The crown was irresistible. It became the only thing I could see. I could tell there was a part of my mind that did not understand why I wanted it, but every other thread of my body cried out in unison to take the crown, take the crown, take the crown. It was so close, all I needed to do was take the crown, take the crown, take the crown.

My hands stretched out to touch it.

And then there was light.

Chapter Fourteen

What Remains

'It's a shame, I liked him,' Captain Deadeye muttered as he trundled back onto the ship. 'I liked his round little head.'

I was bereft of words. All I could do was stare at the monstrous pillar of water that swallowed my companion, and gawk like a fool at the beast who had murdered him.

This act would never be forgiven.

'I will...' I began, taking the time to find the words to this promise through the fogs of my wrath, '...set this foul ship to flame and watch it burn to ashes. I will give image to my justice in the scattered remains of your crew. I will hunt you vermin to the ends of this world, and my pace will not relent until I have given stillness to all your black hearts.' I lifted my gaze to deliver this vow to Deadeye's face. 'Do you hear me, you filthy cretin? This is my promise to you; an agonising end to your worthless lives, death by the hand of Vanclaude.'

Deadeye looked down on me, then cackled and applauded me. 'Aye, that's the spirit! I love it when they have fire! Makes breaking them in for the customers so much more fun!'

Synn elbowed my arm and whispered '*Play it cool*' in my ear.

Deadeye clapped and shouted to his crew 'Righto! Set course for Raider's Rock! Prepare for the switch to seawater!'

Like obedient dogs, his lackeys leapt to work, scattering about the ship to their positions and jobs.

When the beastly captain left us, I leaned over to Synn and whispered, 'What did he mean by '*customers*'? What are they planning to do with us?'

He looked at me, and for the first time since I met him, I saw a hint of sadness in his eyes. 'Don't you know what guys like this do? They're gonna sell us off to slavers.'

'*Slavery?* I will never allow myself to be enslaved.'

'Hold on, I can get us outta this,' he whispered. 'Just follow my lead.'

'I'm *done* following your lead, Synn,' I hissed in reply. 'I will kill them all or die here.'

'Don't be stupid, Vie.'

Just a few feet away from me, there was a pirate with his back turned, focused on tying some knots. He was the one who stole Rosethorn from me. It was attached loosely to his belt, and could easily be parted from him. These imbeciles hadn't tightened the ropes after they took Kiro, so I would be able to slip from them and attack. I braced myself as I prepared to make my final stand here.

But before I could move, there was a deep, bellowing *thum*.

From the seas below, a colossal pillar of holy blue light erupted from the dark waters and shot up into the skies, spearing the belly of the storm. A deafening *boom* ripped through the winds and rain, so deep and mighty it was like the voice of God Himself had sundered the sky. The winds flew wildly from the pillar of light, slamming violently into the ship and knocking every man on board screaming off his feet. The wood of the ship screeched and groaned and shuddered as the *Final Judgement* rocked chaotically in the air. The obsidian clouds swirled around the pillar, as did the seawaters, and its blinding light endured, roaring all the while, forcing all of us to look away and clutch our ears. I screamed from the pain but could not hear myself.

And then it ended. In the blink of an eye, the pillar of light vanished into the dark skies. A dwindling rumbling of thunder echoed in its wake, then settled. The world stopped shaking. My sight was a blurry haze. My hearing was a shrill ringing in my ears. I could make out the dark wood of the ship, and a few of the men sprawling and groaning on the ground.

But even in this condition, I could sense something was wrong.

The ship was not moving.

'*What the hell was that?!*' someone screamed.

The ship halted and wrenched forward, flinging a few men off their feet and one fool overboard. There was a deep, clunky whirring, and many panicked voices. Synn and I were still bound loosely to the mast.

'Look, Captain! Look!' A pirate pointed frantically off the side of the ship.

The spinning twisters were slowing down and growing thin. The rain faded, and the winds slowed and fell quiet. Soon after, the twisters withered and collapsed, the water dropping to the seas.

Then the ship began to plummet.

Deadeye went to speak, but interrupted himself with a hoarse scream as he was lifted from his feet and began to float in the air. The pirates, and Ms Egree, were flailing helplessly in the air, screaming and shouting in panic. Synn and I were kept grounded loosely by the ropes still wrapped around us.

'Now's our chance, quick!' Synn shouted to me. He slipped from the ropes and gripped them as he pulled himself onto the deck. I followed his lead, bending my knees to weigh myself down onto the floorboards.

He pulled out a stubby dagger from his boot and plunged it into the wood with a grunt, gripping onto it tightly. I looked up at the floating crew and noticed the pirate I was about to attack floating directly above me. I reached up and grabbed my sword, pulling it free from his belt and stabbing the deck with it.

'Wait here!' Synn yelled to me. 'I'll get a slowfaller!'

A slowfaller?

'Understood!' I shouted back. I held onto the mast to keep myself on the ground, clutching Rosethorn in an iron grip, ready to battle with the men who were now diving back down through the air. They clung onto the mast and the sails and used them to pull themselves down. I readied myself.

But instead of attacking me, they clambered straight past me and made their way towards where Synn had gone; the cargo hold beneath us. I stood there, confused as they ignored me entirely.

I caught my breath and tried to steady my pounding heart. In a few moments we were going to smash into the water, but Synn was still under the deck. I yelled out his name, but he did not reappear.

And then it occurred to me who I was placing my trust in. A man who was paid to kill me. A man with no loyalty but to that of his own profit. A man who lies and cheats and kills for nothing more than to glimpse at his own reflection in gold coins.

Am I falling for yet another trick?

I preferred to take my chances hitting the water than waiting for him and being crushed along with the ship.

I sheathed Rosethorn, took a breath, and then leapt into the air.

Someone grabbed my ankle and pulled me down below deck.

It was Synn. 'Where are you going, snowball?!'

A man near us climbed out of the cargo hold and slung his arms through two straps of a square bag on his back. He pulled a string attached to it, then flew away as a massive dome-shaped sail burst from the bag and pulled him high up into the sky. Several others emerged from the cargo hold and did the same soon after, Ms Egree among them. Her cackle faded as the wind carried her away.

Before I could question what I had witnessed, Synn grabbed my face and turned me to look at him. 'Hold on tight,' he said, wrapping an arm around my waist and pulling me with him onto the deck. He was wearing the same kind of bag. I wrapped my arms around him.

He pulled the string, and a violent force yanked us up into the air as what looked like a wide, thick flag burst from the bag. A scream escaped me and I clung onto Synn tighter. The sounds of screeching wood and panicking men disappeared in an instant, and a gentle sea breeze filled the void.

I was holding onto Synn, the two of us dangling no more than a few hundred yards above the seawater, floating with a device I never knew existed.

'What'd I tell you?' Synn said, smiling. 'I told you I could get us out of that.'

I peered beneath us and watched the *Final Judgement* snap in two as it crashed into the sea. A tremendous splash of foamy water shot up into the air like a giant spear. A spray of mist tickled my legs.

'Now, not that this hug isn't heart-warming and all,' Synn began, 'but I am going to need to steer us clear of the water, which means I gotta let go of you.'

'What?!' I looked up at his face. 'Don't drop me!'

'Relax, I won't,' he said. 'Just hold onto me real tight, or you'll fall.'

After weighing up the options of letting myself fall and die or hug him, I tightened my hold on him, my head tucked under his chin. It was uncomfortable and humiliating, but slightly better than death. He let go of me and used his hands to steer the so-called slowfaller with little handles on both sides above his shoulders. The wind whistled as we sailed through the air.

The perpetual storm of the Twisted Seas had, finally, calmed. The clouds had quickly dispersed, and now the gulf was shimmering in sunlight under an open blue sky for the first time. The water beneath us had calmed and receded enough to show some soggy grey sand at the bottom of the craggy cliffs. I'm sure it was a sight that Kiro would have rejoiced to see.

There were a few floating slowfallers beneath us, and two above us. I counted five all together. The ones beneath us were flying towards the shores at the bottom of the gulf, where a few of them had already collected. Synn was not aiming for the beach. I was not certain where he was taking us.

'Where are we going?' I asked him.

'See that big hole over there?' He nodded in its direction.

I looked and saw a mouth in the cliff face; a tunnel shrouded in darkness. 'Yes.'

'We're going there.'

'What is it?'

'No idea,' he said. 'But it's better than dropping onto the sand and getting caught again.'

He kept us steady, but my arms were slowly sliding down Synn's saturated clothes. I clambered back up him, ignoring my blemished dignity. His face strained in concentration as he steered for the opening in the wall. 'C'mon, c'mon, c'mon,' he repeated to himself.

I watched as the hole got closer. It seemed we were just about to miss it.

'We're going to miss it,' I told him.

'No we're not.'

He kept gliding. We were getting low fast. Synn adjusted the slowfaller and we flew faster, the wind's forces getting stronger as we soared through it.

'When I say "now", lift your legs up. Got it?' he said.

'Understood.'

We were a few yards away and rapidly approaching. I braced myself for impact.

'Now!'

I lifted my legs, as did he.

The ground swept under us as we flew into the cave. Synn dropped his feet and stumbled forward. I let go of him as my feet met the ground, staggering as I shaped the momentum of our flying into footsteps. I nearly fell over forward but managed to stay on my feet.

I went to speak. 'That was—'

Suddenly I was swept up in the slowfaller. It wrapped around me and whipped me off my feet, sending me to the ground. 'Ow! Blasted thing!' I barked, struggling to free myself.

'Whoops,' Synn's voice said. 'C'mere, buddy.' He tugged at the material wrapped around me and pulled it off. I was expecting him to be holding a knife once I saw him, but all he had was a smile. 'You should consider keeping that, it's a good look on you.'

I ignored his gauche humour. This was no time for gaiety. I was sodden, bruised, and in pain. But far worse, Kiro was dead.

I shrugged off the slowfaller and dragged myself over to the edge of the cave, then sat down on the ledge. There was a serenity to the gulf now. The water was calm, and the waves slow and gentle. The transformation hadn't taken more than a minute or two. I sighed, squeezing my eyes shut to suppress any tears. I steeled myself. Mourning the poor boy would have to come later.

'What happened?' I asked when I felt strength in my voice again.

'I have no idea,' Synn muttered as he walked over and sat beside me. 'A miracle of God?'

It was once a notion I would not have hesitated in believing. But my faith had been tested, and to my shame, my conviction was less so. As I sat there, reflecting, I came to fully appreciate how powerless I was in deciding my fate. If not for that miracle, we would have been on our way to a wretched slum in the corner of the world to be sold off like animals. It was humbling, and disheartening, to know how inconsequential our actions were to our destiny.

'Did you see what happened to Ms Egree?' Synn asked after a while, a hint of genuine concern in his voice.

'I saw her fly away with one of those things,' I said. 'But after that, no.'

He didn't reply. He just looked down at his feet quietly.

'So...' he said, not lifting his face. 'What now?'

A good question.

I had almost forgotten that we were allies purely by circumstances now since passed. I had not killed him because of Kiro's pleas, and now that he was gone, and that we were clear of immediate danger, there was no reason either of us had to work together.

No reason for either of us to refrain from slaying each other.

'I'm not sure,' I said. 'Are we friends now?'

'I don't know. Are we still enemies?'

'If we're enemies, we're quite poor at killing each other.'

Synn chuckled dryly. 'Yeah, you're right.' He cleared his throat and stood up. 'Listen, I know this isn't the best time, but... I do have a job to do. It's not personal anymore, but...'

As I realised what he was saying, I looked up to him just in time to see him point the gun at my head. I hadn't realised he got that back.

'A man's gotta make money. Sorry, snowball.'

But instead of simply killing me or subduing me, he just stood there, waiting for my response. There was a soft look in his eyes that hinted I could persuade him.

So I thought quickly. 'Would you be interested in a counter offer?'

Ever so slightly, he lifted an eyebrow. 'Really? You'd be willing to make an offer to a *commoner rat* like me?'

I stood up slowly, my hands raised to my shoulders. 'Zephelia has promised what is ostensibly a fortune. But her offer is a deception. Have you ever actually met my sister?'

'Well... no.'

'I'd say I know her quite a bit better than you then. Zephelia has no intention of honouring the deal. If you deliver me to her, she will kill us both.'

Synn tutted. 'Do you think I'm a moron? I've considered that. I've made arrangements with her guys so I get my money and get away cleanly.'

'Zephelia was thirteen when she tried to have me killed,' I told him. 'Do you think a woman like that will allow you to live with the knowledge she is a murderous, conniving fraud?'

'She knows that I can't dethrone her. Nobody would believe me.' He smirked, amused by this little game. 'What's the word of a bounty hunter to a regent?'

'Assassins have been trying to find and kill me for eight years,' I pointed out. 'If she was comfortable with letting loose ends like us live, then we never would have met.'

He sucked in his lips. 'Okay. I'm listening,' he said, his eyes following me closely.

'If you help deliver me to Azale, so that I may take my place as regent…' I paused as I gathered the strength to continue. 'I will pardon your crimes, and honour your service with land.'

'Land? How much?'

'Vast acres.'

'No deal.'

I furrowed my brow. 'Land with a small manor, and servants.'

'Nope.'

'I'm offering you a glorious deal.' I was more perplexed than angered. 'Others in your vocation could not dream to retire with such a fortune.'

Synn shrugged. 'I'm a free breed, I don't much like being tied down. I like to keep moving. Don't know why, I just do. So I don't care about land.'

My eyes narrowed on him. 'Then what do you want?'

'Just promise me triple of what your sister offered.'

'Triple?' A small laugh of relief breached my defences. 'If you wanted to make this so simple, why didn't you say so earlier?'

'So thirty thousand prences? We cool on that?' he asked me, searching for surety.

I lowered my hands. 'Certainly.'

He hesitated. '… How do I know you're not going to just kill me, or hand me in once I get us to Azale?'

I took a breath, and summoned the will to say with all sincerity, 'You have my word.'

He paused. He knew the weight of those words had to mean something.

He lowered the gun. 'Okay. We have a deal.'

'Glorious.'

We shook hands.

After a short pause, he glanced around at our surroundings as he fiddled with the gun. 'Good thing this cave was here, huh?'

'If there's no way out, we may have just consigned ourselves to a worse fate,' I said.

'Let's hope not.' Synn twisted the barrel of the gun. I heard a crank and a slip.

The tunnel lit up a light blue as Synn extracted a small glass vial from the gun. Inside it was radiant blue dust, casting a glow around us. 'Ah, much better,' he chirped.

'What is that?'

'Uhh… divination?' He tapped the glass with a finger. 'No idea. My guess is it powers the gun. All I know is that it glows.'

'Splendid.'

He walked ahead of me, lighting up the tunnel with the vial. The light revealed things we hadn't been able to see. Rotten timber arches held up the rocky walls and divided the tunnel every few feet. This was a manmade structure, possibly some kind of abandoned mine. The glow of the vial did not light up much further ahead of us so it was impossible to discern for how much longer the tunnel would go on. 'So this is that magic stuff the kid was talking about,' Synn remarked, studying the vial.

I couldn't shake the instinct that he would eventually betray me, so I kept Rosethorn's hilt in my hand as I walked behind him. I knew after what we had been through, and after making that agreement, I could place my trust in him. And yet, a small voice in my thoughts reminded me to never lower my guard, that I could trust no one but myself. This internal doubt gnawed at my mind. 'What did you think it was?' I asked him, hoping to distract myself.

'I had no idea. I assumed it was some kind of alchemist's powder. Never really thought much about it,' he answered simply. 'It's not like I made it, I just stole it from some weird old guy living in a cave near Meras.'

'I *knew* you stole it.'

'Yeah, yeah, you're a real genius.'

I glanced behind us, and the light from the outside world was now like a window in a hovel. *Why would they dig all the way to the gulf?* I wondered. *Who built all of this?*

We continued forward for what felt like an hour, but it only took minutes for the light of the day behind us to become a tiny patch in the darkness. The air was musty and stale, and only worsened the further we proceeded.

Looking ahead, I noticed a figure in the shadows.

'Stop,' I said, sticking my hand out in front of Synn.

'What?'

'Look ahead. Do you see that?'

He looked forward. 'Oh. I do now.'

I drew Rosethorn and moved forward. Synn followed my lead.

As the light crawled closer to the figure, the details of its body were revealed. It was a man's shape, standing motionless in the darkness, staring at a wall. Once it became clear, the two of us froze in place.

'You there. State your name,' I commanded.

The man did not move. He did not speak.

'Do you hear me, man?' I raised my voice.

No response.

I prompted Synn with a flick of my eyes, and he nodded.

We moved forward carefully, letting the light reveal the figure.

It was a wooden statue.

'What the hell?' Synn murmured to himself.

We dared to inch closer, and the details surfaced in the blue light.

It was some kind of wooden imitation of a man; about Kiro's height, holding a rusty pickaxe in one limp hand. Its body was smooth, with no cracks or bumps on its surface. Its head, which was completely smooth and lacked any face or hair, was dangling lifelessly, looming over its chest as if it was sleeping or dead.

'It's a... doll?' I said, uncertain.

'The question is; is it alive?' Synn asked, leaning down and scooping up a loose pebble.

'What are you doing?'

He tossed the pebble at the figure's head, striking where its ear should be. It didn't flinch or give any response. He may as well have thrown it at a wall.

'Well it's probably not alive,' he said, then he laughed dryly. 'Damn, those sand demons got me scared of wooden dolls now…'

I moved forward, keeping my eyes on the figure and watching carefully for any sign of movement or life. This measure of caution was perhaps excessive, but after the Tyrant Sands, I decided it wise to keep my guard up. I pushed against the wall and shuffled past it. Synn followed after me.

'Creepy thing,' he muttered.

Then the figure's arm moved.

I gasped and staggered backwards, keeping my blade between the figure and myself. Synn flinched, swore, and kicked it over. The figured crashed limply to the ground. It didn't move.

'You saw that right?!' Synn asked me.

'I did.' I drew conclusions in my mind from what I had observed. 'It only moved when the vial was near it,' I realised. 'Hold it out towards it.'

'What? No way. Are you crazy? What if it comes to life or something?'

'That's what this is for.' I indicated my steel, then gave him a nod. 'Go on.'

Synn hesitated. He looked at the vial, then at the figure, then stepped towards it carefully.

I prepared myself.

He got close, then held the vial out towards the figure.

Slowly, its body came to life. Its arms dragged backwards, rearing its elbows and pressing its hands against the ground.

'Wow, look at that,' Synn said quietly, admiring it.

I watched carefully, ready to strike it down.

The figure, powered weakly by the radiating light from the vial, gradually raised itself to its feet at an agonisingly slow pace. Then, once it was standing and facing the wall, it lifted the pickaxe with a faint churning sound that came from its joints. It raised the pickaxe above its head, then brought it down weakly against the rock wall it was facing, a soft *tink* sounding from the contact. It was too slow to make even a dent.

'It's a wooden miner,' I concluded. 'Powered by divination.'

Synn pulled the vial away, and immediately the figure stopped moving and became perfectly still once again. 'Let's get the hell out of here,' he muttered.

We continued through the mine, passing by a few more of these figures in various states. One was lying flat on the ground. Another leaning its face against a wall. All of them were completely lifeless, bereft of motion, until Synn waved the vial near them, bringing twitches of life to their wooden bodies. From what I could reasonably imagine, these figures were likely designed to supplant men as workers. The true enigma, however, lay in the identity of their creators. No city in Advenia would ever employ sorcery to devise and impel these wooden imitations. At least, not in these times.

This mine had to be ancient.

I dwelled on the mystery as we proceeded further into the mine. Eventually, we entered a large chamber, thrice the height of the tunnels and so wide that the glow of the vial could not reach either wall. There were dozens of these figures strewn about seemingly without order. Some were slouched over rusty carts full of jagged minerals as if they had been pushing them before collapsing abruptly. At the end of the chamber, the ground sloped upwards towards a tiny patch of daylight.

We made haste, panting as we climbed up the steep tunnel, passing by more imitations. I was afraid as I neared my freedom, they would suddenly spring to life and seize me, so I quickened my pace. The little square of daylight at the end of the tunnel grew bigger and bigger. The air, I could finally smell fresh air. I pushed on until finally, I reached the top.

The mine opened into the clearing of a luscious, green forest of tall, thin trees. It smelled like rain, and wet leaves and foliage glimmered in beams of sunlight. Birds I could not see serenaded the air with sweet, pretty songs. They were joined by other creatures that croaked and hummed, their sounds echoing throughout the forest. The land was bustling in lush, vibrant greenery, and the air was rich with the scent of earth and leaves. This place looked as if it had gone unsullied by the touch of mankind for many years. If my understanding of geography was correct, this was the Ahnem Forest, north of Azale.

I looked back at the opening to the mine, which was held together more by twisting vines growing on it than the original wood structure. Synn emerged from it, panting. He gazed up and around at the forest and sat down on the grass, whistling a note of relief.

I sat down as well, and all at once as if my body was hiding it from me, a wave of pain descended on me and my posture crumbled. I was utterly exhausted. Pangs of hunger spiked into my belly like daggers. I groaned in pain; this journey was exacting its toll on me, and doubts began to bubble in my thoughts like boiling water.

'Do you have any food?' Synn asked me.

'I have nothing on me but my clothes and sword,' I informed him grimly. 'Those wretched thieves took everything else.'

Synn groaned quietly. 'Then we better find somewhere to eat.'

'Azale is south of this forest,' I said. 'On foot, we'll reach it sometime after nightfall.' I forced myself to my feet, straining against the weakness in my body, distracting myself from the pain by focusing on putting one foot in front of the other. 'We must move now.'

'Hold on, Vie,' Synn said, raising a palm. 'We should just take a second to catch our breath.'

'We haven't a second to spare, Synn.' I continued marching. Synn followed behind me.

It took us an hour or so to proceed through the Ahnem Forest. We were mostly silent, and without Synn's quips to distract my attention, my thoughts were consumed by the memory of Kiro's murder. Knives plunged into my heart whenever I imagined his face, looking back at us for help we could not give him. When my eyes would well with tears, I blinked them back and poured my energy into swinging Rosethorn through the shrubs and bushes blocking our way.

'Hey,' Synn said, with a voice softer than normal. 'That light in the seas. Do you think that was the kid?'

I considered it. 'Perhaps,' I said, unable to resist the vain hope in the notion.

We breached the forest. As we stepped out of the trees, we beheld the sight of vast and sweeping plains that stretched out like an endless ocean of green. Tall, soft grass, adorned by sprinkles of yellow flowers, swayed in the gentle summer breeze under a clear, blue sky. Far in the distance, in the centre of the plains, there rose the tall white walls of the city I once called my home.

'There it is,' Synn remarked.

I took in the image of Azale, its walls of unmatched height, and the looming contour of the White Palace rising within it. My breath shuddered as I fully realised the weight of my mission weighing down on my shoulders.

I went to take another step, but the pain in my body forced me to my knees.

'You okay?' Synn asked me.

'I'm fine.'

'No, you're not. Just sit, dummy.' Synn plopped himself onto the grass across from me. 'Rest for a minute.'

I sighed, but abided.

For a while, we rested in silence.

'I'm sorry about the kid,' Synn said.

That shot a bolt of pain into me. I cast my gaze to the dirt at my boots. I didn't dare let him glimpse at my eyes. 'You don't need to apologise for that.'

'I know.'

The air was heavy and quiet. Synn stirred where he sat then asked me what my plan was. I took a deep breath.

'There's only one person in Advenia more powerful than Zephelia,' I began. 'The King needs to know the truth. I will go to the White Palace and reveal my identity to the world. Once the King and the nobles in his court see my face and hear my voice, they'll remember me, and they'll cast Zephelia out.'

Synn hummed and soothed the bruises on his face. 'You're relying on them believing you are who you say you are.'

'They will,' I said. 'How many others have features like mine? White hair and blue eyes are a distinct trait of my family.' I rested my hand on the hilt of Rosethorn. 'Furthermore, I have my family's ancestral sword. I don't know what lies have been told about it, but bringing it with me is only further evidence of my identity.'

He shrugged. 'I guess that makes sense,' he said. 'Just don't be surprised if they call you a liar. These people aren't idiots. I'm sure they can and will try to spin this around on you.'

'Doubtlessly.'

And then we heard it; a rumbling in the ground, thundering in the distance, getting louder. Getting closer.

Synn lifted his head. 'You hear that?'

I nodded and listened closely.

They were the footfalls of horses, and a lot of them. It sounded like an approaching army.

Synn and I stood up slowly and gazed over a mound towards Azale.

Storming through the grassy fields were a pack of riders in black armour – knights of the Elite Guard. There were probably twenty or thirty of them, with the leader flying a banner bearing the insignia of Azale; a four-pointed star of gold cast against a red background. One of the riders shouted and pointed at us.

I dragged my hood over my hair. 'They saw us,' I told Synn.

'Play along,' he said calmly.

The riders slowed to a halt as they approached us, looming over us from atop their horses.

'Hello there, good sirs,' Synn said in a perfectly imitated accent of an Azalian commoner. He wore the face of a modest man. 'What brings you out here?'

The crowd of riders parted, and approaching us through the centre, atop a mighty white stallion, was a woman in beautiful white vestures laced with gold. She had short white hair, a long nose, and sharp, icy blue eyes. My blood went cold.

'My, my,' said Zephelia Vanclaude, an imperious smirk on her face. 'What have you brought me, Synn?'

Chapter Fifteen

The New Truth

Zephelia had Synn and I shackled and gagged. They confiscated Rosethorn and ripped off my mantle, to be sure I was who they suspected. Before Synn was captured, he hurled away the gun into the forest, unwilling, it seemed, to see it fall into the hands of anyone but himself. For that, he was repaid with a beating from the Elite Guard that left him bloody and bruised.

While Zephelia's men subdued us, she ordered some of her knights-in-black to take Synn and I to the dungeons, while she and the rest continued their expedition to investigate the Twisted Seas.

The knights slung us over their horses like dead game, and carried us to Azale under a sky set ablaze with swirls of orange and crimson by the setting sun. The daylight was all but indigo and dying once we reached the enormous gates to the city. The Elite Guard were clandestine about ushering us through the gates and off to the Protector's Barracks. They shoved us through the jail, then down two flights of stairs into the gloomy, empty dungeons. They consigned us to separate cells at the very end of a freezing, stone corridor, shoving us into the miserable confinements before slamming the iron bars shut behind us. The only light afforded to us was provided by weak, flickering lanterns hanging on the walls outside our cells. They at least had the decency to ungag and unshackle us.

When the men left us, they left us without even a word. We were alone in the dark, filthy, hungry, and battered.

'So,' Synn spoke, breaking the silence. 'That didn't go well.'

In a burst of anger, I kicked the bars of my cell and roared.

'Yeah,' Synn mumbled. 'I get that.'

Fatigued and despairing, I dropped to the ground and sat against the wall. I heard Synn sit against his side of it. 'We're going to die, aren't we?' he asked.

I closed my eyes. 'Yes.'

Synn clicked his tongue. 'Oh well,' he murmured. 'Here's some comfort for you; you were right about your sister betraying me. That's gotta feel good, right?'

I peered up at the mossy ceiling. 'How can you be so relaxed about this? Aren't you scared?'

There was a long sigh. 'No,' he said. 'I never expected to live this long, to be honest. In my line of work, you live every day like it's your last. Because that's the truth of it, snowball; death isn't always a big, ceremonious thing. Death doesn't care. It can happen anytime, anywhere, to anyone.'

My face fell into my hands. 'This never should have happened,' I muttered. 'None of this is how it's supposed to be. I should have been ruling this city. The boy should have completed his journey. You should still be... doing whatever it is you do with your time.'

After a long pause, Synn said, 'Listen, Vie; there is no way that things should be. There's no plan to our lives. There's no grand destiny we will inevitably fulfil. Things just happen because... they happen. There's no greater reason why we're here in this dungeon except we got unlucky.'

I scoffed, shaking my head. 'How can you say that, Synn? Look at what we have been through, all that we have survived. How could we be surrounded by hundreds of those sand demons and live to tell the tale? The Twisted Seas have raged for thousands of years, but the storm collapses at the precise moment to save us? I was meant to be in Azale. I was *meant to rule*.'

'Or... you were meant to travel all this way and die without anyone knowing who you are. Who says your destiny is anything more than that?'

'It is God's will that I rule,' I said with a crack in my voice. 'I am not some common woman. I was born bearing the name Vanclaude. I was raised to one day rule this city.'

'And now here you are,' Synn said, 'rotting away in its hidden bowels.' I heard him shuffle around. 'Here's the thing about destiny, Viella; there's no such thing. It's a concept people made up to feel important. What you do or don't do doesn't matter, because there are no rules in life. Even the King could one day just trip over and break his neck and that would be the end of him. There's no promise of anything in life. The secret is to just do whatever you want, live well, then when you're time's up, have no regrets.'

I wanted to fight the notions in his words, but as he continued to speak, and the repugnant stench of this dungeon singed my nose, the certainty of my future began to wither and fade.

Was I truly meant to see the throne? Or was my life a cruel tragedy, where all this effort to reveal hidden truths and upturn a corrupt, fraudulent rule was all for naught? Am I here to die an abrupt, meaningless death, where my story disappears from the world with my last breath? Was I ever really destined for greatness?

Or was there no such promise at all?

My breathing began to shudder as the resolve in my heart splintered and cracked. I buried my face between my knees as tears rolled down my cheeks. I thought of him. The boy. The boy I condemned to death. The boy I condemned to death because I arrogantly assumed my life was more important, more valuable, than the lives of those I designated a commoner. The boy I condemned to death the day I asked him to come with me. The worst mistake he ever made was agreeing to accompany me to Azale.

'I murdered that poor boy,' I confessed to Synn through shaky breaths.

'Hm?' He sounded awfully calm, like we were merely eating lunch in a garden and I had asked him about his day. 'What are you talking about? You didn't kill him.'

'Of course I did,' I said, my heart aching. 'I asked him to come with me. I put his life in danger by simply being *near* him. If we had never met, he would still be alive.'

'Yeah, but… you didn't kill him, dummy. A bunch of pirates did.'

'But who placed him there on that ship, Synn?' I questioned him. 'It was me.'

I heard Synn stand up, and his footsteps carry him to the bars where he fiddled with the gate, shaking it to test its strength. 'Nope. He did. He made that choice, Vie. If he wanted to, he could have left you and gone solo any time he liked. You weren't holding him against his will.'

'It's not quite as simple as that.'

'Oh, but it is.' Synn grunted as he gave up whatever he was trying to do with the bars. His footsteps paced around idly in his cell. 'Don't blame yourself, Vie, it's not gonna do you any favours. He didn't have to stay with you. He could've left on his own at any time. Same deal with me. I only stuck around with you two because it was… admittedly, kind of fun.'

Synn's excuse perplexed me. 'What do you mean? You had no choice, you were in ropes and we had your weapon.'

He huffed a laugh. 'Trust me, honey, I was going *real* easy on you guys.' He batted the bars with his hands, playing a crude tune with the metal. 'To be honest, once we were done with trying to kill each other, I was enjoying our time together. You guys were a stark improvement over my usual company.' He stopped playing with the bars and moved back into his cell. 'Kiro was the first person I've met in a long time who I actually respected.' Then he chuckled. 'You took some getting used to, though.'

'Such a pleasure, aren't you?' I said dryly.

'You're not the first woman to say that.'

I groaned. 'Yes, I'm sure ladies find you very charming, especially with all the words you have for them.'

'It's hard not to be charming when you look this good.'

'Well, if you wish to relieve yourself of that burden, simply open your mouth and you'll repulse every woman in the region.'

Synn laughed. 'If we somehow make it out of this alive, you should be a jester.'

He managed to get a single, dry laugh from me. 'I think I'd rather be decapitated.'

We sat there, contained within our dirty, dark cells, laughing dryly for a moment before we dwindled into silence. I was starving, filthy, in pain, but above all else, I was tired. So, I dragged myself onto the woefully inadequate bed in my cell, a flat plank of wood tethered to the wall by chains, and curled up into a ball to preserve whatever modicum of heat I could gather. I was exhausted, but sleep did not come easily. I laid there, a pathetic shadow of my former self, bereft of dignity and veneration, wishing for sleep, wishing for something to liberate me from this horrible waking nightmare.

When I awoke, I hadn't a notion for how long I had actually slept. I heard the creaky doors to dungeon swing open, a woman's utterance of a command muffled by distance, and footsteps approaching us. The orange light of an open flame oozed over the stone floor, heralding the appearance of a visitor.

I sat up as a figure in a dreary black cloak, holding a torch, approached the bars of my cell. They slipped off the hood, revealing a smooth, pale face framed by sharp white hair. Two icy blue eyes stared into my own.

'Viella,' my sister said, gazing upon me with some arrogant pity. 'It is a pleasure to see you.'

Rage turned my hands into claws that dug into the wood of this pathetic bed. '"*A pleasure to see me*"? How cruel you must be to say that.'

'Believe me, sister, I am honestly delighted,' Zephelia said. 'I never expected you to be alive the next time I laid eyes on you.'

'Enough. Why are you here?' I questioned her, summoning the last of my strength to face her with whatever dignity I could afford.

'I wanted to speak with you,' she said, her voice refined, cold, and unhurried. 'I want you to understand why I have done the deeds I have done.'

'Be gone, snake,' I snarled. 'I don't care what you have to say.'

'Hush now,' she said with a condescending tenderness. 'This will be profitable for the two of us.'

Her hand emerged from her cloak, offering me a biscuit powdered with sugar. My first instinct was to snatch it from her and devour it, but I would be giving her power over me, and acknowledging the surrender of my humanity.

I took the biscuit and threw it against the wall.

'Come now, Viella, cease this childish insolence,' she said with a touch of annoyance. 'I am offering you some comfort.'

'You mean to kill me, Zephelia. Your charity is an empty façade. You're here to find some absolution for your sins.'

'I am here for your benefit,' she said. 'As a Vanclaude, you deserve to die with some dignity. I will tell you the reason behind my actions so when you are executed, you will at least have some understanding in your final moments.' Zephelia hung up her torch on the wall. 'I'm sure you're curious as to what I have to say.'

I glared at her for a long while. 'I am curious,' I said. 'I want to know this… do you still remember when we were girls? Do you remember our little adventures through the palace? The plays we watched, the drawings we made? Do you remember when we stole a cake from the bakers and blamed it on the baker's son when father found out? Do you remember when we loved each other?'

Zephelia watched the torch's flames. 'Of course I do. And I remember those times fondly.'

I was stunned. '*How dare you…?*' My voice was trembling now, seething with the repressed rage that has simmered in my heart for years. 'How could you say that?'

'I'm not the monster you want me to be, Viella,' Zephelia said shamelessly. 'I am simply willing to do whatever it takes to sustain order and prosperity in Azale.'

'So everything you've done… everything you intend to do to me…' A thin, sardonic smile spread on my face. 'It was all for the *good of the region?*'

'I know you'll choose not to believe me, but it was.'

My hands clenched into fists so hard I thought my nails would draw blood from my palms. 'How could you justify driving me from my home and into a life of hiding? How could you possibly justify murdering your own sister?'

'You were unfit to rule,' she said, a little louder now. 'You *hated* the commoners. You believed your ascension to the regency was a matter of divine edict. You were cruel, improvident, and imperious. You were a *tyrant to be.*'

'I was *FIFTEEN!*' The words came out in a burst of rage and pain that launched me to my feet. Zephelia did not flinch. 'We were *children!* Who were you to decide that!?'

'Yes, we were children,' Zephelia said calmly. 'And even a child could've seen the vain and inept oppressor you were to become.'

'Oh, so you were a prophet?'

'A *strategist.*'

Her arrogance was so repulsive I nearly gagged. I scoffed and tossed

165

my gaze to the floor, scarcely able to endure the sight of her cold, impassive face any longer.

'Do you think I desired this?' Zephelia had the gall to ask. 'I don't dream of murdering you, Viella… but there is nothing I can do to spare you.'

'Yes, there is.' I returned my gaze to her. 'You could free me now.'

Zephelia stared up at me with a placid, indifferent expression. 'I cannot.'

'Yes, you *can*.' I took a step towards her. 'You don't need to kill me. I could live peacefully somewhere, or I could renounce my claim. There's no need for me to die.'

She stared at me pitifully, then shook her head, as if I was a mere child defending a belief in fantasy. 'I pity you, Viella. You were born before me, and that is your curse. Every breath you take is an offence to my rule. It is not your fault, sister, but you must die.'

'It is an offence to your rule because your rule is a *lie*, and I am the truth.' I marched towards the bars and gripped them in my fists as I stared Zephelia in the eyes. 'What would father think of you? What would mother?'

'Mother and father are gone. What they would think of me does not matter,' Zephelia said coldly, staring straight back at me. 'I have gone to great lengths in crafting a new truth, of how you died, of how I came to power. It is the truth this city believes. Your life as Viella Vanclaude would set flame to this new truth. It would burn down my rule, it would destroy everything I have accomplished for this city. Even if you renounced your claim, it would tarnish my authority and invite chaos and instability. Because of that, I cannot spare you.'

'Heyyy,' Synn's voice croaked. It sounded like he had just woken up. 'Is that you, Your Highness? How ya doin'?'

Zephelia turned her gaze at him, the contempt on her face clear. 'Synn. Thank you for bringing yourself and my sister to Azale for me.'

'No problem, snowflake,' he said boldly. 'Can I get that ten thousand prences, please?'

Zephelia was not amused. 'Curious you believed I would ever honour a deal with the likes of you,' she said dryly.

'Ah, of course. How could I forget? You have none to spare.'

She returned her attention to me. 'I don't want to end your life, Viella,

I *must* end your life. I do not derive pleasure nor regret from it, because my duty is to protect the order of Azale, and a good leader must always do her duty.'

'Yes, of course.' I nodded along. 'You wouldn't want me unravelling your web of lies, would you?'

'Not lies. A *new truth*.'

Synn spoke up. 'Hey, can you tell these guys—'

Zephelia raised her voice to silence him. 'Criminal, if you open your mouth again in my presence, I will have your tongue ripped out with pincers,' she said slowly and calmly.

Synn fell silent.

'Zephelia,' I said, my voice now drained of strength as the last of my hope finally flickered out. 'At least tell me this much; how do you intend on murdering us?'

She turned her cold blue eyes to me. 'You two will be burned at the stake.'

My blood turned to ice in my veins. I stepped back, aghast at her cruelty. 'Burn me? How can you condemn your own sister to such a horrible demise?'

'Oh Viella, if you ever held real power you would understand you must make horrible decisions to keep your control,' she said pitifully. 'Synn's legacy of crimes have made such an extravagant execution necessary. Anything less, and the law would not be respected. You, dear sister, will be called Satanya Black, his criminal lover. You'll burn alongside him at noon today, and finally, your threat to the new truth will end.'

I stared at her, unwilling, unable, to believe her. 'Why not escort me somewhere quiet and peaceful and give me a poison to take me painlessly?'

'Because that leaves a trail of clues, dear sister, and then your threat to the new truth endures. Executing you as Synn's harlot means your death does not provoke anyone's suspicion. No one will remember who burned alongside the infamous Synn.' She thought for a moment, then the faintest hint of a smirk curled her lips. 'And I suppose it's also befitting of the tale I weaved for the people of how you perished eight years ago. The world believes that after father died, you, in a fit of grief, set flame to your bedchambers and let the fires swallow you and your pain. We were quite committed to the theatre of it all. We burned your room in the

White Palace. We even plucked a peasant girl from the fields to become a charred corpse for your coffin.' She gazed at me, a thin, cruel smile on her face. 'You must at least respect the extent of our efforts. We handled it with competence and class, nothing clumsy or inept would be good enough for you.'

My lip quivered as I fought back tears. '…Why? Why did you do all of this?'

Zephelia donned her hood. 'Because, sister, this city deserves a leader who will do whatever she must do to see it prosper. Power is not given, it is *taken*. There is a price you must pay to rule, and I have paid it.' She grabbed the torch from the wall. 'Goodbye, Viella.'

Then she turned and walked away, taking the only light with her. Her footsteps echoed through the cold air of the dungeon until they disappeared, leaving us to be swallowed in darkness and silence.

Chapter Sixteen

Alone

I awoke to the sight of stars in the night sky, wreathed by leafy treetops.

I groaned as I sat up and looked around. I was alone in a forest at night. My satchel, my staff, and my ring were all missing. I had nothing but my clothes, and something I was gripping in my hand.

When my eyes focused, I realised I was holding the crown.

I gasped and dropped it and clambered away.

Everything was slowly coming back to me. I was kicked into a twister, then I woke up in a vast, dark ruin. I found that crown, and then...

And then there was light.

'Viella?' I called out weakly. 'Synn? Are you there?'

There was no reply.

I pushed myself up to my feet and looked around. I was in a lush forest of tall, thin trees. The flora was dense and flourishing, and the scent of earth and leaves was thick in the air. It was beautiful, but now was not the time to appreciate it.

'Viella!' I shouted, my strained voice echoing through the trees. 'Synn!'

Every time I shouted their names, I was met with silence. And every time, the panic jittering in my chest grew all the more frantic.

'Viella! Synn! Ms Egree! Can you hear me?!' I yelled as I ran through the forest. 'Is anyone there!?'

Wind. Trees. Moonlight. That was all.

My breathing quickened as desperation settled in. I was trembling, from the cold and the panic.

The crown, said a thought in my head. *Take the crown.*

I remembered I had left the crown behind and abruptly I was calm, which was strange. I knew I could not simply leave the crown here. It needed to be contained and studied. There was only one place in the world where a conduit of that power would be safely kept, and it fell to me to take it there.

I retraced my steps then found it, the blue godstone glimmering through the grass blades. Carefully, I picked it up. I could still vividly remember how great and terrible its power felt on my body. But now, its energy was absent, as if lying in wait. I stuffed it into the pockets of my trousers.

Viella, Synn, and Ms Egree were still on the ship when I was thrown overboard. To find them, I needed to find the Twisted Seas. I suspected this forest might have been the one that we were approaching on the ship, the one we saw on the other side of the gulf. If so, that would mean the seas were to the west.

So, I looked up at the sky and searched the constellations for the Southern Star, the glimmer of light that always hangs over the south. I spotted it, then turned to the right of it and began heading west through the forest.

After some time of walking, I reached the edge of the trees and found a gulf. It was the Twisted Seas, but to my shock, the storm was gone. The twisting, rising columns of water were all gone. Now it was just a vast, colossal gulf bathing in moonlight, where seawater washed against a beach that was miles below the cliffs. There were no ships flying through the air. There was nothing and no one here.

I shivered as a cold wind soared past me. There was so much land that I could see, and not a single living thing in sight.

I had never felt so alone.

I turned my back on the seas, trying to forget the horrors I witnessed there, and began slowly trudging through the forest, heading east.

With no knowledge as to where Viella and Synn were, I had no means of finding them.

Am I ever going to see them again?

I shook my head, as if doing so would fling the horrible thoughts from my mind. But still, they remained, tormenting me as I walked alone through the moonlit forest. I sniffled, at first because I was cold, and then because I was crying. There was only one thing left I could do – continue my journey east, on my own.

We should have tried to fight back when those men attacked us. We gave up without any struggle, and though we were tired, we were capable fighters. I had the power of divination at my disposal, but because I was too scared, too weak, I didn't use it. And because of that, we were beaten, humiliated, and I was thrown to my death. I lived only by the will of unknown forces that I could not explain. I wiped at my eyes as my crying turned to sobbing.

Maybe Viella was right. Maybe, sometimes, the only solution to save lives was to take others. Of all the living beings I had met so far in this journey, so many have tried to kill me. Was life truly precious? Maybe the Order was wrong, and evil could dwell in the hearts of humanity, and I had never suspected such because I had never known anything different. Was this the ultimate truth I was seeking?

Pulling me from my reflections, I came across something strange; a southbound path, cutting through the trees. It was subtle, and I had almost missed it, but I noticed some shrubs and bushes were lopsided and shredded, forming a makeshift, invisible corridor through the forest.

It was like someone had slashed through it with a sword.

I gasped.

Maybe it was them.

Chills rippled through my entire body. My heart started beating faster. An ember of hope sparked a tiny fire in my chest. *Maybe it was them. Maybe they escaped. Maybe they're alive.*

My sluggish trudging morphed into a staggering run through the trees as I poured all of my hope into the chance that Viella and Synn were alive.

But as the trees dwindled, so did the shrubs and bushes, until the forest widened enough that the trail faded and I was lost again.

I swept my gaze through the forest. I searched through the swaying trees drinking in the moonlight, searching for anyone, anything. I called out their names, I called out for anyone.

But the wind carried back no response.

As I was giving up hope, I saw something under a leafy shrub. A shape and material that was not natural. Something like the hilt of a sword. I crouched down and pushed aside the leaves.

It was Synn's gun.

I was afraid to believe it, but once I held it in my hands and felt its weight in my palms, I knew it was real.

'Synn!' Hope lifted my voice into the night. 'Synn! Viella! Are you here!?'

There was no response but a flutter of leaves as an unseen animal I scared dashed away through the forest. I stuffed the gun into my robes, tucking it under my belt.

I searched through the trees for any other clues. Finding none, I continued south. If the path through the trees led me to the gun, then the two of them, or at least Synn, was heading south.

And as I continued, I reached the edge of the forest.

Before me were sweeping fields of green that seemed to stretch on forever. In the distance, resting in the centre of the grasslands, there rose the tall white walls of a city, surrounded by farms and a tiny town, and crowned by a towering, white palace within. That city must be Azale.

I left the forest behind me and entered the plains. If Synn and Viella were here, they would have been heading towards Azale.

But why would Synn drop the gun? Did he drop it accidentally? Did it break? After studying it closely, I could not see any obvious faults.

But as I looked down on it, I noticed the ground I was standing on. It was a mess; the dirt was torn up and flung around, and littered with dints. After looking closely, I realised the imprints were made by hooves.

Then I saw it, trampled and covered in dirt. I crouched down to reach it, wiping away clumps of soil and taking it in my hands.

Viella's mantle.

I gazed around me, searching in the land for any other clues, any bit of knowledge that could tell me what happened and where Viella and Synn were. There was hope, now that I knew they escaped the Final Judgement and travelled here.

But what I had found was strange. The imprints of hooves suggested that horses were involved, and a lot of them. And if Viella's mantle was discarded here, then maybe her true identity was discovered. She would not throw it away without reason. Neither would Synn throw away the gun. Was this struggle an attack on them? Were they hurt? Were they killed? Were they taken?

I looked out towards Azale.

If Viella and Synn were alive, they would be there.

I stood up, rolled my shoulders, and began walking towards the city.

The journey took me hours. I followed a white dirt road that carved through the grasslands all the way to the city. As I walked, my stomach cried out in hunger. My body, still bruised and aching from the violence I suffered on the ship, pained me with every step I made. I couldn't even hold myself up straight. But my pace did not waver. I continued walking, one step at a time, towards Azale. I could not give up. I *would not* give up.

After many long, gruelling hours, the plains around me turned into walled meadows and farms. I entered a small town, named Cherry by a sign hanging over a wooden archway that welcomed me into the settlement. Just beyond it lay the towering walls of Azale.

Cherry was a humble place. The houses were simple buildings; small stone and wood cottages, not necessarily made well, arranged along branching dirt paths that carved weaving lines through the grassy plains. Most homes had four walls of horizontally aligned planks that were topped with sloping, mossy tiles. Some of the larger dwellings clutched onto chimneys made of grey bricks and had one window or none at all. The town was empty, its people all asleep inside their homes.

But when I had reached Cherry, my body was finally beginning to falter. I could only push through this pain for so long. Azale, as prominent as it was now, was still far away, and my gait has been reduced to a shamble, my every breath rugged and heavy. The pains in my body had not dulled on me, but worsened, until I was pushing through a fog of agony dragging invisible claws through my flesh and bone.

By the time I had come close enough to the city walls to truly appreciate how tall they were, the light of dawn was spilling over the land from the east. And as light returned to the world, I finally reached a barbican. The walls loomed over me like I was standing at the feet of a giant. Atop, men in metal armour patrolled the walls and stood vigilantly. Massive banners of red and gold, bearing the symbol of a four-pointed star, hung over the city walls and fluttered with the breeze. It was an impressive sight, but walking here had cost me the last of my strength.

As a man in armour called out to me from the city gates, I fell to my knees, then collapsed in the dirt.

Chapter Seventeen

The Execution of Justice

I couldn't move my body. I could barely comprehend what was happening around me. I could feel my face pressed against pebbles and dirt. Arms lifted me by my shoulders and dragged me through the city gates. A pair of voices, male and female, talked nonsense to each other above my head. I could just barely lift my eyes to take in my surroundings. At one point, a door was opened and closed, and the air around me became warm. I was laid down on a soft surface, then left alone.

'There, there, you're alright,' said a woman's voice. 'Drink up, lad.'

I woke up to someone pouring a skin of water into my mouth. I hadn't even noticed I had fallen asleep. I drank the water in eagerly, quenching a desperate thirst.

'Good heavens, what happened to you?' asked the woman.

It took a moment for my mind to understand my eyes. I was in a stone room framed by thick wooden beams, laying on a bed by the wall. A woman with dark hair, tired brown eyes, and a scar running down the left side of her face was looking down on me from my side. She was wearing the same armour as Azale's guards, but her helmet was on the floor. She was a protector. I tried to sit up. Her hand pressed me down.

'Easy, lad,' she said. 'Pace yourself.'

I looked up at her. 'Where am I?'

'You're in the Protector's Barracks,' she said. Her accent was similar to Viella's, but it had a rougher twang to it. 'You collapsed at the north gate of the city. What brings you here, and what happened to you?'

It occurred to me that telling her the whole truth may not be a good idea. 'I am on a journey to the Edge,' I told her, being as honest as I could. 'I was going to stop here in Azale to rest.'

Her brow furrowed. She stood to retrieve something across the room. 'Alright. And why are you in such a poor state? Is that blood on your trousers?'

I peered at the trousers Ms Egree gave me, and the bloodstain that had splashed across my legs.

'On my way here, I was attacked by bad men,' I said simply but truthfully. 'They robbed me, beat me, but one of them... one of them was murdered in front of me by their leader. I managed to escape them but... I am not sure how.'

The protector returned to my bedside, knelt, and offered me some bread. I took it and thanked her. She asked me where this attack occurred, and I said on the road north of here. As I did, I heard a man announce something down the hall, then a group of men celebrate with hearty cheering and applause.

'What was that?' I asked the protector.

She glanced over her shoulder, out the door. 'That was the commander telling the protectors the good news,' she said with a weary smile. 'We finally caught Synn.'

The news sent chills rippling down my back. He was here. 'Really?'

'Yes,' she said, herself joyed by the news. 'After all these years, we finally got the bastard.'

My heart started pounding. 'Is he still alive?'

'That's the best part, we got him and his partner alive,' she said. 'The execution is set for noon today.'

I tensed up at the word *execution* but held back any expression on my face that would tell my objection to that. 'I... didn't know that Synn had a partner.'

'Neither. Her name's Satanya Black,' said the protector. 'You ever heard of her before? She's not mentioned in the stories.'

Her?

Could that be Viella?

I shook my head. 'No. Where will they be taken?'

'You want to watch, eh? It'll be in Cathedral Square. The Grand Speaker promised a very public punishment for all that he has done. I'm sure it'll be a spectacle.' She stood up, picking up her helmet from the floor and putting it on her head. 'Now, are you feeling better?'

My body was still in pain, but having food and water made a huge difference. 'Yes, I am.'

'Good. I'd offer you to stay here as long as you need but, sadly, I can't. This is a barracks, not an inn. Can you stand?'

I sat up, then swivelled my feet off the bed and onto the floor. Pushing through the pain was made easier knowing where Viella and Synn would be, and what would happen to them if I couldn't endure some aches. 'Yes. Thank you for everything, madam.'

'It's my duty, sir,' she said, before stepping aside and gesturing to the door. 'Now, stay out of trouble, young man.'

The protector followed me as I walked down a dimly lit corridor towards the exit. We reached the entrance hall, but before I left, the protector seemed to remember something.

'Wait,' she said, grabbing my shoulder to stop me. 'I forgot to give back that thing you had.'

I looked down and noticed Synn's gun was missing from my sash. It must have slipped out when I collapsed.

'Oh, I didn't notice,' I said with a nervous laugh. 'Thank you.' Slowly, I laid my hand over my pocket, to check if the crown was still there. It was, thankfully.

She turned to go back the way we came. 'Wait here.'

I did as she said, my gaze wandering over my surroundings. The same banners I saw hanging on the walls of the city were adorning the walls in here as well. There were two doors on my sides, and the one on the right was slightly ajar. Curious, I peered through the gap. Inside it appeared to simply be storage, but as I turned away my eyes, I caught a glimpse of a golden hilt.

I looked back and that's when I saw it; Viella's sword, laid on a table in its sheath.

As I suspected; Satanya Black was a name assigned to Viella. She was here, with Synn. If she was being called that name, it must've meant she was captured by people who knew her true identity and wanted to keep it a secret.

My first thought was to take Rosethorn, but I hesitated. To steal from this city's law enforcement would make me a criminal. They would hunt me down and put me in chains, just like those assassins.

But how truly righteous are laws that dispense death and call it justice?

'Here you go,' the protector's voice surprised me. She was holding the gun out towards me, unaware that she could instantly kill me with it.

'Thank you,' I said as I took it and tucked it under my sash on my hip.

'What is that thing anyway?' she asked, cocking her head to glance at it.

'It's... a trinket,' I lied. 'My father made it for me as a charm of good luck for my journey.'

The protector glanced at me with a sharp, sceptical look. 'It's very good quality. Looks quite strange though.'

'My father... is a strange, talented man.'

The protector seemed suspicious, but there was a softness in her brown eyes that told me she wasn't going to question me any further. 'Right then.' She nodded to the door. 'Stay out of trouble.'

She didn't move to leave me, so, surprising myself, I came up with a bold lie. 'Pardon me, madam, but...' I put on an embarrassed face. 'I also had a purse with me. It's not in my pockets, so I think it's in the other room.'

She jutted out her chin. 'You did? I didn't see anything else when I went back.'

I shrugged. 'Maybe it fell out of sight?'

Her gaze narrowed on me, that softness fading as suspicion stirred. 'Right,' she said, her voice hard. 'I will check for you.'

She turned to leave. Once she was out of sight, and I was alone, I did not hesitate. I pushed open the door to the storage room, my heart pounding, and grabbed Rosethorn.

I went for the doors, tucking the sword under my sash.

'You there! Boy!'

There was a man in armour a few paces behind me. He drew his steel. 'Stop! Put down that sword!'

I bolted.

When I burst out into the streets of Azale, I was stunned by the size of it. Houses and workshops and other buildings, crammed within looming white walls, all towering over narrow, brick streets branching like veins through the city. I ran into the first one I saw, sprinting as I heard metal clattering and heavy, thumping footsteps pursuing me. I spotted a narrow alley that connected with another street, and ran into it. The gap was so small I had to shuffle through it on my side, with no more than an inch of space in front of my face. When I reached the other side, I saw my pursuer, the armoured protector, wedged in the gap. He was yelling and barking at me to come back this instant, until he gave up trying to squeeze through, and instead retreated the way we came, yelling for other protectors to come and help.

I ran further into the city, into the streets.

It was still the early morning, and only a few people in the city had emerged from their homes to begin their day. They did not pay any attention to me as they went about the motions of their morning. There was a certain joylessness about them. Nearly all of them had creased faces smeared with dirt and sweat. Their heads were bowed low, their gazes fixed to the ground. The only people who stood out were a group of knights in black armour, striding through the quiet streets. They were escorting a small but lavish carriage pulled by white horses. I breathed out my tension and walked past them, my gaze downcast, preparing to run if the protectors recognised me. But they simply ignored me, and continued heading in the direction of the barracks.

When I felt I was far enough away to be safe, I relaxed and took in my surroundings. A thick, vaguely unpleasant smell hung in the air, a potent mix of scents and odours merging into one, unique smell. The size of the city reminded me of Adven. Unlike Adven, however, the streets here were cramped and flanked by buildings that were like two houses stacked on top of each other. The architecture here was completely different; it lacked sophistication and elegance, and the buildings were clearly raised to fulfil a purpose and fill it quickly. An exception to this was the palace in the centre of the city. It was elaborate and magnificent, and it rose over the city like a god. It was built of white stone and protected by four bastions that faced the four directions. The palace itself was crowned by a central tower that reached into the sky like a spear. It was the tallest building I had ever seen. I had noticed it on the road to the city, but it was even more impressive when I could see it clearly.

I wished I could've experienced this new place in the company of my friends. I wished I could've enjoyed exploring this elaborate city on a full stomach, and without the weight of lives pressing down on me. Instead, I am a fugitive, a liar who exploited the kindness of a protector. *Am I doing the right thing?* I had once been so sure of my perspective, and of the Order of Light's philosophies. But venturing through Advenia made me question if the world below the mountains was misguided, or if we were.

As the sun climbed higher into the sky, the streets filled with more people. I had been looking for any sign of a cathedral or a square, but quickly I was overwhelmed by the cacophony of noise and motion. Footsteps, countless footsteps battering the stone streets. People bartering, arguing, talking, yelling. Wooden carts rolling on the roads. Horses puffing and their hooves clopping as they trotted about. All these sounds, all at once. There were more people here than I had ever seen in my entire life. The streets were bustling with people of different shapes and sizes, all moving through the streets like a slow, wriggling river of flesh. I was awestruck. There were so many people I didn't know; so many individual lives, full of memories and experiences as vivid and complex as my own, all moving through the streets like an invisible sea of stories that I will never get to know.

I was running out of time, and I still had no idea where to go. The streets were like a labyrinth, and nothing like the natural world I grew up around. I never thought much on my height, until now, I was surrounded by people who were mostly taller than I was. I could hardly see the streets around me through all the people passing by. I struggled to wade through the crowd, and the ceaseless, jumbled noises gave my mind no chance to centre myself. Anxieties made a fist in my throat. It felt like I couldn't breathe. When I stood still to steady myself, a man bumped hard into me and swore in anger as he shoved me out of his way. Before I could apologise to him, he was already gone, swallowed by the crowd. The endless momentum and noise of the city surrounding me pulled and tore at my attention in every direction. It felt like I was drowning.

I couldn't handle it anymore. I stumbled into a clumsy run, pushing past people who swore and yelled at me until I clung to the wall of a bakery like it was a riverbank. Finally, I found stillness, and sucked in gulps of air, only now realising I was hardly breathing.

Once I calmed down, I entered the bakery and asked the man inside where Cathedral Square was.

'It's in front of the Haphasteon Cathedral. Go left until you reach the Smiling Lion, then right and you'll see the square,' he said, before gesturing to a selection of baked goods arranged behind him. 'Anything you want here?'

'I'm sorry, I don't have any money.'

'I'll take that sword off your hands.'

I turned to leave. 'No, thank you, sir.'

The baker mumbled something sharp and foul as I left the shop. I followed his directions, weaving through the crowd, until I found the Smiling Lion, a large inn on the corner of two intersecting roads. I went right, passing through a corridor of colourful market stalls until I found a wide clearing.

The Cathedral Square was an open, flat clearing in a city that desperately needed more space. Stepping into it was like escaping a cage, like the first breath of air after being held underwater. The square was lined with slender trees planted in stone boxes and adorned in the centre by a sparkling fountain. Across the square was the Haphasteon Cathedral. It was a dark, brooding building, with many high arches, spires, intricate stone carvings, and ornate windows. I found myself wondering how one city could contain such beautiful buildings like the palace and the cathedral, alongside poorly organised streets overflowing with rickety, lopsided houses and shops.

In the shadow of the cathedral, there was a timber stage surrounded by a crowd of onlookers. On the stage were two wooden stakes, and protectors were amassing a clumpy pile of sticks beneath them.

It looked as if they were preparing to start a large fire.

The grim realisation of the pyres' purpose sent chills rippling through my skin. They're going to execute Viella and Synn by burning them alive.

My nails dug into my palms as I balled my fists. *What barbaric minds would burn people to death and call it justice?*

'*Make way! Make way!*' called a man's voice.

Behind me, a horse-drawn cart was riding into the square. The rider called for people to make way as his four horses dragged in a big, iron cage. Inside it, there were two miserable prisoners. I did not recognise them at first. I gasped when I realised it was Synn, and beside him, garbed in a tattered black cloak and white bonnet that hid her hair, was Viella.

A swarm of angry people following the carriage poured into the square, joining the crowd who had been waiting there in hurling rotten fruits and insults at the cage.

Both of them were bound and gagged, but Synn made an effort to retaliate against the crowd with his own muffled barrage of insults. Viella stared bleakly at her feet and made no indication she was even alive. I followed the carriage up towards the stage, merging with the crowd. I wracked my mind trying to think of a way to save them, but as I sifted through hopeless imaginations, the bitter reality of my powerlessness was slowly becoming clear to me.

The carriage pulled up next to the scaffold, behind a long line of protectors who held the crowds back. One of them opened a lock on the cage with a key, then swung open a latch. Four protectors went inside and took hold of Synn and Viella, dragging them out and up the steps to the stage. They wrapped ropes around them, tying them to the stakes. A thin man in solemn black garments stepped forward on the stage to address the crowd. He did not try to silence the people before speaking, as if he knew it to be futile. So he spoke over them.

'On this day, the justice of the King shall be made manifest in the execution of the infamous criminal Synn, and his villainous lover Satanya Black. The guilt of these blasphemous, ruthless killers was made known in trials for which neither of the two convicted chose to attend...'

As impossible ideas continued spinning in my thoughts, a thick dread churned in my stomach. I stared at Viella and Synn, bound to wooden stakes, their glistening, frightened eyes darting around. If only I had my ring. If only I had divination to save them.

But I had nothing. I was powerless. Without that ring, I was just a person. The only plan I could think of was to rush the stage and free them, but I wasn't strong enough to take on the combined force of the protectors.

I don't know what to do.

I don't know how to save them.

My hands were shaking. My breathing slipped out of my control and panic seized every muscle in my body. *They're going to die*, I realised. *They're going to die because there's nothing I can do.*

Then my hand went to the gun tucked under my sash. I was tempted to use it. It was a powerful and shocking weapon that the people of Advenia knew nothing about. If I used it to strike down at least one or two men, then maybe I could convince the crowds I could destroy them all if they did not free Viella and Synn.

But that would mean to save lives, I would have to take others.

Could I really do that?

I already knew the answer to that. I couldn't kill another human being. That would make me no better than the twisted laws of this place. I was terrified of what I was becoming by even considering that.

I was pulled from my thoughts by a sudden silence in the crowd. They had stopped talking when the thin man receded, and an old man in flowing white robes stepped forward. He looked similar to Master Shien, but he wore a tall white hat and had a saggy, beardless face. He stretched out his arms.

'Here we stand in the sight of the Haphasteon Cathedral, to see the will of God made real. These two criminals have committed many odious sins, and for which I, as your Grand Speaker, will deliver them to their ultimate punishment…'

Viella and Synn squirmed in their binds. Two protectors stood beside them, holding flaming torches.

The execution was imminent.

I had to do something.

But what?

My heart was pounding against my chest, and I was so scared it made me sick.

'…And now, by the fires of justice, their sins shall be purged from the world…'

Desperate, and unable to stand by idly another second, I did the only thing I could.

'*Please!*' I pleaded, interrupting the Grand Speaker. Tears welled in my eyes and my voice cracked as I wailed, '*Please don't kill them, I beg you!*'

Viella and Synn's eyes fixed on me, then widened. The crowd all around me, who had been silent for the Grand Speaker, stared at me with utter disgust and contempt. All their glaring eyes on me felt like a thousand knives piercing me at once. They erupted in collective outrage, shoving at me, forcing me out of the crowd and away from the stage as they barraged me with fierce insults and curses. I was being shoved around like a leaf caught in a storm, crying as hatred and anger lashed me with blow after blow until I was thrown to the ground, my head hitting the stone hard.

'Peace, peace,' the Grand Speaker urged the crowd. 'He is but a boy, crying out for mercy. Do not punish him for his compassion, I implore you.'

The words of the Grand Speaker moved the crowd to silence and stillness. No one helped me, but they left me alone. As I brought myself up to my feet, I noticed the crown had spilled from my pocket and was on the ground in front of my face.

The crown.

Maybe I could use the crown.

Quickly I snatched it before anyone could see it, and stumbled away from the crowd, into the shadow cast by one of the trees in the square.

This crown was far more powerful than the ring. I may not even be able to control it. But if I did manage to use it, in my current condition, it could destroy me.

To save lives, I would give my own.

I was fine with that.

I glanced over my shoulder. The Grand Speaker was still rambling to the crowd, who listened on quietly. Viella and Synn were watching me, their eyes unblinking and rimmed red. The Grand Speaker concluded, then gestured to the protectors holding the torches, who moved to the pyres and pressed the flaming torches to the sticks.

Fires were born, and the people cheered. Viella and Synn began to thrash and panic helplessly as the flames spread, and black smoke wafted up into their faces.

Without a second to think, I clutched onto the crown with an iron grip. I shut my eyes and called upon the power within.

The divination in the crown ran much deeper than I anticipated. It felt like there was an ocean of power contained within this little godstone.

If I had to command an ocean, then I would do so.

Wake, I compel you, wake and rise to my will.

Then I felt it; the ancient power, responding to my call. It stirred and flickered. I summoned every fibre of my being, every thread of my soul, to take control.

There was resistance. The power shrieked and convulsed at my intentions. I strained and fell to my knees as I wrested for control. The power was pouring into my flesh from the godstone, coursing and flourishing through my body. The marks appeared in my skin, burning bright as they carved their way up my arm and into my chest.

My entire body was shaking. It felt like I was being crushed. I fought on, clenching my jaw so hard I thought I would crack my teeth. I held a purpose firm in my heart and soul, and dedicated every ounce of my willpower into turning that purpose into the reality of the world.

But even with everything I had, it was not enough. The crown was powerful, deeply powerful. I was losing myself to its influence, and soon my body would splinter and break apart. I couldn't control it.

Screaming. Muffled, horrified, screaming. I reared my head through tremendous pressure to see two blazing fires on the stage.

Viella and Synn, two very dignified people, my friends and companions, were screaming in pure fear. The gags muffled their wails, but the horror behind them was not lost on me. The crowd cheered and clapped.

I looked down on the crown.

I refused to be defeated by a piece of gold. This arrogant ring of metal would not stand in the way of me saving the people I love.

I will fight.

I will rage.

I will give my life for them.

And then, a fire. Deep within, burning and raging and screaming, its roar echoing from the furthest depths of my being, and soaring all the way up from the depths of my soul and into the strength of my body.

The crushing pressure weighing on me lifted, and my muscles burned with divine power.

I had it.

I conquered the crown, and now, an ocean of power was surging through my flesh and blood, all at my command.

I gazed up into the sky. Gripping the crown in one hand and stretching out the other up into the air, I commanded a storm to arise. I envisioned clouds darker than night, swirling in the sky and engulfing the light of the sun. I envisioned thunder that could be heard across the world. I envisioned bolts of lightning that could split mountains with their strikes.

And the divination obeyed.

The wind around me quickened. In seconds it had morphed from a light breeze into surging, screaming gales. It howled through the Cathedral Square as the light of the sun disappeared. Swirling dark clouds formed in the sky, rippling out to engulf the whole city in darkness. First came thunder, rumbling in the black clouds as it did in the Twisted Seas. Then came lightning, flashing in the oppressive dark looming over the city and crashing into the earth. People in the square were looking up in terror, pointing and shrieking at the blackened skies.

I slammed down my hand as I commanded the storm to pound the earth with rain.

There was a crack of lightning so powerful I felt the ground shake, then rain fell from the skies. I focused it onto the stage, drowning the fires until not a single ember remained. People screamed and fled and cowered. I roared as I fought to hold myself together through the flood of energy rushing through me.

I saw the fires flicker and die.

And I let go.

I let go of the crown, and the divination in my body returned to the godstone. The rain faded away, and the thunder dwindled into crackling then into nothing.

I fell to my knees, and then onto my back, utterly drained of strength and energy. I rasped as my body tried weakly to draw in breath. It felt like I was about to die.

But before I did, I turned my head to the stage. Viella and Synn were still alive, now drenched and horrified and confused. The Grand Speaker, fluttering his arms, declared this a sign of God's wrath at an unjust execution. He demanded the prisoners be let free, shouting at hesitant protectors to cut them loose.

I had done it. It was over. They were safe.

I closed my eyes, and exhaled slowly, agony leaving my body with the expelled breath, and a peaceful warmth taking its place. I didn't mind that I was going to die here, that I was never going to see the Edge and complete my journey. Even if I did, I already knew now that I wanted to leave the Order. I didn't want to spend the rest of my life in the Sanctuary. I wanted to explore the world. I wanted to help people. That was what I wanted. Not that my decision mattered anymore.

My friends were alive. That's all that mattered.

As eternal sleep caressed my face and lured me to let go of the world, quick, pounding footsteps neared me, then I felt hands lifting me up. Arms wrapped around my shoulders and back.

My eyes opened. Viella was hugging me.

'*I thought we lost you*,' she whispered, her voice shaking.

I was barely able to lift my arms, but as Viella laid me back down, I managed to move my hand enough to lay it on the hilt of Rosethorn and tilt it towards her.

With just enough strength left for a whisper, I said '…For you.'

Then my eyes closed and I fell into nothing.

Chapter Eighteen

Resurrection of the Truth

I cradled the boy in my arms as I wept.

The burns in his flesh flourished and danced up his right arm and all the way up to the right side of his face. At his limp hand, a gold crown adorned by a single sapphire was on the ground. *No. Not a sapphire, a godstone.* The storm that saved us, it was him.

Synn approached from behind me, laying a hand on my shoulder.

'Is he still alive?'

I took a breath and stifled my sobbing. 'I don't know.'

He leaned down and hovered his ear over Kiro's mouth.

'He's still breathing, just barely.' He slipped his hands under Kiro's back and legs, lifting him from my arms. 'We gotta get him somewhere safe.'

I wiped at my eyes and stood, taking the crown from the ground and hiding it under this awful cloak that was thrown on me. The crowd that had cheered for my death were now gathering around Synn and I, watching us with wonder and fear in equal measure. The Grand Speaker approached us through the mob.

'Synn and Ms Black, by the providence of God you are hereby

pardoned for your crimes,' he declared. 'Go freely.'

A protector approached with others behind him, their armour clattering as they shoved through the crowd. 'Halt,' he barked. 'You do not have the authority to pardon these convicted criminals, Your Holiness.'

'It is not by my authority that they live, knight,' replied the Grand Speaker. 'It is by divine decree they shan't be executed. This transcends the law of man.'

'That is not for you to decide.'

'Are you mad, boy?' the old man snapped. He stabbed a finger at the grey sky. 'If you try to apprehend these two, God's wrath will crash upon the land! If we defy Him, the city will fall! Now, let them pass!'

The protector shifted where he stood, clearly hesitant to arrest the leader of the Holy Church. The Grand Speaker turned to the crowd, a trembling hand raised into the air. 'In life, God gives signs for us to interpret, and never has a divine call for mercy rung a more resounding toll than this.'

The crowd mumbled in agreement, nodding their heads and muttering to each other. As the Grand Speaker indulged himself in a long, rambling sermon to the people, Synn elbowed my shoulder to get my attention, then signalled me with a jerk of his head to follow him. He led us into the choked, filthy streets, pushing past commoners and threading our way through rivers of people. He seemed to be following a very exact path, and the further we went, the fewer people we saw. We turned left, then right, then left again, then slipped into a mossy alleyway that seemed to lead to nothing more than a dark wall. But when we reached it, I realised it was actually a thick curtain of vines. Synn pushed past it, and I followed him, wincing as many leafy tendrils dragged across my face and neck like cold fingers.

Beyond them lay a quiet, shaded street of decrepit, empty buildings. The street was small and seemed to have been sealed away behind a brewery and a library apparently by accident. There was no one around, and it seemed like no one had been here for many years. It was empty and forlorn – an island of silence amongst a sea of ceaseless noise.

'What is this place?' I asked.

'Oh, right, yeah, I almost forgot – don't tell anybody about this place,' Synn said. 'This is an abandoned street, sealed away God knows how long ago. Nobody knows this is here, except for me. I've used this place to hide from the protectors a couple of times. It's safe.'

Synn went to the door of what looked like an abandoned house and kicked it open. Stepping inside, the dust in the air was almost thick enough to choke me. There was nothing in here except for some broken glass and pottery on the floorboards. Synn laid Kiro down on the dust-laden floor, beside the square of light on the ground where the daylight spilling through the window fell.

'So that was all him, huh?' he asked me.

I knelt beside Kiro, watching his chest rise and fall with slow, raspy breaths. 'Of course it was. And look – it nearly killed him.' I looked up at Synn. 'He did this for us.'

He folded his arms, but for once in his life, he didn't have a clever little quip or remark. Instead, he simply made a weak little laugh of disbelief and stared at the boy. I took Rosethorn from Kiro's sash and stood up. I hadn't the faintest notion of how he possibly could have taken this from the protectors, nor why he would undertake such a severe risk to return it to me.

'How do we help him?' Synn asked softly.

I studied the marks on Kiro's face, and took in a deep breath. 'I don't know,' I said. I recalled what the boy had told me in Dagger Peaks. 'He needs to rest. I don't think there's anything we can do for him but keep him safe.'

Synn rubbed his stubble and paced around the room. 'This place isn't much good for anything except hiding,' he said, looking around with clear frustration. 'This is no place for him. He needs a bed and a nurse.'

'And where do you suppose we get him that?'

'...I don't know.'

I sat down, leaning against the wall while Synn stood, arms folded, staring out the window. For a long while, we said nothing as we slowly came to fully grasp all that had happened, and waited for Kiro to wake. On the edge of the silence, I thought I could hear the snap and crack of the wood burning as waving, flaming arms crawled up the pile, reaching closer and closer until the moment black smoke smothered me, burning my eyes and nose and throat. My heart pounded in my chest, and my hands trembled uncontrollably.

And yet, this battle was not over.

'So…' Synn broke the silence. 'What now?'

I took a breath to steady myself, and grabbed my hand with the other to hold them still. 'Once Zephelia realises we're still alive, she will do whatever she can to kill us. She will never allow the Grand Speaker to pardon us.'

Synn hummed. 'Seems to me we only have one option here.'

My fingers curled around the grip of Rosethorn.

'Yes,' I agreed. I stood up, fastening Rosethorn to the belt on my hip. 'I'm going to the White Palace.' I took out the crown I had hidden and handed it to Synn. 'Here.'

It was strange to give a famous criminal a priceless, mysterious treasure and have no doubt I could depend on him. He inspected it with a thief's awe. 'Whoa. What is this?'

'It was on the ground next to him. I presume it may have been the source of power he used to conjure the storm. So, we will keep it for him.' I went for the door. 'Stay here, keep Kiro safe. I will return.'

When I opened the door, Synn called out my name. 'Viella.'

I glanced back at him over my shoulder. He smirked and gave a nod of encouragement.

'Give her hell.'

I returned the gesture with a nod of my own, then left.

I passed through the curtain of vines and returned to the odorous, crowded streets. I gazed up at the magnificent White Palace looming over the city and made my way towards it through the winding, bustling roads. Infiltrating the palace may seem impossible to any commoner who spends each day living under its shadow, but I was not a commoner. I had a childhood in that palace, and many adventures through its countless winding halls and corridors. I could still recall the wonder and fascination I felt as a young girl when I found a secret passage in the cellars that led to a canal beyond the pale stone walls of the palace.

All I needed to do was find that canal. My memories of it were vague, but I recalled it was beneath an overhang close to the White Palace. Thus, it would be in the noble district. I proceeded towards the centre of the city, clutching at the disguise thrown on me. Until the King knew the truth, I could not wear my true identity as armour. If one of Zephelia's puppets sighted my face and white hair, then I would die as merely another common woman with a slashed throat in the gutters.

I crossed the Wellgate Bridge that ran over the city canals, entering the noble district. It was refreshing to walk through clean streets empty of barking peasants, but I needed to be careful now. My wretched appearance stood out here, and if I drew too much attention, I would be thrown out. I went down the path clinging to the side of the canal, avoiding the attention of the strolling nobles. The canal branched off. One stream went further into the noble district while the other continued to flow around it. I followed the canal inwards, approaching the looming figure of the White Palace. Gradually, the land beside the canal pathways lifted until I was enclosed by raised stone walls. Ahead there was an overhang at the end of the canal.

This sight certainly seemed familiar. As I approached the damp, dark end of the path, I brushed my hand against the wall, blindly feeling for the fake stone that would open into the passage. I was beginning to wonder if it had been sealed away.

But then I found it.

The door was a section of fake bricks that, from simply observing, would not raise one's suspicion. I pushed into the door until there was a click. Then, as I released my hand, the door swayed open, revealing a narrow, dusty passage.

I stooped down and stepped inside, closing the door behind me.

Completely engulfed in darkness, I proceeded carefully, guiding myself by pressing a hand to the wall. The air was stale and difficult to breathe, and it became a labour to draw in breath. Occasionally the passage winded up like a stairwell, and other times I'd trip over steep, ill-formed steps. I was grateful this tunnel still existed. I never did learn who built it or why. I had suspected it was built in secret by the 14th King, so he could have his commoner lover smuggled in and out of the palace at a whim. Thank God for his lechery.

My footsteps and rugged breathing echoed through the impenetrable dark. I heard rats squeak and I wondered if anyone would hear me scream if one of them grazed by my ankle. After what felt like an hour, I began to question if there was any end to this tunnel. As those doubts surfaced, however, I spotted tiny beams of light, peeking through the slits in a metal latch.

At this point, I was nearly crawling on my hands and knees. I pushed against the grating.

It was locked.

Despair thickened in my throat as I shook the latch to no avail. It seemed loose but I couldn't rip it off.

I took a slow breath in, then shuffled around awkwardly until I was lying on my back. I reared my knees up to my chest, prayed to God that no one would hear this, and then kicked the latch as hard as I could.

My feet crashed through, breaking the tiny door off its hinges, and sending it scattering against a cold stone floor. Despite my prayer, it clattered loudly, the harsh noise ringing off the walls. I winced and gritted my teeth, waiting for any sound that could mean a guard rushing to investigate. After a long silence, I crawled out.

I was in the musty cellars of the White Palace, standing in a corner beside shelves of barrels. It was just as I remembered; quiet, cold, dark, and with a low roof held up by a lattice of stone archways. It was gloomy, lit sparingly only by a few lanterns. I thanked my younger self for being insolent enough to ignore my father's commands and venture down here all those years ago.

I made my way to the stairs, following the vague map of my memories that guided me through the dimly lit underground. I found them, a creaky wooden staircase leading up to a door in the far corner of the room.

Opening it slowly and discretely, I peeked through the gap.

Beyond the door were the white stone corridors, illuminated by light pouring through tall, narrow windows. A red carpet edged with gold trimmings laid a path through the hallway. From memory, the Elite Guard patrolled through here with two men roughly every quarter-hour.

So, before I stepped out and risked my discovery, I closed the door and waited. After only a small delay, I heard metal shuffling and a pair of footsteps marching through. I waited for the sound to fade, then I emerged.

Finally, the memories of my home merged with sight for the first time in eight years. Tall and quiet hallways of white, lined with looming windows on one side, then on the other, gorgeous canvas paintings depicting previous Kings, Regents, and historic scenes from the Old Times. I remembered, distinctly, that the painting of Lord Regent Baragus Vanclaude, a bald ancestor with a bushy moustache that always amused my younger self, was the one that was closest to the Royal Hall. I went left, moving just swift enough that I would be prompt but not noisy, checking the paintings on my left. I recognised them all; *Lord Neevus of Ceren Surrenders to Lord Haphasteon of Azale*, *The Battle of Frostgard*, *The First Petition Festival in Meras*, *Portrait of Vanclaude the Rose Knight.*

I turned a corner, and the hallway continued only a short way to a pair of wooden doors bolstered with iron. I remembered those doors – they led to the foyer before the Royal Hall. On my left, the paintings became portraits of former regents, as I knew they would. The stern and solemn faces of my ancestors stared at me the way they always had as I marched under them.

As I approached the doors, they opened before I could reach them.

A pair of elite guards stepped through them.

I bowed my head and, without allowing the jolt of panic to falter my footsteps, I gave modesty and duty to my gait, just as a servant does. I walked like I had duties to attend to, and that I was sad and meek.

And it succeeded. In the corners of my vision, the guards' black armour walked straight past me, and I resisted the temptation to glance back at them.

But as I reached the doors, I heard their footsteps stop abruptly.

'You there, wait.'

I threw open the doors and rushed through. The guards gave chase.

I would not be stopped this close to my freedom.

I ran into the foyer and followed the red carpet to the grand, arching doors of the Royal Hall. I charged through them, flinging them apart with a thunderous crash.

The Royal Hall was just as I remembered it; an imposing and splendorous chamber that was twice as tall as it was wide, lined on both sides with rising, milk-white pillars and tall, elaborate stained windows. It was bustling with the nobility, men and women draped in sumptuous and colourful fabrics, chatting among themselves in the court. The Elite Guard stood by each of the lofty pillars that supported the high, arched ceiling. The red and gold carpet stretched from the door, through the crowds, all the way up to the steps of the raised slab atop which the four thrones of the Regents sat, the preludes to the dais where the tall throne of the King rested. The 33rd King, a blond, clean-shaven man, was sitting there, sprawled in it lazily, leaning his crowned head into a palm propped up by an elbow. Beneath him were the smaller thrones of the Regents. Only one of them was occupied today; the one to the immediate right of the King, where the Regent of Azale sat.

My sister was sitting on that throne. She was dressed in fine, white vestures embroidered with flourishing gold threads that weaved around her waist and arms like vines, granting her an august appearance that was a worthy rendition of her vanity. Our mother's precious ruby necklace hung around her throat.

The sight of her there, lavished in riches, atop the throne that belonged to me, sitting comfortably, invoked the wrath that had stirred within my core for eight years. Suddenly, it was all coming up. The heavy dread for unseen enemies, the rage of being denied a life that was rightfully mine, the humiliation of being hunted like an animal by the people who should have been protecting me. All these rose up from somewhere deep within me, and poured power into my voice as I bellowed through the hall the name of the one who had orchestrated my suffering.

'*ZEPHELIA!*'

Silence ruptured the hall, and every head in the room turned to face me. No one dared to speak or move.

Zephelia gazed down on me from atop my throne, and when her blue eyes found me, the colour drained from her face.

The guards who were pursuing me latched their gauntlets tightly onto my arms and tried to drag me out. I planted my feet and fought back.

'We're very sorry, my Lady and my King,' one of them said. 'We'll remove this trespasser at once.'

'Unhand me!' I commanded them.

'Who is this insolent woman?' cried out the angered voice of a noblewoman somewhere in the room. Her question ignited the outrage of the other nobles, who began to clamour and bark like a pack of dogs.

'That's Satanya Black!' someone else shouted.

'Who?'

'A criminal's harlot. Throw her out!'

'Remove her!'

Each time they spoke of me as if I was nothing more than a criminal, a flush of hot anger pulsed through my veins. Another lie for the subjects, another insult to my heritage.

No more. No more lies. No more false names. The new truth would die with me.

'Enough! I am not Satanya Black!' Years of smouldering resentment carried my voice across the hall. 'I am not some criminal's harlot! I am not guilty of any crime except that of being born the eldest of two daughters!'

I elbowed one of the guards in the face and slipped out of their grasp. While the two of them were stunned, I stepped forward and ripped off the disguise that had been thrown on me, throwing the bonnet and tattered cloak to the ground. I dragged Rosethorn from its sheath and slashed the air as I raised it above my head. I stood tall, as myself and nothing less, and addressed the world.

'*Bear witness!*' I bellowed. '*I am Viella Vanclaude! I am the eldest daughter of Avaric and Camelia Vanclaude! I am the truth that has been kept from you! I am the true and rightful heir to the Regency of Azale!*'

Shocked gasps and exclamations rippled through the nobility. I sheathed Rosethorn and watched my sister and the King, waiting for them to respond. The 33rd King's hazel eyes recognised me, and he stood up, his face painted with disbelief. Zephelia was still frozen, afraid that any movement of hers would make this all real.

'What is the meaning of this?' asked the King. He looked at Zephelia with wide, unbelieving eyes. 'Your sister is alive?'

Zephelia, who had been petrified and speechless, retrieved her wits. 'My King, I am as shocked as you are,' she said with a façade of outrage and confusion that mirrored her words. 'My sister has long since departed this world. This woman is an imposter, desperate and mad enough to attempt this ridiculous affront.'

All I could do was laugh in disbelief. 'Do my senses fool me? Or am I to believe you are staring at the face of your sister and calling me a stranger?'

Zephelia gritted her teeth. 'My sister is dead! You are brazen to barge into the Royal Hall and bear her name like it was your own, deceiver!'

'*Deceiver*, am I?' Fury catapulted my words through the hall. 'You call me deceiver while you sit on the throne you stole from me? You, the conniving snake who condemned me to burn under the name of some criminal's harlot? You *hypocrite!*'

Zephelia reached her limit. 'Guards, remove her! Now!' she roared.

An upheaval of angry voices clashed in the air. The nobles declined into a clamour of outrage, some flinging insults at me and calling for my head, while others who believed me vainly urged the guards to stop. Obediently, four guards seized me, snatching my arms in iron grips as they roughly dragged me towards the doors. I fought back, resisting, yelling, but it was fruitless.

A single word halted them all.

'Cease!' roared the King.

And the guards stopped, and the crowd fell quiet. The men stopped dragging me out, and stood there, waiting for orders.

The King took a step forward, his heavy and opulent vestments of red, gold, and purple draping down to his feet, and was wordless for a moment. His silence gripped the hall, keeping it as still as a painting.

'Unhand her,' the King commanded.

The guards released me, and I brushed down my shoulders.

'Approach me,' the King said to me.

I did so, walking through the silent hall, the crowd parting before me until there was nobody standing between the King, Zephelia, and I. I stopped a respectable distance away from the thrones. The King studied my face for a moment before blinking. 'It really is you, Viella,' he said softly. 'Where have you been?'

I bowed. 'Your Majesty,' I said formally, before lifting my eyes to meet his. 'I have been hiding in the far west from assassins and cutthroats sent by Zephelia to kill me. It took me years to amass the skill and courage needed to travel here. On many occasions through my journey, I have nearly been parted from my life. I have returned to claim my throne and perform my duties to Azale and the region.'

Zephelia spoke up. 'My King, this woman is a skilled manipulator, who—'

'Silence,' said the King, glaring at her.

Zephelia pursed her lips and obeyed.

He gestured to me and asked me why I disappeared all those years ago. I told him, and the hall, everything – from how Gerard Crow heard whispers of ill intent and smuggled me out of the city, to the moment "God" invoked a storm that quenched the unjust flames rising to consume me. I even produced from my pocket the letter Zephelia had written to Synn and gave it to a senior knight who read the contents aloud to a dismayed hall. As I explained my story, the King's eyes slowly darkened as anger built behind them. When I concluded, he merely said

Zephelia's name with a grave tone.

She turned to him, kneeling.

He asked her, 'Is what she professes true?'

There was a long and painful pause, then Zephelia raised her head and her disguise melted away, revealing her true self; cold, unflinching, and shameless. 'Yes, my King.'

People all around me gasped, and quiet muttering clamoured in the air for a moment before dissipating once again.

'You are appallingly unapologetic, Vanclaude,' The King remarked in a low voice.

'That is because… I am not sorry.'

The King's eyes widened, a flash of anger at her boldness. 'You're not sorry for deceiving me? For trying to murder your sister, you offer no regrets?'

'No, my King,' she said, unabashed. 'If I had not done all this, then I could not have become regent and done all that I have for this wonderful city. I could never have served you as well as I do now. If I had the chance to stay my younger self's hand and spare my sister from all the tribulation I have caused her,' she paused, then said without an ounce of doubt, 'I would not change anything.'

Her words struck me hard, like a blow to the stomach robbing me of breath. I blinked, unprepared for the pain driving a knife into my heart.

The King shook his head, a frown carved into his face. 'Disgraceful,' he mumbled, his anger softening into something sorrowful. 'You should be ashamed of what you've done, Zephelia. Your deceit has befouled the honour of the regency, and now all your works are put to shame.' The King sat down and rubbed his face. 'Do you understand the position you've put me in now?'

The warmth of my growing confidence was suddenly snuffed out when I realised the King's feelings on the matter. Instating me seemed more like a terrible obligation than a just correction. He should be delighted to discard a liar and a murderer from the regency, and yet, his eyes exuded regret, and his words were reluctant. A heavy dread stirred in the pit of my heart, weighted with trepidation that I had yet to finally take back what I have sought tirelessly for so long.

'I understand, my King,' Zephelia said, 'but you will not need to remove me.'

The King, and the hall, were stunned.

'What did you say?' he asked.

Zephelia stood. 'I have ruled Azale as its regent for eight years, my King,' she began. 'I have earned the love of the people. I have decimated crime and I have quashed dissent. I have brought prosperity and order to the region. I will not see myself and my achievements cast aside so easily.' She turned to address the hall, and myself in particular. 'Of course my sister has a rightful claim to the regency, but as do I. I refuse to surrender my position without as much as an objecting breath. This is a contest of claims, and I intend to resolve it in the honourable way.'

Murmurs in the crowd simmered in the air as Zephelia walked down the steps until her standing was level with mine. She raised her voice, silencing the hall.

'Viella Vanclaude,' she said, staring into my eyes, 'I challenge you to a duel.'

An outburst of astonished chatter lifted into the air and filled the hall with speculation and interest. My heart sank. The challenge was a cunning play. Even if the King desired it, which I suspected from his tolerant silence he did not, he could not overrule it. Zephelia had just saved herself from being immediately deposed. I studied her face – it was pale and still, betraying nothing of her true emotions, if she had any at all. All that was evident was her conviction, her despicable commitment to her own treachery so egregious that she would sooner forfeit her own life than to see herself punished for her crimes.

But I would not yield. I had not come this far to let her win. If she called for a battle, I would oblige her.

I put aside my fears and hopeless longing and met Zephelia's gaze with my own.

'I accept your challenge.'

Chapter Nineteen

A Dance of Blades

I woke up to the sound of humming.

There was a moment or two before I realised I was alive. I remembered my body and its senses. A dull, throbbing ache was pressing against the bone of my forehead. I was flat on my back in a soft, warm bed, with heavy blankets up to my chin.

A raspy groan slipped through my dry, cracked lips. I squinted and pushed myself to sit up. A hand gripped my shoulder and held me steady.

'Easy, Kiro,' said a man's voice. He sounded familiar, like I knew him. 'You're finally awake, huh?'

A fog in my vision finally cleared. I could see again.

Peering down on me was a handsome man with long blond hair. It was my friend. His name was Synn.

'Synn…' I said, my voice bone dry. The effort to rake the words up my throat prompted a few hoarse coughs. Synn left my side and returned a moment later, holding a round canteen, which he pressed to my lips. Clean water flowed into my mouth, as sweet as honey to my parched tongue, and I drank it in eagerly.

'Good to see you're alive. You've been knocked out for two days, kiddo,' he informed me. 'How you feeling?'

I groaned, rubbing my brow with a palm. 'Not good,' I replied weakly.

'Yeah, I figured. You hungry?'

Once he asked that, I became aware that I was, in fact, so hungry it was painful. 'Yes. Very much so,' I said.

He smiled. He had a nice smile. 'Well, you're in luck. We have some of the best food in Advenia where we are.'

That raised a question. 'Where are we?' I asked.

'You're not gonna believe this,' Synn said. 'We're in the White Palace.'

I looked around. I was in a small, cosy room made of smooth, pale stone, and illuminated by light pouring through an arched window to my left. Peering through it, it seemed like we were in the sky. All I could see was the white of clouds. Across from the bed I was in, there was a mirror. I gazed into it, and I could hardly recognise myself. My eyes were sunken into a pale, gaunt face. Coarse, dark stubble wrapped around my jaw and under my nose. There were faded marks and lines on the right side of my face. I touched them carefully with my fingertips. I had never experienced divination's effects in such a drastic manner. Seeing the marks unfurling on my face was scary, and a reminder of just how lucky I was to be alive.

'Where is Viella?' I croaked.

He gave me a piece of dry, firm bread. Something fierce came over me and I sunk my teeth into the bread like an animal.

'Wow, you are hungry, eh?' Synn said, noticing it. 'She'll be back, kiddo, don't you worry. Go back to sleep. You need to rest.'

He stood up and swirled a hooded green cloak around himself.

I swallowed the last bite of bread. 'Where are you going?'

He donned the hood, concealing most of his face. 'I'm gonna go get some more food for when you wake up. Ham sound good? Maybe some cheese?'

I smiled and closed my eyes, nodding slowly. I was still exhausted, and weak, but his words were comforting. 'I would appreciate that greatly,' I said slowly.

'Awesome. I'll see you on the other side, buddy.'

A door creaked open, then was gently closed. I nestled my head into my pillow, and let the warmth of the bed and the knowledge I was being cared for soothe me until I was asleep.

The next time I woke up, the world outside was dark. A sprinkle of stars glimmered out the window.

'Synn?' I said.

There was a rustling of clothes, as if someone turning their head.

'Kiro,' said Viella's voice. 'You're finally awake.'

I flinched, realising it was her, and swung my head to see her.

Viella was sitting on the floor in a pool of moonlight streaming through the window, leaning her back against the wall. Her disguise was gone, and her long snowy hair flowed freely down her shoulders and half of her face. She was staring at me with wide eyes.

I went to sit up so I could get out of the bed, but I strained with the effort. Viella forwent her usual, regal stride as she swept across the room to help me. 'Tenderly, Kiro,' she said, laying her hands on my shoulder and chest. 'Don't strain yourself.'

I sat up but stopped there. 'It is good to see you again, Viella.'

'Likewise,' she said quietly. 'I thought you were dead.'

'So did I.'

Her eyes wandered over my face and neck. 'The marks have faded.'

I touched my face, and except for the coarseness of a budding beard, I couldn't feel any marks. 'That's good. It means my body is healing.'

'Are you well? Do you need anything?' she asked me.

I licked my lips. 'Water, please. Do we have any water?'

She retrieved the same canteen that Synn had, and gave it to me to drink. I asked her where he was, and she clenched her jaw at the mention of his name. 'He's gone, Kiro.'

I blinked. 'Gone?'

She knitted her eyebrows as she glanced off somewhere. 'He disappeared yesterday. There was no word or warning. When I returned here, you were alone. I'm afraid he's taken that crown of yours as well.'

I took in a sharp breath. The crown. I only then realised it was missing from my robes. 'He stole it?'

'Presumably, yes.' Viella's lips curled into a scowl and her gaze dipped. 'I have searched this room thoroughly and found no trace of it. The gun is missing as well. It is my fault – I was wrong to pour my trust onto a man like him. Even after everything we have been through, I was a fool to think scum like him could ever change for the better.'

I couldn't believe her. I refused to believe her. His kindness to me when I first awoke was genuine. He was not the same man he was when we first met him. 'He was here. I woke up before and he was at my side,' I told her. 'He gave me water and bread, and he left to go and get some more food.'

She sighed and paced around the room, stopping at the window, through which she peered up at the stars. 'He lied to you. He lied to me,' she said without passion. I found myself expecting her to explode in an outburst, yelling and storming around and vowing to exact revenge. But instead, she was subdued and calmly disappointed. 'He is a convincing liar, but a liar nonetheless. People never change, Kiro. If they are destined for a life of vice then they are eternally bound to it.'

I shook my head. 'That's not true. Everyone can change for the better, madam,' I said, ignoring the sting in my eyes. 'Maybe he got lost or got in trouble. Maybe he didn't return because he couldn't, maybe—'

'Please, Kiro, you know he is very much capable of handling himself,' Viella said flatly. 'My presumption is he seized the opportunity to take that crown and flee the city while he still could. For both our sakes, discard him from your thoughts.'

A new pain joined the dull aches in my body. My voice wobbled. 'But... he...'

Viella glanced at me pitifully. 'It is a cruel truth of this world. People are evil, and selfish, and foolish. You cannot hold them to any expectation of overcoming their flaws. In the end, they're only people.'

After everything I had done, I wasn't good enough to help him. I knew I should be feeling furious. Instead, I just felt like crying. But I couldn't. Maybe it was because I was too weak, or because my mind would not allow me to believe it. No matter how much I tried, I just couldn't comprehend why he would do that. It just didn't seem possible to me, so surely it couldn't be true. It just couldn't be true.

Viella sat down at the end of my bed, and we talked for hours into the night, telling each other what had happened after our paths diverged in the seas. She was shocked by my story of Adven and the crown, and seemed unwilling to believe me but unable to deny that it was the truth. After we realised the burst of light we both saw was one and the same, I had no doubts that Adven was buried under the Twisted Seas, and the crown was the source of the world-bending storm that had raged there. Knowing that Synn now had that crown, oblivious to its true power, made me ill with anxieties. I tried not to think about it, grimly accepting the fact I had no means of finding him and recovering it.

Viella then told me about what happened after I saved her and Synn.

'A duel?' I repeated her words. 'What does that mean?'

Viella's gaze settled on her sword, resting across her lap in its sheath. 'There is a law in Azale that allows contests of claims between two noble parties to be resolved by means of a duel. It means we are going to fight.'

'To what end?' I asked.

'It's to the death, Kiro,' she said gravely. 'The victor will be the one who kills the other.'

My jaw dropped. 'What? You're going to kill your sister?'

'Of course not,' Viella said quickly. 'It won't come to that. I will defeat her, and once I have her at the end of my blade, she will know better than to choose death over surrender. She will yield her claim, and I will finally be where I belong.'

'But what if she beats you?' I voiced my concern.

'She won't.'

I stared at her, wordless for a moment as I tried to imagine how I could talk her out of this. Viella's face was stern but I could see a glimmer of doubt in her eyes. 'Madam, why do you want this fight?' I asked her. 'Do you yearn for power so greatly as to risk your life in a battle?'

'It is more than that, Kiro,' Viella said, with a slight hint of offence. 'I am fighting for my destiny. I am fighting for the life I was promised. I am fighting to end a reign of duplicity and injustice.'

'But to cross blades with your own sister,' I said, sadness sapping the strength from my voice. It took me a moment before I could speak again. 'Is sitting on a throne truly worth killing your family?'

She said nothing for a moment. 'I will not need to kill her,' she said slowly. 'She will surrender when I defeat her.'

'*If* you defeat her,' I said, 'and *if* she surrenders. What if she refuses?'

Viella looked away and pursed her lips. She stood up to leave. 'If she refuses,' she said, turning her back on me, 'then I will do what I must.'

~

The day of the duel came a week later. On that day, sullen grey clouds, swept in by an easterly wind, veiled the skies above the city.

Viella and I were escorted downstairs by two tall men garbed in black armour and rigid silence. I was recovering, but still slow and stiff. Viella had given me a cane made of coiling wood to help me walk. The taps of the cane on the tiled floor rung through the long, opulent hallways of the White Palace. Rich paintings and tapestries adorned the walls, depicting in meticulous detail historical events that I didn't recall ever reading about in the Order's archives. Solemn portraits of stern, stoic figures gazed down on us as we walked beneath them. We descended a stairwell for a long time until we reached a foyer that preceded the Royal Hall, as Viella called it. I could hear the muffled mumblings of a crowd behind the two arched doors. Viella and I approached them, and the guards opened them.

The Royal Hall was a grand and lofty chamber, bustling with noble spectators and the clamour of their eager, speculative chatter. They were grouped on both sides of the hall, staying clear of the middle. Viella's sister was standing at the end of the hall, atop a slab where the other three Regents reclined in their thrones. Zephelia was a short but intimidating young woman. She stood with a perfect, upright posture, and a transcendent air of elegance and dignity that was unabated by the wickedness of her actions. Her pale hair was cut short and sharp, falling just past her chin. She was eyeing us carefully from across the hall, her steady gaze icy with contempt.

Viella was approached by servants carrying a padded vest for her. She lifted her arms parallel to the ground and allowed them to strap it onto her.

I went to her side. 'There is still time to turn back, madam,' I whispered to her. 'You don't have to do this.'

'And be marked a coward?' She shook her head. 'No. I will not run.'

'*Please*, Viella,' I begged her softly. 'It doesn't matter what people call you. I know you are good with a sword, but you could *die* today. Don't throw away your life for pride. Renounce your claim and leave this all behind you, I'm begging you.'

'I must do this, Kiro,' she said quietly but with heavy words. She gazed right into my eyes. 'I will never flee from my destiny again. If she strikes me down today, so be it. But I *will* fight for what is mine. Now please, *stand aside.*'

I stared at her, yearning to do anything I could to stop this. But I knew I could not change her mind. This was out of my hands. I shut my eyes and took a breath.

'Be careful,' I said finally, before receding into the sidelines.

A door behind the thrones creaked as it swung wide, and the voices of the crowd dwindled to lowly hums then to nothing as the 33rd King strode into the room, a long and heavy cloak of red and gold dragging behind him. Zephelia stood aside as the King marched up the steps of the dais and took his throne. The bejewelled crown on his head leaned to the side as he rested his chin on his fist.

A plump man with a pointed beard and wavy brown hair, dressed in a green doublet, stepped out from the crowd and stood below the stairs to the thrones. 'Today, the contest of claims between Zephelia Vanclaude, Regent of Azale, and her sister, Viella Vanclaude, shall be resolved with a duel,' he announced to the room. 'Heed these binding rules; the contestants will wield swords of their choosing. There will be no respite or pause, and the duel will conclude only when one contestant falls, or if one chooses to surrender her claim.' He paused, then glanced from Viella to Zephelia. 'May God bless the worthiest contestant with the strength to overcome her opponent.' He made a bow, then slinked into the crowd on the side.

Zephelia, who had been glaring at Viella from the regents' stage, began striding towards her sister, down the steps and into the clearing in the centre of the hall. She stopped some distance away, facing her sister. Once the air was heavy with silence, she spoke. 'To be clear with you, dear sister, and with everyone in this room,' she said calmly and clearly. 'I do not regret what I did.'

Viella narrowed her eyes. 'Even now, Zephelia? Even now, at the edge of your life, you refuse to admit your own evil?'

'I would never disgrace my honour like that,' she uttered coldly. 'You were unfit to rule, a tyrant fool in the bud. Because of my actions, however heartless they were, I have brought prosperity to Azale. I have served my duty and my King well. You may proclaim whatever you like about me, but the goodness of my deeds is irrefutable.' She extended an open palm outwards, and from the sides, a servant approached her and unsheathed a thin, elegant sabre. He bowed his head as he offered it to her. Without sparing even a glance to the man, she took the blade and walked forward until she stopped a few feet from Viella. 'Because you are a Vanclaude, and I am a merciful woman, I will grant you one final dignity. I will allow you to die here, in this beautiful palace.'

She slashed the air with the sword's tempered steel as she raised it parallel to her face and body.

Viella, without a word, slid Rosethorn from its sheath and entered a poised stance.

The King gave a small flick of his hand to a servant beneath the thrones, who then shouted into the hall, 'Let the duel… begin!'

The Vanclaude sisters began to move slowly in a circle, their eyes fixed on one another. I did not know what thoughts were flowing through their minds, as the expressions of their faces betrayed nothing, but it seemed they were studying each other's composure and form, designing predictions and estimations.

Finally, Zephelia lunged her blade at Viella, who quickly repelled the attack with a swing of her own steel. After a few moments, Viella jabbed at Zephelia, who caught the attack and deflected it away from her.

This went on for a few more minutes; an exchange of quick and precise stabs and lunges. There was a certain restraint in their attacks, suggesting that there was no lethal intent driving the swords forward. Rather, they were attempts to stir a reaction that could be studied, to gain a critical understanding.

Eventually, their contacts became longer and harder to follow. Their fighting serenaded the air with the sounds of clashing metal and sweeping footsteps. The two of them would slash and cut at the other, who would repel the strike effortlessly, then move forward with their own attack that would be diverted and then countered. These exchanges flowed like poetry. They both displayed a mastery of will and talent that was almost like a form of art. Their movements were blindingly quick and precise, and neither one could properly seize an advantage over the other. They were locked in a dance of steel and death.

Eventually, however, Zephelia feinted a strike and, once Viella's sword was clear of the way, she thrust the tip of her blade at her sister's face. Viella saw it coming and jerked her head to the side, but was not fast enough to escape injury. A thin cut opened across her left cheek, just under her eye. A tiny cry escaped her and she dashed backwards. My heartbeat quickened, and anxiety quivered in my chest.

Zephelia pressed the attack, unleashing a torrent of vicious yet precise strikes at Viella, who was now entirely on the defensive. She could not find a pause between Zephelia's attacks that would allow a retaliation, and was now forced to catch her sister's strikes where they came. I held my breath, frightened that this might mean the end of her life. Even if I had any source of divination with me, I would be too weak to use it to intervene. I felt a strong urge to step forward and shout for this to end, but Viella urged me to stay out of this, and I knew the effort would change nothing.

But even though I was afraid and uncertain, Viella showed nothing on her face. It was impossible to tell if she was feeling any fear at all as she met Zephelia's sword with her own, again and again. Not for a moment did her composure ever waver. Even after Zephelia's strikes laid a few more cuts and wounds along her body, she did not falter. She was patient and calm. I realised that she was not losing. She was waiting. Finally, after a long assault, Zephelia's pace began to wane, and that was when Viella took the offensive.

And then, the tide of the duel changed.

Zephelia's air of dominance began to waver as her composure slowly crumbled. It was subtle at first; a stutter in her step, an expression of surprise at a counter or a lunge that got closer than she was comfortable with. Eventually, she spiralled. Her breathing became heavy, and she showed strain in using all her strength in attempts to kill her sister. Viella's face was like stone, steady and unflinching. The crowd around me were taking notice as well, making quiet little observations to each other.

Finally, Zephelia's rapid pace began to slow. She had exerted so much energy that she had exhausted herself. Even still, her determination did not falter as her body did. In her lethargic slashes and strikes, she was carried by a momentum driven by a profound desperation. Viella was not hesitant. When her sister showed weakness, she seized the advantage and drove her to the edge of the clearing with a barrage of complicated attacks that demanded Zephelia's full attention. But ultimately, Zephelia was fatigued. She could not keep up. A slash at her face surprised her and she became unbalanced. Viella lunged, and as Zephelia blocked her sister's blade, she tumbled to the floor, her pained cry echoing through the lofty hall. Gasps and shrieks scattered through the crowd. Viella stomped a boot onto Zephelia's wrist, pinning the hand gripping the sword to the ground, while she held the tip of Rosethorn against Zephelia's throat.

The scene was held for what felt like an eternity; Viella peering down on her defeated sister, holding the sword to her throat. Neither moved. Neither spoke. Viella needed only to push her blade forward to take what she had longed for, but yet, she did not.

To her sister, she whispered, 'Surrender.'

Zephelia gazed up at her, confused. It was as if she had never considered this circumstance to be a possibility. 'What?'

'Surrender the regency, and I will spare your life.'

Then, Zephelia's face changed. The corners of her lips curved into a cruel smile. 'No,' she whispered.

Viella paused, her breathing beginning to quiver. '*Surrender*,' she hissed again, but this time she sounded as if she was pleading with her, begging her to save herself.

Zephelia, however, would not give in. 'As long as my heart beats, that throne is mine,' she declared, her voice firm. 'I will *never* surrender that seat. I will rule this city until my last breath.'

Viella tried to remain invincible, tried to seem unshakeable and in control, but her composure began to crack like glass. Tears shimmered in her eyes. She wanted to plead with her, but she knew she could not change Zephelia's mind. She opened her mouth, but could only manage to quietly mutter with a shaky voice, '*Why, Zeph? Why? Why?*'

Zephelia said nothing. She just kept staring into Viella's eyes, watching for any sign in her sister's expression that would indicate her fate.

Viella sniffled and blinked back her tears. Then her face hardened with resolve, and she took a deep breath to steady herself.

Slowly, she sheathed her sword and lifted her boot off her sister's wrist.

Zephelia's eyes widened.

'It's yours,' Viella muttered.

There was a pause.

Zephelia stared at her in disbelief. 'You're sparing me?'

Viella shut her eyes and, with a sombre heart, said, 'If you're willing to kill and die to be called the regent... clearly, you yearn for the title more than I. If killing my sister is the price of power, I will not pay it.'

'Then you concede your defeat?' Zephelia asked.

'I refuse to stain my honour with the blood of my family,' Viella declared. 'If that is defeat, then I welcome it eagerly. There is nothing in this world that can compel me to slaughter my kin. No title is worth murdering my own sister.'

Zephelia's emanating superiority faded. Viella had given her what she wanted, and yet there was not a trace of joy or pleasure on her face. She took a moment to compose herself on the ground before rising to her feet.

'Just promise me this, Zephelia,' Viella said weakly. 'Leave me in peace. Do not come for my life or try to interfere with my affairs. Likewise, I will stray far from you.'

Zephelia nodded slowly.

There came a voice from the thrones.

'Viella,' said the King, 'are you forfeiting?'

She looked up at him. 'I am, my King.'

He exhaled softly. He seemed relieved. 'Then make it so,' he urged her gently, waiting for a sworn promise.

For a moment, Viella said nothing. Then she turned to the room and, without a word, lifted Rosethorn. She held it in the air for a moment before she dropped it to the ground. The loud clatter of its steel echoed through the silent hall.

People began to murmur, their chatter slow and unsure. They looked to the King for certainties, and he provided them. 'Viella Vanclaude has made her intentions known,' he remarked solemnly. 'Let it be written that this contest is ended. Viella Vanclaude has forfeited her claims, and Zephelia shall remain the Regent of Azale.'

There was a heavy silence that hung in the air. No one was sure how to react, of what to say.

Viella wiped the blood from her face, then ripped off her padded vest and tossed it carelessly to the ground. She turned and went for the doors without a word as the crowd watched her. I followed her out, hobbling along with my cane. As I left the hall, I glanced over my shoulder at Zephelia. I saw her penetrating blue eyes watching us, a faint frown on her face. She and her reign had survived, but with all her lies laid bare, she, and everyone in the room knew, this was not her victory.

Chapter Twenty

Reparation

A pair of knights escorted Viella and I out of the palace. We crossed a bridge over a deep and empty moat, walked under a massive portcullis, and entered the streets. It was here when I noticed an immediate difference in Viella. She was quiet and lacking her usual confidence. Her gait, which had once been a direct and dignified stride, was loose, slow, and aimless.

'Viella?'

She did not respond. She glanced up at the White Palace behind us, then turned and walked away.

'Viella, wait.' I staggered into a painful dash to get ahead of her, hammering the road with my cane. The sight of her face was tragic. Her blue eyes were dull and heavy-lidded, staring into nothing. The cut Zephelia had carved along her cheek had trickled a curtain of blood down the right side of her face. I took her limp hands in mine to steady her arms, then noticed more bleeding wounds along the back of her right hand and up her wrist. Her gloves had been slashed open, and blood was seeping through the cuts. The vest had done well to protect her from death but the battle had left its mark.

'You're hurt,' I pointed out. 'We need to take care of your wounds.'

She ripped her hands from mine. 'I can take care of myself.'

'You're bleeding, madam. Please, let me help you.'

She stood there, her eyes downcast. After a little while, she sighed. 'Fine.' I could hear the fatigue in her voice. 'Let's just… go somewhere quiet, alright? Somewhere without people.'

'Alright.'

I surveyed the streets as we hobbled wearily through them, grazed by passing glances of curiosity and contempt from the men and women in fine garments who noticed us. The stares stopped as the buildings around us became cramped and shoddy, and the streets dense with people in humbler fabrics. I found a place I knew to be an inn, the Smiling Lion, and led Viella inside.

Inside was a long room filled with tables and chairs, and a polished wooden bar that stretched from wall to wall. The smell of hot meat and beer wafted in the air. Behind the bar, a woman with curly ginger hair was polishing a glass with a cloth. There were a few small clusters of people sitting at tables; a trio of sunburnt farmers, some colourful actors, and a pair of relaxing protectors eating mutton by a hearth. The bartender saw us enter, and went to smile before she noticed Viella's face. She blinked in surprise, her smile disappearing as she put away the glass and swept around the bar to approach us. 'Oh dear, what happened? Are you hurt?' she asked us.

I had not expected anyone to come and help, so for a second, I forgot to speak. 'Oh. Yes, she was in a fight. Is it okay for us to rest here for a moment?'

'Of course,' replied the bartender. 'Here, let me help you.'

'I am perfectly well,' Viella insisted. 'Don't fret over me.'

'Don't be silly, love. You're bleeding.' The bartender gently took her hand. 'Come this way, darling. I'll fix you up.'

Viella weakly objected. 'You don't have to do this.'

'I insist.' The bartender dragged out a chair by a round table. 'Sit here.'

At her insistence, we sat down. Once Viella found the seat, it was like everything holding up her body gave way at once, and she collapsed into a sprawl on the chair.

'Are you alright, darling?' the bartender asked Viella, who simply shut her eyes and nodded. She then went to press a cloth to Viella's face, but

I noticed it was the same rag she was using to clean the glass.

I stuck out my hand to stop her. 'Wait.'

The bartender seemed confused. 'What's wrong, young man?'

'We can't tend to her wounds with a dirty rag,' I told her, remembering the old texts on human care in the archives. 'A wound must be clean to heal. Dirt and filth will cause them to fester and worsen. Trust me.'

The bartender cocked her head, and looked at the rag. 'I've never heard of that,' she remarked curiously. 'Alright, wait here.'

She left to find a clean cloth. In the meantime, I sat down and assessed Viella's injuries. The cut across her face was, fortunately, not too deep. Her hands and arms, however, were of concern. Delicately, I slid the gloves off her fingers, revealing a nasty cut on the back of her hand. A pained cry hissed through Viella's clenched teeth as I peeled the glove off. 'This is exactly what I didn't want, Kiro,' she muttered.

'I know,' I said, 'but you *need* help.'

The bartender returned, holding a wet cloth. 'Good God, you poor thing,' she murmured, dismayed by the sight of Viella's hands. 'Here.'

She reached out with the cloth to touch Viella's face, who winced and stiffened as the bartender's hand neared her.

Gently, the bartender dabbed the cloth on Viella's cheek, wiping away the blood.

'You're going to be fine, darling,' the bartender assured her.

Viella studied her carefully with wide, unsure eyes. Her lips parted ever so slightly, but she did not say anything.

A man's voice that I didn't recognise spoke. 'Excuse us, Bonhilde, is everythin' alright?'

I turned to see a farmer who had approached us, with two of his friends behind him.

The bartender, Bonhilde, looked at them. 'Hello, Ket. Truth be told, this fine lady is in bad shape.'

'Is there anythin' we can do to help?' Ket asked.

Viella groaned quietly and squeezed her eyes shut.

An idea came to Bonhilde's mind, and she said, 'Come to think of it, you could help me wrap up her wounds. Go look for something behind the bar to stop the bleeding, there should be some wrappings we can use.'

'Got it.' Ket and his friends leapt to action, heading to a door behind the bar.

'You know where the spare stuff is, yeah?' Bonhilde called out.

'Think so,' Ket's voice said from behind a wall.

Viella groaned miserably. 'Must we do this… so visibly?'

'It's not there, Bonny,' another man's voice called out from a room behind the bar.

'It should be, keep looking,' Bonhilde replied as she returned her focus to Viella, pressing the reddening cloth firmly into Viella's hand.

Watching these strangers work together to help Viella was deeply moving. I could feel tears welling in my eyes, and I smiled. *See*, I thought to myself, *there are good people in the world*.

The farmers returned to the table, looking sorrowful. 'We couldn't find it,' Ket reported, scratching his neck.

'Surely it's there?' Bonhilde stood up, then looked to me. 'Here, young man, hold the cloth to her hand. Just like that. Keep a firm hold. I'll be back.'

I took hold of the cloth and pressed it firmly onto the wounds. Viella scrunched up her face. The farmers discussed amongst themselves what they knew about treating wounds and how to go about fixing up Viella. Bonhilde returned a little while later, also empty-handed.

'Bugger me,' she sighed. 'I can't find it either. Mister Dawble must have tossed them out.'

One of Ket's friends, a lean, bald man, stood up and drew a dagger from a sheath on his hip. The sight of the steel immediately spun images of violence in my mind, and to my bewilderment, I expected him to attack. But instead, he held it to the end of his own tunic and began to cut through the yellow fabric.

'What are you doing, Bennick?' asked Ket.

'I'm cuttin' off some fabric for the lady,' he answered. When he finished, he handed me a strip of his clothes, and gave a flick of his chin. 'Here, lad. Put it to good use.'

I thanked him and took it, then wrapped it around Viella's hand, tying a little knot to keep it in place.

Viella opened her eyes and peered at the cloth wrapped around her hand. She inspected it curiously, then looked up to Bennick, the man who had given it to her. 'Is this from your clothes?'

'Yes, madam,' he answered with a polite nod.

She was stunned. 'You cut off your clothes for me?'

'It was only a strip of it. I won't miss it.'

Viella had no words. She just blinked at them, as if she could not believe he had done it. 'Why are you doing this?' she asked him. Her eyes darted between them. 'Why are you all helping me? Do you want something from me? Money? Favour? Are you trying to indebt me?'

Bonhilde and the farmers were taken aback by her suspicion. 'Of course not, madam,' she said gently. 'We're helping you because you're hurt.'

Viella blinked a few times and stared at them. 'What do I owe you, then?'

'Nothing at all, madam,' Ket said.

Viella paused. It seemed she simply could not believe their kindness to be sincere, to be unspoiled by secret motives. She was silent for a time, her eyes staring downwards into nothing while she collected her thoughts. After we had bandaged her other wounds, she finally said with a quiet voice, 'Thank you for all your assistance.'

'Happy to help.' Bonhilde smiled. 'Do you have a room with us?'

I spoke up. 'No. We don't have any money.'

Bonhilde hesitated, then said, 'That's alright. Let's just get you a place you can lay down, how does that sound?'

I smiled. 'That sounds wonderful, thank you.'

Bonhilde and I helped Viella stand. Once she was on her feet, Bonhilde led us to a spiralling staircase in the corner of the room. We followed its creaking steps up to another floor where a long corridor lined with doors awaited us. Bonhilde went to a particular door down the hall and on the right, which she opened for us.

Inside were two neatly made beds, a small table between them, and a rug of fur on the floorboards. On the wall between the two beds was a window overlooking a bustling street; abundant in movement but entirely soundless here. It was cosy and warm, and exactly what we needed. When Viella sat down on the bed, Bonhilde asked us to inform her if we needed anything else before she left the room.

Once we were alone, I turned to Viella. 'Do you see how good people can be?'

She was staring at the cloth wrapping on her hand. 'I had not expected such kindness from commoners,' she remarked softly.

I sat down on the bed across from her, laying the cane across my lap.

'How are you feeling?'

She sighed quietly. 'Utterly exhausted.'

'Your wounds don't seem too serious, I think you'll recover well.'

'It isn't that,' she said. 'It's what I've done.'

She seemed sombre, so I sat down next to her and asked her what was on her mind. For a while, she said nothing. I let her find the time to speak. When she finally did, she simply said my name. 'Kiro.'

'Yes, madam?'

'Did I do the right thing?'

'You did.'

She rubbed at her temple, then ran her fingers through her pale hair, pushing it off her face. 'Why does it not feel like I did?'

I took a moment to ponder, reaching for an answer from my own experience. 'The right choice is not always an easy choice to make,' I said. 'And sometimes, it is not clear if the decision we made is right or wrong until well after we have made it.'

She regarded my advice with a meek nod, but her eyes did not lift from the floor.

'Tell me what's in your heart,' I encouraged her gently. When she did not say anything, I added, 'You don't need to walk this journey alone, Viella.'

Without lifting her eyes, she mumbled, 'I… I don't know what to do.'

'You don't need to, madam,' I told her. 'If you're living and breathing, you're doing all you need to do.'

Her eyebrows lifted and a faint smile surfaced on her lips for a brief instant. 'I thought my place was here in this city, in that seat. That was my destiny, and fulfilling it was all I wanted.' Her chest heaved and sank with a heavy breath. 'And now, I have no home. No family. Nowhere to go.'

'You do have family.'

'What, in *her*? That cruel girl…' Her brow fell into her hand. 'I yielded my claim. I had her at the end of my sword and I *yielded*. You understand what that means in a contest of claims, Kiro?'

I shook my head.

'It means I have nothing now,' she said. 'When two people duel to resolve a contest of claims, only one of them will hold the righteous claim by the end. Either by death or surrender does the other forfeit her claims.

Do you see? That means I can't go back to my family, even if I wanted it. I have no wealth and no entitlements. My name is meaningless. What remains of my honour now?'

'Have you forgotten why you spared her life?' I asked her, craning my head to look in her eyes. 'Do you remember what you said? You said that there was nothing in this world that could compel you to slaughter your kin, that no title was worth murdering your own sister. And you were right. If mercy is not honour, then honour is evil.'

'But what am I to do now, Kiro?' She leaned back and tossed her hands into the air, letting them fall on her lap. 'My destiny was that seat. Every day since I was born, I was taught that, one day, the regency would be mine. When I was young, I was told it was God's plan that I would rule. Every day was spent in preparing me for one thing; the day I would finally bear the weight of the regency upon my own shoulders. It was my duty, my honour, my *purpose*. And what have I done? I have thrown it all away, and consigned myself to a life of... *mediocrity*.'

I thought carefully, then spoke. 'You are not consigned to anything, Viella. You are free. You have always been free, since the moment you were born.'

She looked up at me with lost, sad eyes. 'What do you mean?'

'The world, there is still so much to see. So many new friends to meet, so many new places to explore. There's food to eat, music to hear, mysteries to uncover, triumphs to be had.' The hope in this message lifted me to my feet, and I stood as I spoke, propping myself up with the cane. 'You are free to go where you wish, to do as you wish.'

Viella pursed her lips. 'Yes, yes, it's a very pretty world to see,' she said sadly. 'But what is my place in it, if not the throne? Where in this very pretty world do I go?'

I sat back down on the other bed. 'You're uncertain,' I said. 'That's okay. Why did you want to rule?'

The question was simple, but it puzzled Viella. 'What do you mean?'

'Why did you want to become regent?' I asked again.

Her chin dipped. 'Because... it was my destiny. It was my duty, to my family and to Azale, to rule.'

'But did you have any personal desire to rule? Did you have a vision of how you wanted Azale to be?'

She paused. 'I... I wanted to meet the expectations that were set of me. I wanted to make my father, my mother, my ancestors… proud.'

'So… did you want to rule, or did you want people to feel proud of you?'

She was silent for a moment before she made a half shrug and said, 'I suppose I'm not truly certain anymore.'

I nodded. 'It's normal to be unsure of yourself. Personally, I'm not sure what I'm going to do.'

She lifted her chin. 'Oh? Do you not have your Sanctuary to return to?'

'I do,' I said, 'but I've changed my mind. I don't want to be ordained and live up in the mountains for the rest of my life. I want to see the world. I want to help people. That's the destiny I've chosen for myself.'

That last sentence returned a frown to her face. 'Destiny is beyond our will, Kiro,' she said, defeated. 'We cannot change our fate. Zephelia's destiny was to take that throne. Mine was to be forgotten.'

I paused, then asked, 'May I share a lesson with you?'

She gave a small gesture with her hand to continue.

'I don't know what they teach you here about the world's beginning, but we in the Order of Light know this; the world was created by three gods, and all life was created by Orisaea. When She made us, She gave us souls, so that we may be free. Do you know what that means?'

She exhaled. 'What?'

'It means there is no greater purpose to your life than the one you choose. Destiny is not beyond your will, it *is* your will. Humanity was not created to be pawns of a divine plan. We are free to choose our own path in life. It is all up to you. That is why life is beautiful. Do you see?'

Viella was silent, but slowly her eyes lifted to meet mine. There was a glimmer in them, something bright and hopeful building behind them. 'If I told you that Synn said something similar, would you still think that was clever?'

I laughed. 'I'd say Synn was cleverer than I thought.'

A small smile appeared on her face. 'You're quite a wise young man, aren't you? Wiser than most boys your age.'

I smiled, too. 'Thank you.'

'No, thank *you*,' she said sincerely. 'You are right, about a lot of things. I used to think you naïve but… perhaps that word is more befitting of me. You've given me much to ponder. Now, I just need time to…' she sighed, '…contemplate everything.'

'Of course.' I stood up, tapping the floor with the cane. 'I will leave you to reflect. If you need anything, I will be downstairs.'

'You have my thanks, Kiro.'

I pulled the door open and noticed something on the floor, which stopped me.

Viella noticed my hesitance. 'Is something wrong?'

I glanced back at her. 'Someone left this outside our door.'

I knelt and scooped up a plate of food, a fresh serving of bread, mutton, and cheese.

Chapter Twenty-One

Parting Ways

Viella and I stayed in Azale for another week. The Smiling Lion was hardly a place to call home, but it began to feel like one after a while. Bonhilde became a good friend of ours. She was kind enough to offer us work in exchange for money. She handed me a broom and I swept every room in the inn. Then, I graduated to cleaning the kitchen, the bedrooms, the chamber pots, and the cellar.

Viella assisted Bonhilde and the inn's owner Mister Dawble with their written records for a day or two then found another good use for her literacy. She would go out into the streets, find a nice spot, and then read aloud stories she had memorised to paying spectators. I never realised that most people in Azale were uneducated and that my ability to read was a gift. As Viella earned more and more coppers and silvers, her confidence grew, and she began to tell her own story. Every passing day, her energy and theatricality grew all the more practised and entertaining, just as the crowds who came to watch her grew all the more larger.

One day, after I had finished all my little jobs, I went to watch Viella tell her story as the day drew to a close. She was even better than when I last saw her. A large audience had gathered and were entirely captivated by every note and beat in her story. She noticed me in the crowd and smiled. As she finished delivering a colourful account on the peril we faced in the Tyrant Sands, she sketched a bow and the crowd applauded her. People tossed coins, coppers and silvers, into an open pouch at her feet.

But as she leant down to pick up the bag of money, there was a blur of blue and the pouch was gone.

A thief in a blue cloak had snatched it, and was bolting through the streets.

'Thief!' someone cried.

'You! Stop!' Viella shouted.

But the thief didn't get far. As he dashed through the crowd, heading towards an alley, an arm swung into his way and collided with his face, knocking the thief flat on his back.

Viella and I ran up towards the scene. Viella grabbed the pouch, while the man who had intervened lifted the dazed thief by his collar and threw him stumbling towards some protectors who were running over to us.

'Thank you, sir,' Viella said to the man.

I looked up at the stranger. He was tall and draped in a green cloak that hid most of his face. Before he spoke, I already realised who he was, and my heart skipped a beat.

'No problem, snowball,' Synn said, poking a finger under his hood to reveal his cool grin and striking green eyes.

Viella's grateful smile went cold when she saw his face, and she stared at him for a moment.

Then she punched him in the stomach.

Synn made a sputtering laugh and staggered back from the hit. '... I deserve that.'

'You do,' Viella said, her voice hard and unfriendly. 'It takes a rare impudence to show yourself after what you did.'

I could see under his hood that Synn's long hair had been cut short, and his face cleanly shaven. He scarcely looked himself, but not in a bad way. I approached and placed my hand on his shoulder. 'It is good to see you, Synn,' I said.

He smiled. 'Good to see you too, kid.'

'What do you want?' Viella questioned him.

'To talk.' Synn drew the hood tighter over his head. 'Somewhere private, preferably.'

Viella and I noticed the large crowd watching us in great interest. She put on a sunny smile and again loudly thanked them for listening to her tale, then led the two of us to a quiet, shadowy alley while the people dispersed.

'You have our attention.' Viella folded her arms. 'Go on. Explain yourself.'

Synn glanced over his shoulder at the street, to check if anyone was watching, then pulled out the crown from his cloak, handing it to me.

'Seems you lost this,' he said sheepishly.

A heavy weight in my heart lifted when I saw it. I took it carefully from him. 'It seems I did,' I said, then smirked, happy to play his little game. 'Thank you for finding it for me.'

'Yeah, you're welcome, pal.' He stood there for a moment, his hands on his hips, digging his heel into the ground and glancing at his feet, at the street, and anywhere that wasn't our faces. He clicked his tongue, sighed, then raised his gaze to meet ours and said honestly and plainly, 'I'm sorry.'

For him to say those words was stunning. Viella and I listened on eagerly.

'Look, let me be real with you for a second,' he began. 'For a long time, my life was kind of... uh... boring.' He shrugged. 'When I say "boring", what I mean is... I wasn't really living. I was alive, sure, but I didn't enjoy anything. I didn't believe in anything, or anyone. It felt like... like something was missing, you know?' He seemed uncomfortable, as if it was embarrassing to talk about his emotions. 'So anyways,' he continued, 'for a long time, I was looking for something that would bring back that spark I was missing, the spark I needed to start enjoying things again. I thought all that meant was I just had to take on more risky jobs, do more dangerous stuff, get more money, but... I don't know if it's because I'm just too damn good, but it just... got stale. And ramping up the stakes didn't really do anything either... until I met you two.'

Viella raised an eyebrow. I restrained my giddy excitement as best I could.

'I think, when you knocked me out in that forest, a part of me was happy that I lost for once,' Synn said to Viella. 'It was like... I wanted to lose.'

'Not that it matters.' She smirked. 'I beat you because I'm better than you.'

'Yeah, sure, whatever,' he said with a little grin of his own. 'Anyways, when we were together, and I was getting to know you guys more, I...'

And then, again, he fidgeted and stirred, scratching the back of his neck and hesitating.

'I... I actually began to feel something.' He winced then shook his head. 'Ugh. This is so pathetic.'

'No, it's not,' I said, giving him a nod. 'Keep going.'

He seemed encouraged. He cleared his throat, lifted his chin, and continued. 'When Kiro here got kicked into a twister, I actually felt... upset.' The word seemed strange for him to say. 'Sad? Just... I felt *awful*, you know? Which was weird. Then when I saw you again, I felt happier than I've been in years. I've got a lot of reasons to be happy, kiddo, trust me. Look at me. Look at this.' He waved a hand over his face and body. 'I'm hot as hell. And the ladies know it.'

Viella's eyes rolled skyward and she swivelled on her heels to leave.

'No, no, wait.' Synn stuck his hand out. 'Hear me out.'

Viella stopped and returned her attention to him.

'When I started thinking about all this, I panicked. I thought that was weakness,' he admitted. 'I thought it was stupid of me to get attached, and once I was sure you were alive and gonna be okay, Kiro, I ran. I took the gun, and your crown, because I knew a guy who would pay big for it. I was gonna go back to my old life.' He sighed. 'But, as I was heading to the city gates, you know what I felt?'

'What?' I asked.

'Nothing,' he said. 'I didn't feel clever, or satisfied, or relieved. I felt that same emptiness I'd been feeling for years again.' He shrugged and cast his gaze aside. 'That's when I realised what I was looking for – people who treat me like I'm a person. People I like hanging around. Not cutthroats and thieves trying to leech off my reputation or kill me for it. Actually decent people. Good people. A good, honest life.'

I couldn't help smiling.

'So I decided I was going to change. I'm gonna live a good, honest life, and make some good, honest friends.' He held out his hand for me to shake. 'And the first step towards that life is admitting I'm wrong. And saying sorry.'

I looked at his hand, then stepped past it and hugged him.

'I'm proud of you, Synn,' I said to him truthfully. 'I knew you could change for the better, and I'm so glad you did.'

He patted me on the back. 'Thanks for treating me like a human being, kiddo.'

We let go, then he extended his hand towards Viella.

She squinted at it, then narrowed her eyes on him. 'You're sorry, yes?'

'Very, very sorry.'

'What are you sorry for?'

His nose puffed and he hesitated. 'I'm sorry for... being an ass.'

Viella hummed, pleased so far. 'And?'

'And for... calling you mean names. And beating you up. And trying to kill you that one time.'

'Two times.'

'*Two times*, yeah.' He smiled briefly, then without a trace of mockery or sarcasm, he said, 'I'm sorry, Viella.'

Viella studied his face.

Then she shook his hand.

'I accept your apology,' she said.

'Great,' Synn said, a big grin on his face. 'Whew. That felt good. Is this what you feel like all the time, kiddo?'

I chuckled. 'I guess so. What's your plan now?'

'Now?' He gazed out into the street. 'I'm pretty hungry. You guys want some dinner?'

We went back to the Smiling Lion as the sun set. The inn was bustling with people, chatting, laughing, and enjoying the company of their friends. Glasses clinked. The fireplace crackled. Bards filled the air with cheery melodies. Synn paid for our meals, and we talked, exchanging jokes, stories, and our theories of some of the strange things that happened in our journey.

After our plates were empty, I asked Synn what he was going to do now.

'Well, first thing's first, I have some business to finish up in Ceren,' he said. 'After that... not sure. Start a farm? A brewery? No idea.' He took a swig of his beer, then brought the mug back down to the table. 'I'll figure it out.'

He stayed the night in the Smiling Lion, in a room a few doors down from ours. The next morning, we ate oats for breakfast with him at one of the many empty tables. We talked, but there was a certain bittersweet air about us, born from the shared and unspoken awareness that it could be the last time we ever saw each other.

Long after we had finished our meals, Synn stood up. 'I guess this is it, then.'

Viella and I stood up as well. 'It's been a pleasure, Synn,' I said.

He winked. 'But it wasn't always, right?'

I shrugged. 'We had our moments.'

'We did.' Then there was a flash of shock on his face, as if he just remembered something important. 'Oh, I almost forgot.' He reached into his cloak and pulled out the gun, contained in its leather pouch, then held it out towards me. 'This is for you.'

I hesitated. 'You're giving me the gun? Why?'

'It has divination in it, so I thought it would be of use to you. It's better off in your hands anyway. I don't need it anymore.'

I took it carefully, holding it in both hands. He gave me a few instructions on how to use it.

'And if you're going to kill someone, aim for the head.'

'I'm not going to kill people with it. I'm going to study it.'

He chuckled and slapped my shoulder playfully. 'Yeah, yeah, I know. Have fun.'

'Take care of yourself, Synn,' Viella said, giving a respectful nod.

'You too, Vie,' he replied, returning the gesture.

I extended my hand to him. 'Farewell, Synn.'

He shook it firmly. 'Goodbye for now, Kiro. I'm sure we'll meet again someday.'

'I hope so,' I said honestly.

He pulled open the door. Before he stepped out into the light of the street, he gave us a wink and a smile. 'Take it easy, dummies.'

Then he turned around and walked out, the door swinging shut behind him.

That was two days ago.

Tonight, when Viella returned to our room, I was already in my bed waiting for her so I could blow out the candle.

'Good evening,' I said.

'Good evening, Kiro,' she said cheerfully. 'And what a splendid evening it is.'

The energy in her voice piqued my interest. 'Why's that?'

She put down a canvas sack full of things by her bed. 'I have enough coin to leave the city tomorrow.'

'Oh.' I paused. I didn't know she was leaving. 'Where are you going?'

'I will be travelling south to Meras,' she answered as she unbuttoned the top of her blouse and gestured me with a flick of her head to avert my eyes.

While staring at the wall, I asked her why she was going to Meras.

'Meras is a beautiful city, and it's the heart of culture and art in Advenia. The finest artists, performers, and bards all employ their craft in Meras, and with the unexpected success of my street stories, I feel compelled to pursue a vocation in theatre.'

'I see. I'm surprised you're drawn to acting,' I said.

'Some of my fondest memories of my childhood are attending plays with my father and sister,' she said wistfully. 'I've always had a penchant for the performing arts, ever since I was a child.'

'How will you get there?'

'I will be boarding a carriage tomorrow at first light. Don't you worry, Kiro, I'll keep my wits about me.' She paused, then added, 'You can turn your head now.'

I looked over to her. Her head was resting on the pillow, poking out from under the covers of her bed. When she saw my face, concern spread on hers. 'What's wrong?'

I was confused. 'Oh? Nothing. Why do you ask?'

'You look... sad.'

I touched my face. 'I do?'

'Are you well?'

'Of course, it's just... I'm surprised you're leaving so suddenly.'

Her gaze broke away from mine. A moment passed without a word. 'Forgive me, it truly was a spontaneous decision, inspired by your words on controlling our destiny,' she said. 'There is nothing here for me in Azale. I could not endure living here with the White Palace always looming over me, so I will find somewhere else to shape my future, and I want to begin as soon as I can.'

'Are you prepared?' I asked.

She made a little laugh and shrugged. 'Not really,' she admitted. 'We are never prepared for the journey of our lifetime, not until we take the first step. Because that is how a journey is walked, one step at a time.'

I smiled helplessly. 'You remembered.'

She smiled, too. 'You are quite wise for a young man. I am grateful for all of your advice.'

The comment was touching. 'I am glad to have been of service.'

Her smile wilted a little bit. 'Will you be alright on your own, Kiro?'

'I will.'

There was a pause as she read my face, some unspoken worry in her eyes. 'What's your next move?'

I thought about it. 'I was going to wait here for a little while longer, enjoy the shelter I have, then continue past Azale.'

'So, head further east?'

'Yes, until I reach the Edge.'

She cocked her head. 'You're going to continue your journey? Have you changed your mind on leaving the Order?'

'No.' I peered up the wooden ceiling as I imagined what the end of the world might look like. 'But I've come so far already. I might as well see this through to the end. I want to know what's at the Edge that's so enlightening.'

The next morning, Viella was already tightening the belt around her waist when I awoke. She was awake early so the carriage she was taking could leave the city before it got too crowded. Viella asked me if I would like to come and wait with her outside. I said I would.

The city was empty and silent, and the whole world inside the walls was coloured a faint blue as the morning light emerged in the sky. The air was cool and crisp, and our breaths created little clouds that vanished in the same second they came to be. We were standing outside the inn, waiting. We were the only two people I could see. It felt like we were the only ones in the whole city. The rest of the world was still quiet and asleep.

I wanted to fully appreciate this moment, so I took extra care in absorbing the sights of the silent streets, the feeling of the chill air on my skin, and the smell of the clear morning. I wanted to remember this moment so I could cherish it later, because I knew this may very well be the last time I would see Viella.

It was strange; our partnership was only a matter of getting to Azale.

It had never really occurred to me that it was only a matter of time before we would say goodbye and part ways.

'This is where we say goodbye, then,' Viella said. She must have been thinking the same thing.

'I hope we meet again someday,' I told her in earnest.

'As do I.' After a short pause, Viella stirred where she stood then said, 'One last time, I wish to thank you, Kiro. For years, I lived in fear. I ran, and I hid. I was afraid to face the world. You… You helped me build the courage I needed to begin my journey. You followed me through the mountains, through the desert, through the seas, and you bent the heavens themselves to save my life. You've shown me the world in a light I've never seen it. You didn't have to be, but you were there for me, by my side. For that, you have my unyielding gratitude.'

Her words stirred something in my chest, and I could feel I was about to cry. It was here when I realised just how much this was going to hurt.

'And I thank you Viella,' I said, trying my best to stay composed as I looked in her eyes. 'You have taught me and shown me so much about the world, more than our texts ever could. You gave me guidance, led me through a land I did not know, and protected me. If it were not for you, I would not have made it this far.' I paused, then added, 'Thank you for everything, madam. I enjoyed our time together.'

She smiled, her blue eyes twinkled, and she said, 'I'm going to miss you, Kiro.'

My heart swelled, and welling tears stung my eyes. 'I'll miss you, too.'

Disrupting the silence, a carriage appeared in the streets and rolled toward us, pulled by two horses driven by a rider clad in brown leather. Viella turned and took a step forward as the carriage drew near. It came to a stop outside the inn. The rider greeted Viella, who hesitated before she boarded. She turned to face me and said, 'I hope you find peace in the destiny you carve for yourself.'

For a wordless reason, I felt it was right to step forward and hug her. She seemed surprised, then after a moment, wrapped her arms around me. Her hand gently rubbed the spot between my shoulders, and I felt a tender warmth in my chest.

'Goodbye, my friend,' I said.

We let go. She bowed her head and took a moment to wipe her eyes. She cleared her throat, took a deep breath, then raised her head and picked up her things. She opened the carriage door. Before she stepped inside, she peered over her shoulder to look me in the eyes. 'Be well,' she said.

Then she shut the door. The rider flicked the reigns, and the horses took off, riding out of the city. I watched the carriage go, getting smaller and smaller as it progressed down the streets until it turned around a corner and disappeared.

Chapter Twenty-Two

The Edge

After Viella left, I returned to our room in the Smiling Lion. As soon as I entered, a sudden and heavy melancholy descended on me. The room did not look any different to when we had left it, but now there was an inexplicable loneliness to it. It was overbearing, and memories of our conversations echoed here. I could not endure it for long.

So I gathered my few belongings and waited downstairs. When Bonhilde arrived, I told her I was leaving the city. I had not planned to leave Azale this early but I could not stay any longer. I thanked her graciously for her kindness and tried to pay her for the last night I spent here, but she refused to accept my money. She seemed disappointed I was leaving but wished me safe travels.

I wandered through the city's winding streets, watching it slowly rise from its slumber and come to life, filling with people beginning one of their many days. I made my way to the east end of the city, passing around the White Palace and the beautiful noble district. As I progressed further to the east, the buildings became shoddy and the streets grimy and narrow. There was an unsavoury feeling in the air here, moulded by aloof frowns on people's faces and the suspicious glares they delivered me as I passed by them. I felt safer when I arrived at the massive Eastern Gate of the city. The protectors had no problems in letting me pass through.

Beyond the city walls, a dirt road led into more grassy plains and farms dotted by cottages and huts. It was the afternoon now, and the farmers had been working in the fields since dawn. I passed through a town like Cherry, called Apple. It was full of farmers and common folk working hard. No one paid any notice to me as I passed through. I had grown used to the stares but now there were none.

I crossed over a river on an old stone bridge and passed through the last of Apple. Here, I walked through empty fields of long, swaying grass under rolling white clouds. The image of Azale's walls and towers became smaller and smaller on the horizon behind me until they were gone. The hours melted away as I walked, lost in my thoughts and absorbed in the sweeping sights of the world around me. I was concerned I could get lost, so I stayed strictly eastbound and resisted any temptation to explore the world around me. At one point I stopped to rest, and to simply drink in the motions of the natural world; the sway of the sweeping grasslands caressed by the wind, and the tumbling, billowing passage of the white clouds through the vast blue sky.

As I walked, a pensive sadness fell on me, coming from somewhere in my mind. It slumped my shoulders, weighted my footsteps, and bowed my head. At first, I didn't realise what it was. This feeling had no words or image to it. I began to understand that it stemmed from a bitter realisation; the world was not as beautiful as I thought. Violence seemed as natural to living things as hunger and thirst. Nearly every living being we came across on our journey wanted to kill us. There was no justice in Azale. While the nobility revelled in overflowing riches, the commoners withered in the streets. The people cheered as they watched Viella and Synn burn to death. I knew people would be different to how we were in the Sanctuary, but I was truly unprepared for what I had seen. I felt like a fool for ever having believed what I did.

But I reminded myself to have faith. People could change for the better, given compassion and time. That much was true. Synn was living proof of that. I still could not stop a smile from spreading across my face when I thought about the moment he came back to us. I wished the two of them could have come with me to the Edge for one last journey. I missed them so much it hurt.

Gradually, as the sky turned a blazing orange, the plains around me began to rise and fall, becoming lush, rolling hills of green. I passed by a stout, sturdy tree that was alone on the side of the path. Apples were growing on the branches, and I swiped at the lowest branch I could reach to knock an apple free. It took me a few tries. If I still had my staff it would have been much easier. I curled up under its shade, the only shelter I could see for miles, and admired the stars as I fell asleep.

I awoke the next morning, sore and hungry, and pressed on through the open expanse of country. After some hours, I found packs of sheep and cows grazing in grassy paddocks, then farmers working in fields of wheat. They were part of a small, pleasant village named Maycott. The warm scent of fresh bread wafted through the air. No one carried swords or armour. Azale's banners rose here, but none of the buildings could even reach the height of the Smiling Lion. The tallest building Maycott had was a chapel made of stone bricks, situated near a running stream of water. Even the chapel was small, hopelessly dwarfed by the size of the Haphasteon Cathedral. I still liked it though. It did not need to be an extravagant palace to be something to appreciate; its simplicity was enough.

By the time I had arrived at Maycott it was already well past noon. A growing hunger was barking in my stomach, so I visited a bakery and used the last of my coppers to purchase some hot bread; some to eat now, some to eat later. The accent of the people here sounded different from the one I heard in Azale. The people here had a rougher twang to their words, a cadence that frolicked up and down just like the hills that surrounded their cosy home. It was fascinating to listen to them speak.

I asked the baker how much further away the Edge would be.

'Just continue heading eastward 'n' ye'll be getting claise tae it. Wance ye see th' Old Towers, ye'll know yer nearly thare.'

'Thank you.' I went to leave, then the baker spoke up.

'Pardon me bit, dae ye mynd if ah ask ye how come ye'r gaun thare?'

There was a dash of worry in her voice. I said I was travelling to see the Edge, then to return home. She hummed a note of acknowledgement but seemed uneasy.

'Alright, tak' care will ye?'

'I will, thank you.'

I wondered what could have made her concerned.

As I left the bakery and continued through Maycott, I passed by many of the townsfolk. They were friendly, and when I would pass by them they would bid me good day with a warm smile, regardless of the fact I was an outsider. I crossed a bridge running over the stream and encountered fewer and fewer villagers the further I walked. Here it was mostly just farms that lay in the smoother, flatter parts of the hills. I pressed onward and eventually, the farms ended and I was alone again, walking on a road through empty, grassy hills. Grey clouds gathered in the skies, and not long after I was walking in the rain. The wonderful scent of earth and water lifted and mixed in the air, and it became a delight just to breathe.

As the rain dispersed, the hills began to wane and flatten and the terrain became rocky and bare, a craggy mirror of the grey skies above. The path I was following dwindled into patches of dirt amongst the grass and rocks.

And then I saw them, looming ahead in the distance. Tall, upright columns. As I got closer, their overwhelming size became apparent and I saw more and more of them.

Stretching for miles in a line through these barren plains were massive, looming towers built of sturdy, brown stone. These must have been the Old Towers that the baker had mentioned. I had seen them from quite a distance away, but it took me hours to even reach them.

I approached the one closest to me to study it, delicately placing a hand on the stone to feel it. The stone was old and rough, and there seemed to be indented lines dividing the tower into sections. I then realised they were actually stacks of around twenty identical blocks of stone, each about twenty feet high and wide. Their size was utterly astounding. I gazed up and watched the towers rise for hundreds of feet into the sky, far exceeding the walls of Azale and the White Palace. I peered north and south and counted the others. From what I could see, there were about thirty of these towers. I was awestruck, and baffled. *How could anyone build towers so high?*

The surroundings were barren. There were no trees nor any sign of civilisation. Azale was the nearest city, and it had taken me two days to travel from there. Whoever built these dragged the stone from elsewhere, gave them this shape, then stacked them atop one another for hundreds of feet into the sky, thirty different times.

My only guess was the ancient Advenians, aided by divination. But if so, then the Order would surely have written about the towers in our texts. I supposed I placed too much faith in our archives. It was hard to believe I never doubted the knowledge in the Order's library, never considering that there was more to the world than what those old writings told.

I remembered the words of the baker; that I would be close to the Edge after I reached the Old Towers. I moved on as I pondered who could have built them, and for what purpose.

After another hour of walking, the sun was already slinking down to the horizon behind me. The rain faded and the wind became stronger as I approached the end of the land; the Edge.

Here, the world was barren and grey. There were no people, no trees, no hills, no houses, and no roads. The grass was pale and riddled with thick, stubby clumps of shrubs. It felt like I couldn't be any further from any other living person than where I was now. The wind was cold and fierce, and my robes whipped at its gusts. Right ahead of me, the land extended like the bow of a ship outwards over a sea of clouds that merged seamlessly with the sky at the horizon. The sight was breathtaking. It was what I imagined the cosmic heavens to look like.

At a cusp, the land extended like a balcony over the clouds. My excitement building, I walked towards it, the mainland receding behind me. As I approached the end, I realised I could count the last of this long journey's steps on my hand.

I pushed against the wind, putting one foot in front of the other until I planted my feet on the last inch of Advenia's land.

It was finally done.

I gazed over the edge of the world and saw the white cliff face plunge into the mists below. I could not see the bottom. The clouds all below were like an endless sea of mist. The only sound there was to hear was the unending whistle of the winds flying past me.

I surveyed the sweeping view of the cliffs at the edge of the world, searching for something, anything that could be what Master Shien spoke of. I couldn't see anything that could fit the description of the ultimate truth. Besides the amazing view, there was nothing here.

'Hello there,' said a voice from behind.

I turned and spotted its owner; an old man, short and hunched, wearing a green, woollen waistcoat. He was hobbling towards me. 'How are ye, lad?' he asked. He spoke with the same accent as the people in Maycott.

'I am well, sir,' I replied, raising my voice over the wind. I stepped away a few paces from the cliff. 'I did not see where you came from.'

'I came from Maycott as well,' he said with a smile. He pointed his thumb over his shoulder, and beyond him, in the distance, a brown horse was waiting. 'The ol' girl took me here.'

'I see.'

He stood a few feet behind me. 'Beautiful view, innit?'

I took in the vast sea of white and breathed in the clear air deeply. 'It is indeed.'

The old man was quiet for a moment before he spoke. 'Ye know, some say... that the Edge was not always the end of the land.'

'No?'

'No. Some say that, long ago, there was more land that connected here. It was cursed land, full to the brim with monsters. They say those monsters wanted nothin' more than to feast on the flesh of man. But man fought back and won. We beat those beasts back into that land and once we did, it broke away and sank into the mists, and none of those creatures were ever seen again.'

'That's quite an imaginative story.'

'Aye.'

'It seems specific, what makes them say this?'

'Well, ye saw those towers on yer way here, aye?'

I nodded. He asked if I knew what they were and when I said no, he explained for me.

'Those are the Old Towers. No one knows who built them or why, but whoever did, they built them bloody well. Thirty men have charged those towers with rams and not once could they bring it to even budge. We couldn't tear them down even if we tried. Some say they used to be the parts of a wall that separated the land of man from the land of monsters.' Then he chuckled. 'But, ye know people, they like to say all kinds of things.'

The old man spoke of these things as if they were merely tales and he did not expect me to believe them. But from my understanding of the Unbeings, it was not implausible. 'Those stories may be true,' I said, gazing out over the clouds.

The old man shrugged. 'Aye, maybe. There's no way to tell.' He paused, then chuckled to himself. 'Ah, where are me manners? Me name is Caragen.'

I offered my hand. 'My name is Kiro.'

He shook it firmly. 'Pleasure to meet ye.' He smiled. 'I hope not to offend ye, but ye don't look like yer from around here.'

'I am not offended, sir. I am from the Gentle Mountains.'

'Aye, the Gentle Mountains!' His face lit up. 'A truly beautiful place.'

His excitement brought me a smile. 'You have been to the Gentle Mountains?'

'Aye, when I were a younger man, many years ago.' He stared off into the distance, his eyes twinkling as he revisited memories of bygone days. He looked to me. 'That's a faraway place. Did ye travel all that way here by yerself?'

'No, I met some friends.' I told him. 'I travelled with them for a while.'

'Aye, I see. I hope ye don't mind me asking where they are now.'

'The three of us, we parted ways. One of them is travelling south to Meras. And the other is going to Ceren.'

The old man hummed. 'So the three of ye travelled on foot? Horseback?'

'Mostly on foot, yes.'

'That's quite an effort!' he marvelled. 'What brought ye here, lad?'

I hesitated, then told him about the Order of Light, and the task given to me by Master Shien, and why. He nodded along all the while, listening patiently and with sincere interest. A part of me worried that the revelation I was of the Order of Light would prompt a historic distrust, but he didn't seem to know who we were.

'Ah, I see. I'm glad ye came here for a good reason, lad.' He seemed relieved. 'I had another dreadful thought as to yer coming here.'

I was confused. 'What do you mean?' I asked him. 'Why else would I come here?'

A sparkle in his eye dwindled and he became grim. 'Well, unfortunately, lad, not everyone shares our appreciation for the world. Some come here to... to throw away their lives.'

His sentence gave me pause. 'Really?'

He continued. 'Some folks, they're tormented by ill thoughts. They foolishly believe their lives to be worthless, so they come here to toss themselves off the Edge and be gone in the clouds.'

I was shocked. 'That's terrible.'

He nodded wearily in agreement. 'Aye. That is why I come here, lad. When we see travellers or any sullen folks heading eastward, we get worried. We always see them passing by, in Maycott. I come here to try and talk 'em out of it. That's why I followed ye, lad. Bessie told me about ye askin' about the Edge, and we both agreed we didn't want to take the risk of lettin' ye go alone.'

Bessie must have been the name of the baker. That would explain why she seemed concerned. 'I would never think of that,' I swore honestly. 'Why would anyone willingly throw their life away?'

'They all have so many reasons, lad. All of them different. But mostly, they feel like there is no joy in their lives, no hope for better days. They'd rather toss it all to the winds then see it done. Tis a regretful thing indeed. Their hearts are bleedin', and they think there's no other way to stop it.' He turned to me and reached up to grab my shoulder. 'Might I share some advice with ye, Kiro?'

'I would be honoured, sir.'

'I've walked this world for seventy years. I've buried a brother, a sister, a wife, and a daughter. Never once was there a time I could not get back up after getting knocked down, lad. Never once.' He took his hand back and gazed out over the vast expanse of clouds. 'I'm lucky to have lived so long. Not many get to be as old as I do. My time has come and gone, and now I spend my last days giving back to the world by making sure other young folk don't throw their time away.'

We were silent for a while, listening to the winds as I reflected on his story. 'Do they change their minds when they listen to you?'

He hummed. 'Most do, thank God. Most just need someone to talk to. Someone who'll listen to them.' Then his gaze drooped to the ground. 'But some… they cannot always be reached. I ache for them, I do; the ones I couldn't help. But I always try, lad. I always try.'

A new weight sank into my heart to carry. I could not imagine yearning for death, to ever think of choosing it over life. 'That is quite a burden to willingly bear.'

'I wouldn't consider it a burden – more a service. A heavy one at that, but one that I shoulder nonetheless.' He nodded slowly, his lips pressed, his eyes creased and looking off into a world of memories that only he could see. 'Our time here is so short tis almost cruel. We only get one chance to experience the world and there is nothing to gain in ending it so quickly. I have lived a full life and seen so much, and I feel eternally fortunate for it. I want to spend these few years I have left helping others find the will to see their time through. I feel it's the right thing to do, a way to give back to the world.'

'That is noble of you, sir,' I told him. 'I admire your compassion.'

'Thank ye, lad.' He smiled. 'I'm glad ye got to see yer task through to the end. Listening to ye talk about it, I can tell it would've been hard.'

I thought about it. 'It was… enlightening.'

'Aye, there's no substitute for experience, lad. The world wasn't created to be read about in books. It's there for ye, my boy. All its beauties and hardships.'

And that was it; the sentence that shined a light of clarity in my mind. The words that gave rise to a realisation, the answer to the many questions that swirled in my thoughts.

I had finally found it,

The ultimate truth.

Epilogue

Shien was in the gardens when he felt the energy of a familiar soul.
He had returned.

Shien went to the gates and heaved as he pulled the lever to open them. Standing on the other side of the massive doors, atop the stairs, was a young man who he did not recognise at first. Upon settling his gaze on him, Shien realised it was his student, and was astonished by how much he had changed in the two months he was gone. The young man's face was made rugged by the scraggy beginnings of a beard. Short brown hair had grown over his head. His robes, which had once been white, had endured much of the elements and been rendered a vague grey by various coalescing stains. His eyes, once wide, quick, and curious, were now relaxed and certain.

'Welcome home, Kiro,' he said, clasping his hands together and bowing.

'Master,' the student replied, giving a respectful bow. His voice was slower and deeper than it had been. It was calm and assured.

'Did you complete your journey, my student?'

'I did, and I have learned much. My eyes have been opened to new perspectives the scrolls could not show me.' He bowed his head. 'I am thankful I had the chance to see the world.'

In the student's soul, Shien could sense the strength of certainty where there had once been doubt. Everything about Kiro was bolstered and deepened. He had grown for the better.

In the candlelit eating hall, the student reunited with his former peers and teachers over tea. He told stories of his journey. He described a beautiful forest of endless colours. He weaved a tale of jagged, barren mountains haunted by screaming, winged beasts. He described a vast and shifting desert of oppressive heat, and a monster that inhabited the sands and compelled its grains into the forms of men. He told of a storm of unfathomable wrath that raised and twisted the seas, and the incredible creations of man used to soar through its gales. And most curiously, he spoke of the buried, ghostly ruins of Adven, conjured and sustained by divination. He gave the masters a small, leather-bound book to transcribe to the archives, brimming with vivid descriptions of all these lands, discoveries he made of the world, and the events of his journey.

After the pleasantries were over, the young man and the wise master who had raised him walked the balcony of the Sanctuary. They gazed out over the valley, listening to the wind and the delicate songs of the chimes that it swayed.

'So tell me,' Shien began, 'did you find the ultimate truth?'

'I did.' Kiro smirked, then said, 'The ultimate truth is... there isn't one.'

Half a smile appeared on Shien's face, and he stopped to listen to Kiro.

The student rested his hands on the balcony and absorbed the view of the mountains. 'After thinking about it for a while, master, I began to question if such a thing existed. Only after reaching the Edge did it occur to me what your plan had been from the beginning. There was no ultimate truth I needed to find.' He glanced back at his teacher. 'You just wanted me to see the world.'

Shien made a small, inward laugh and joined the young man at his side. 'Very good, Kiro,' he said, pleased. 'You are right. The Masters and I knew you would pass the ordainment test, but we could not allow you to make the choice of becoming a master without first seeing what you would be sacrificing.' Before Shien asked the next question, he already knew what Kiro's response would be. 'Now that you have proven yourself, and that you have seen the world, are you ready to be ordained?'

After a brief pause, the young man answered, 'No.'

Shien nodded slowly.

He explained himself. 'At least, not yet. There is still so much more in this world that I must see, that I yearn to see. I want to travel across Advenia, helping people find their way in life. I want to make the world a better place.'

And from Shien's heart, a song of pride.

'Your destiny is your will, Kiro,' the wise master said. 'Wherever you may go, always remember that you have a place in our Sanctuary. You may return here whenever you please. We will always welcome you.'

The following dawn, the old teacher stood with his former student at the gates of the Sanctuary.

'It was wonderful to see you again, Kiro,' Shien said. 'I wish you good fortune in your journeys to come.'

Kiro gazed out over the world beyond the steps of the Sanctuary. 'Thank you, Shien.' Then he looked back. 'Before I leave, there is something I need to give to you.'

From his bag, Kiro pulled out a wreath of smooth gold. It was bejewelled with a single, heavenly blue godstone. When Shien asked what it was, Kiro explained to him it was a crown taken from the ruins of Adven. He warned Shien of the crown's deep and terrible power and urged him to keep it contained and studied here in the Sanctuary. Shien took his warnings seriously and promised him they would do so.

'Thank you for everything, Master,' Kiro said, offering a final bow. 'For now, this is goodbye.'

Shien returned the gesture. 'Farewell, my student.'

As Kiro turned to face the world illuminated by the rising sun, he glanced over his shoulder, and left his master with the parting words,

'Be well.'

Acknowledgements

It is often said that your first draft is a 'vomit draft', and this book was no exception. Writing *Journey Advenia* was itself a journey, one where I made many mistakes and learned much, and one that I did not walk alone.

I want to give a big thanks to Mum and Dad for their continued support. A big thank you to my friends, Callum and Alex, for reading the manuscript and giving me their feedback. And of course, I want to thank you for choosing to read my novel. I hope you found it was worth your time.

I appreciate you, whoever you may be.